Praise For
KILLING TIME

"An inspired piece of historical fiction that takes me right back to my childhood in Charlottesville."
—*Rob Coles, Charlottesville, VA*

"The characters in *Killing Time* are wonderful! A *must read* for all!" —*M. Wolman, Philadelphia, PA*

"Killing Time is great. The action is tight and unpredictable. The characters are well drawn and credible. It is an accurate exposition of the legal process in a Virginia criminal jury trial, and provides an excellent portrayal of the social mores and thinking of folks in late 1950s Virginia.
—*H. Watkins Ellerson, Byrd Creek Farm, Hadensville, VA*

"Killing Time provides us a glimpse into our past— and shows us how we're still struggling."
—*Ellen Osborne, artist, Charlottesville, VA*

"I couldn't put this book down. *Killing Time* is gripping and the historical perspective added meaningful context. Another winner from Alden Bigelow!
—*Dr. Beverly Joyce, Clinical Psychologist, Charlottesville, VA*

KILLING TIME

IN A SMALL

SOUTHERN TOWN

by Alden E. C. Bigelow

BE Unlimited Publishing • Palmyra, VA

Also by Alden E. C. Bigelow:

Growing Up with Jemima
From the innocence of the early days as the Lone Ranger, Tonto, and his trusty cocker spaniel sidekick making Charlottesville safe and happy, to the coming of age in Richmond with the hard truth, these are the early adventures of a boy who learns early on that life may be overrated, but a good dog will never let you down.

Norton's Lament
Norton's Lament is the sometimes fictional autobiographical life struggle between faith and reality, love and hate... you know, life. It may be your struggle, too.

I Have My Reasons Audio CD
A musical celebration of some of Bigelow's favorite people and in honor of some of his favorite dogs.

I Have My Reasons Celebration Booklet
A 32-page celebration. Contains 15 poems and prose excerpts from *Norton's Lament.*

www.ABigelow.com

KILLING TIME

IN A SMALL

SOUTHERN TOWN

Author's notes:
This is a work of fiction. Any resemblance to persons living or dead is largely unintentional.

Although I have endeavored in most cases to be historically accurate, I have made a few embellishments. For example, the Lincoln Continental with suicide doors referred to did not come along until 1961, and the Gaslight Restaurant did not open its doors until 1961, but because I love the car and the restaurant I gave them birth two years earlier. Further I borrowed the name of Donald Stevens as the judge in this story. In fact, he was a well-known business man and entrepreneur who possessed some of the same qualities as expressed in the character of Judge Stevens.

A BE Unlimited Book
© 2012 Alden E. C. Bigelow

Layout and Design by Ellen Moore Osborne, www.TrinityArts.com.

First American Edition 2012

ISBN 978-1480128347

Many thanks to Rob Coles who was my reader and supporter throughout; to John Conover who provided valuable research and encouragement; to Ellen Osborne, my production director and designer, for great work and friendship; to Kevin Quirk who provided editing and great consultation; to Wat Ellerson who arrived just in time to add historical perspective; and to my wife Marjorie, my chief editorial consultant and close personal confidant.

Killing Time in a Small Southern Town
Table of Contents

Chapter 1: A Hot Southern Night

Roy slapped his foot down on the Lucky Strike wrapper. WHAP! "Ain't gonna have me no bad luck for a long time, Lucius. Betcha that means a good time tonight with Charlene."

Lucius was not impressed. "Where's your sense, boy? Steppin' on a cigarette wrapper ain't goin' bring you no luck with Charlene. 'Sides, you don't need luck with her. Just a little courtin' money and Red Eye '52."

"Now YOU crazy, Lucius. You know all those gals want is my bodacious body."

"The hell you say," came Lucius' quick reply. But he couldn't hold back the grin that was gurgling within. Both boys laughed as they ambled down Peach Street. They were walking slowly toward Charlene's house as Roy was working up his courage. Lucius never got to her house. And Roy was to wish he hadn't for the rest of his life.

It was one of those hot July nights small southern towns like Charlottesville are noted for, when everyone was killing time and trying to stay cool while wishing for the evening breezes to bring some relief. And there was old Miss Cora Lee Jones sitting on her porch, furiously fanning herself as she watched Roy and Lucius walk by. She turned to her sister Florence. "Those boys are up to no good tonight. Just look at the way they're giggling an' carryin' on. Why, it's a disgrace! They should be home doin' their chores. I declare!"

"No, Cora Lee," answered Florence patiently. "You mustn't be so hard on them. They's good boys with a touch of the wild oats on such a hot night. But they don' mean no harm."

"Hmmmmmmph," retorted Miss Jones, to emphasize the end of that particular dialogue. "Wild oats, indeed!"

Another hot July night, like so many Julys before in Charlottesville. Usually the conversation centered on the weather and neighborhood gossip. But in 1959, there was something even more volatile than the recent Independence Day fireworks in the all-white and all-black neighborhoods. Integration. Desegregation.

"Those damn Pinko liberals from up north are trying to tell us what to do," said Mrs. Baldwin Lee III to her sister whom she was calling in New Orleans. "We didn't have any trouble with the coloreds until that Communist Supreme Court stepped in. And now even President Eisenhower has rolled over and forced those Negroes into Little Rock High in Arkansas. Gracious, even my house servants are starting to get uppity, talking about integration. Why, can you imagine, my cook suggested that wouldn't it be nice when her little Leroy would be going to first grade with my grandson Jefferson Lee? It's outrageous! Why, I'll have my daughter take him out of school before I see that happen! Or I'll send him to private school!" Mrs. Baldwin Lee III continued. "First the schools, then the movie theaters. Why, before you know it, they'll probably want to use the same bathrooms!"

Nevertheless, Mrs. Lee, and those of her class knew that they had one ingredient that allowed them to resist integration, or at least mold it to their liking: money. For little Jefferson Lee there was private school, an immediate and effective alternative to the desegregation his grandparents disdained.

But for the father of Mickey Courage, desegregation was anathema, yet seemingly inescapable. There was no money for private school. What they did have, what they had struggled for, was a place in the pecking order: a nice all-white neighborhood of little two- and three-bedroom clapboard cottages, well trimmed lawns, a sprinkling of picket fences, the odd shade tree, flower gardens, and all-white neighborhood schools.

* * * * * * * * * *

Mickey found himself leaning against a parked car and listening to his father's speech at a neighborhood Irish tavern two blocks from his home. "This damned desegregation would change all we've worked for if we let them invade our schools with their little pickaninnies. Next thing they'll want to shop in our stores! Then they'll want to swim in the public pool! Next thing you know they'll be trying to buy into our neighborhoods, even going to our churches! I'll fight with everything I have before I let that happen! I don't have no money for private schools or moving, and we've got to take our stand here and now!"

Mr. Michael Courage's speech rambled on, but the basic text was, "Keep the Negro in his place," and the underlying theme was, "If you don't, then the next thing you know he'll be in *your* place."

Young Mickey Courage and Billy Sprouse listened to what they wanted to hear. They were both seventeen, couldn't care less about schools or neighborhoods, but were always eager to have a little fun, maybe cause a little ruckus. They were both strong and tough. Most of the town labeled them trouble and no good, and they were proud of it. Only the previous month, they had been permanently banned from the city pool. They had beat up the head lifeguard because he had told them to quit hassling the visiting girls' swim team from Farmington Country Club.

"You know, Mickey," said Billy, "this would be a good night to go coon hunting. Let's stash a bottle of my dad's Wild Irish Rose, then go on down near

Coon-town and kick some black ass."

* * * * * * * * * *

Jack Forester, Charlottesville's youthful common-wealth attorney, loved his town but understood its complex dimensions. Charlottesville in the mid fifties was a largely self-contented university town attractively located in the Virginia foothills of the Blue Ridge Mountains. Charlottesville had a population of about 25,000, of which 5,000 were black. Among the whites there was the following pecking order, bottom to top:

White trash: These families lived from hand to mouth. The father, if he was around at all, worked enough to buy booze and stay drunk for a while. His personal liquor supply, or lack thereof, determined his willingness to work at a variety of odd jobs: hauling, yard work, the kind of general labor he could always pick up by getting to the general employment building by 7 o'clock on any morning but Sunday. The white trash wife was discouraged from making any real effort to keep a neat house. With more kids than she wanted underfoot and the hog pen outside surrounded by mangy hound dogs on chains, her only abiding concerns were coming up with enough food for her family and hoping her husband would be kind to her whenever he returned home. The kids grew like weeds in an untended garden. They learned how to survive early or not at all. They learned to hunt and fish and kill for food. They learned how to steal, first from each other and then from their neighbors. They grew up tough, so they grew up mean. For them it was the only way to *get* grown up. White trash were lowest on the white man's pecking order. It was very important to them to have someone to look down on: the coloreds, the Negroes, or, when angry, "them niggers." They would do anything to keep them in their places.

Rednecks: The redneck worked with his hands and with the strength of his back and legs. He was different from white trash in that he worked long and hard and regularly. Unlike white trash, he could write a little and read some more. He was proud of the little clapboard cottage that was almost paid for. As he and the missus sat on their porch swing every Sunday afternoon, he surveyed his neatly mowed lawn, spreading out from the little flower garden to the sidewalk where his four children had gathered to start yet another episode of kick-the-can. It was true, he thought, that he drank a little too much Irish whiskey last night, but a hardworking man is entitled to a little drink now and then, just as he is free to pick his neighbors and his schools. Rednecks did not hate the black man if he stayed with his own, knew his place and didn't get uppity, but they would fight with anger, determination, and rage if outsiders or blacks tried to push into the community environment they had worked so hard for. This was what Mr. Michael Courage Sr. was telling his neighbors on that hot July night.

Merchant Men: The merchant man in 1959 was quite pleased to be doing business in Charlottesville. Ever since General Eisenhower had won the presidency in 1952, his common-sense business philosophy had been to let business get on with it and feature less government meddling. That is actually what the merchant man had done, and done well, too. In Charlottesville he had built up sizable assets, was taking vacation trips to Washington and Virginia Beach, and, what made him proudest, was sometimes sending his son to college. For the first time in all his knowledge of his ancestors, his son was going to be a college man. The merchant man's only major political concern in July 1959 was the fear that he would be forced to put his two younger children in private schools if that Communist traitor, Supreme Court Justice Earl Warren, finally forced desegregation on Charlottesville. The merchant man had nothing against colored people, but his kids weren't going to school with them. It just wasn't right. The cost of private school for his other children would mean not enough money to send his oldest son to college. And all because of the colored question.

Nouveau riche and *wealthy transplants: nouveau riche* had a lot of company in 1959. Charlottesville's economy had been good in those early Eisenhower years. Many industrious Charlottesvillians, by dint of work and foresight, earned and saved in real estate, banking and general speculation. *Nouveau riche* was now wealthy, yet still between classes. He struggled

to get into the snobby Farmington Country Club but
often had to settle for the more bohemian Fry Springs
Club. He sent his oldest son away to Choate, accepted
on grades since there was no clout, with the hope that
the son would one day be completely accepted into the
upper class that *nouveau riche* could never quite attain
for himself. Wealthy transplant was somewhat more
acceptable to the old-liner Charlottesvillian. Whereas
the origins of the *nouveau riche* were easy to place
and discern by Charlottesville society, the wealthy
transplant could project whatever he wanted to be
and possibly had been, as long as he had money and
manners. The wealthy transplant was never completely
accepted into the inner circle by the old-liners, but as
long as he was useful to them and could provide new
blood to the endless dinner parties, wealthy transplant
was admitted into homes and onto the cocktail circuit.
The *nouveau riche* and the wealthy transplant, with
their money and mobility, were not overly concerned
with the Negro question. They *were* concerned about
coming down on the right side of Charlottesville
society's opinion.

Old-liner: The Charlottesville old-liner was
special not only to Charlottesville, but to Virginia
and the rest of the old South. He traced his roots to
Thomas Jefferson and Robert E. Lee, to Stonewall
Jackson and John Marshall. In his veins ran the best
blood of Virginia, of the South, and of the country.
Old-liners did not have to have money, but it helped.
It was important to own land, preferably land that

had been in the family for generations. Many of the old-liner farms around Charlottesville had been in the same family since before the War Between the States. The old-liner was well educated, starting with a sprinkling of elementary public school to learn about other people. He usually went away to private school at eighth grade, and came home to college at the University of Virginia or attended one of the acceptable Ivy League schools, preferably Princeton. He often obtained a graduate degree toward some vocational pursuit, but, whether trained as doctor, lawyer, banker, or professor, his primary function was to maintain, continue and protect longstanding family traditions and property. The colored servants and field hands who lived on the family estate had been with him for generations. He frowned on big-city society, such as that in Richmond or Washington, as too shallow and too fluid. Though he rarely said so, it was essential to maintain the easily definable class system of which he was the leader in Charlottesville.

For Jack Forester, this was the basic breakdown of Charlottesville society through which he had to navigate carefully if he were to continue to be successful as the city's commonwealth attorney.

Chapter 2: Kidnapping

"Hey Roy, why ya want me with you anyway if you gonna step out with Charlene tonight anyway? 'Sides, I got better things to do den watch you foolin' 'round and spoonin' with her."

"Now just tighten up, Lucius. You could use the education. And tonight's the night. You know why? 'Cause bodacious Roy done looked out for poor old Lucius tonight! See, Charlene has got her cousin up from Gum Springs stayin' with her. Now, you know all those country girls do is watch the bulls play around with the cows. And you know she just ready for one of her own! Tonight is your night!"

"Wow," was about all Lucius could muster. He knew Roy talked big when it came to the girls. But he also knew that Roy was far from a virgin, and Lucius still was. Like so many young men before 'getting experienced', Lucius was convinced that getting laid was the single biggest hurdle to be jumped on the road to manhood. He started walking faster as he contemplated the prospects with Charlene's cousin.

"Slow down, Lucius. You movin' like a hound dog in heat! The girls'll wait, and we don't want to get there too early." Roy said this as he grinned knowingly at his friend.

Lucius forced himself into a slow, ambling gait, but his heart continued to beat with the thunder of anticipation.

Meanwhile, Mickey Courage and Billy Sprouse were making their way down Rafferty Lane, a road that intersected Peach Street. This intersection divided the all-white redneck neighborhood from which Mickey came and the all-black neighborhood of Lucius Johnson and Roy Amery. Charlene's house was on the edge of the black neighborhood, almost exactly at the intersection of Peach Street and Rafferty Lane, and all four boys, with distinctly different purposes in mind, were headed toward Charlene's house.

"You know, Billy, what the ol' man said about them niggers and this integration business, well Pop is usually full of hot air," said Mickey, "but he's right this time. Those coons'll try to come where we live. Hey, you know, I bet some of 'em might even think about dating our white girls. Could you imagine that?"

"Shit!" came Billy's comprehensive reply. "Pass the bottle over here."

"Well, anyway, it's gonna be fun tonight," Billy

said as he took another quick swig from the Red Eye '52 and passed it back to Mickey. "We'll teach 'em a lesson 'bout even thinkin' about white girls!"

Talking and drinking, the two boys convinced themselves that every black buck in Charlottesville was just waiting to get a white girl. Fortified with courage from a bottle, they felt reckless on that hot July night; they felt that their anger was righteous.

"We ought to break down every shack south of Peach and Rafferty!" shouted Mickey.

Billy looked at Mickey hard. "I ain't never liked no nigger no how. I'd just as soon cut one as look at one. Maybe I'll do it tonight." With that he pulled out a razor-sharp ten-inch switchblade and watched the fading rays of the sun glint off the blade's steel edge.

"Now go easy, Billy. We don't want to kill nobody, just have a little fun and scare a few coons." Mickey walked nervously as Billy tilted the bottle up and gulped down the last of the wine. Billy pointed the open switchblade at Mickey.

"You get a nigger, you do what you want. I get one and I think I might cut him up some." He looked idly into parked cars as they walked along. Suddenly, Billy stopped and grabbed Mickey by the arm. "Hey, let's take this car! Some rich-ass fool left his keys in it. Maybe we'll take a couple coons for a li'l *freedom* ride tonight."

Mickey stood as if frozen to the ground. He watched Billy jump into the car and start the engine with a roar. He had never seen the usually silent Billy talk so much or so recklessly. Now he was stealing a car. Maybe now would be a good time to back off before it was too late. After all, they'd both been picked up by the cops for fighting, various shopliftings, and thefts, and they had always gotten off with a stern warning because they were still juveniles. But this was different: stealing a car and Lord knew what Billy had in mind for any colored boys they picked up.

"Get in, Mick. Hurry up. We ain't got time to wait for the whole neighborhood to come out and see if this is their car we're stealing." Billy threw open the passenger door. Almost automatically Mickey climbed in. It was too late to turn back. All the hatred and violence he had heard about coming from the white trash he was seeing for the first time in his friend, Billy Sprouse. Mickey's hands began to tremble involuntarily. He shoved them in his pocket so Billy wouldn't see.

"Say, listen Billy," he said, "maybe this ain't such a good idea. Let's ditch the car and I'll go back home and sneak some more of the old man's wine."

"Shut up, Mick. Here, take a few sniffs of this and you'll really get high. Then we'll get some niggers." Billy shoved a large tube of airplane glue at Mick, who took a few sniffs, tentatively at first, and then, as he watched how Billy snorted it, he began deeply inhaling noxious fumes. The effect was almost immediate.

Suddenly Billy pulled the car over right at the corner of Peach and Rafferty. "Look," said Billy.

"Those two right there. I betcha they're holding some loot, too, from the way that one's dressed. Probably after some colored whore. Let's get 'em in the car."

"Wait a minute, now, Billy," said Mickey. "We can get in real trouble for this. I don't know--His thoughts drifted off in the haze of the glue fumes he'd sniffed. As Billy jumped out from the driver's seat, Mickey found himself lurching out of the passenger side to follow him.

"Hello, niggers. See this knife? Now don't say nothing, and don't do nothing but what I tell yuh, and yuh might not get hurt." In an instant Billy was holding the switchblade right under the exposed neck of the totally surprised and petrified Lucius Johnson. Roy looked behind him only to find Mickey standing there. Nobody moved.

"That's real good," Billy said. "Now you get in the car first, boy, and I won't cut the gizzard out of your friend here." Roy's skin tingled as he looked into the car he was supposed to get in. His palms were clammy. He wanted to run. He didn't want to leave his friend, but everything in him told him to run—now—while he still had a chance. He looked behind Billy Sprouse once more to measure the power, the strength, and the resolve of Mickey Courage.

"See my friend with the knife?" Mickey said to Roy in grisly lyrical tones, as he lurched closer. "He's gonna kill your friend if you don't get in. He'll really do it, you know."

"Listen to him!" rasped Lucius with the pressure

of the knife blade. "Please do what he says. Please get in the car." Tears were streaming down Lucius' face, and his whole body shook in convulsions. Roy crawled into the back seat of the yellow 1955 DeSoto Billy had stolen only minutes before.

"Alright, that's real good, nigger. Now Mickey, you get in and drive. I'll get in the back with this ol' boy, and if he and his friend don't do 'zackly what I tell 'em, I'll slit the neck on this one, and then get the other one! Hooooo-eee! We gonna have some fun tonight!"

Billy pushed Lucius before him, always with arm and knife around his neck, then shoved him into the back next to Roy and jumped in behind, quickly reapplying the knife blade to Lucius' neck.

"C'mon, Mickey. Let's go. Just get in and drive. I'll tell you where to go. This is gonna be the best time of our lives, ain't it niggers? You do just like we say, and we'll have a real fun time. If you don't, you're dead."

Mickey climbed into the driver's side and pulled away. Even through the haze of his drugged stupor, Mickey felt his head pounding, and he was perspiring heavily.

Chapter 3: Accidental Death

"Just keep goin' down this ol' road til I tell yuh to stop, Mick. We're gonna show these boys the sights." As Billy finished speaking, he searched in his pocket with his free hand for the tube of glue and began to sniff it again. His left shoulder and arm were wrapped tightly around Lucius Johnson's neck, the knife pressed against his jugular vein.

"Now which of you guys been trying to go out with our white girls?" said Billy, as he pressed the knife more tightly against Lucius' neck.

"We ain't nevah dated no white girl, and nevah even thought about it," pleaded Roy. "We ain't done nothing to you. Just let us go, will yuh?"

"Hmmm, well how much money you got, niggah? You know, Mick, I know where we can go party all night, long as we got enough money, say about six dollars." Billy smiled at Mickey, then glanced back at Roy. "How much money you got, boy? Ah ain't gonna ask you again!"

"Two dollahs, two dollahs and two bits," mumbled Roy as he held out two dollar bills and two shiny quarters. "Just take it and let us go." He was somewhat over his initial shock, and the fear he still felt for himself and for Lucius was coupled with anger and a growing rage at being addressed as 'nigger' and 'boy' and treated like an animal by this white trash holding the knife. Fear and caution controlled the rage for now.

"That all you got, boy? Well how 'bout our friend here?" Bill let up the knife pressure just enough to allow Lucius to speak.

"All's I got's fifty cents," rasped Lucius, who began trembling again as tears glistened in his eyes.

"Yeah, so here's my money," said Roy, handing over his two fifty to Billy. "Let us out here. We'll walk back to town, and we won't tell nobody nothing."

"Well shit, we still need three dollars, and you boys gonna get it for us. Slow down here, Mick. That's right. Now turn off at this fork onto that dirt road. Now keep driving 'til yah see a little old broke down farmhouse on the right. Cuz that's where we all be goin' for a little party."

Mickey did as he was told, but he was confused now, not so sure, and wishing tonight's adventure had never started. He, Mickey, had always been the instigator, and the leader, of the twosome. He had done the talking while Billy had been meaner, more vicious, in the numerous brawls they had gotten in, but that was because Mickey started the fights and Billy finished them for him. Now it was different; Mickey was no longer in control. As he drove the DeSoto up the rocky red road of Albemarle County clay he wondered what Billy had in mind. For the first time he was frightened of Billy and of what he might do.

"Hey Billy, what're we gonna do when we get to this house, anyway? Look, we got all the money they got on 'em. Let's throw 'em out of the car and head back to town. We can buy some good cheap wine with the money, and you know these boys are too smart to say anything—"

Mickey slowed down as if to stop and let Roy and Lucius out.

"Damn it, keep driving 'til we get to the house!" growled Billy. "You always think you know better'n me, don't you? Just because I didn't have no schoolin' after second grade, you always thought you were smarter. You start a fight an' I finish it. You start the trouble, I pay for it. Well, tonight is different! You do like I say. I tell *you* what to do. You understand, Mick?"

"Sure, sure, Billy. We'll do it your way. Just tell me what you want me to do. Let's have a good time, though. Let's have fun. You're still my friend, aren't yuh?" As Mickey Courage looked into those hard-glazed eyes he was trying to reestablish some rapport and gain some measure of control over this different and menacing Billy Sprouse.

"Yeah, I'm still your friend, I guess. Long as you do what I say tonight. I'm the boss. Billy chuckled ominously. I'm the chief and you're the injun. Right?"

"Right," said Mickey slowly.

As they approached the collapsing white house, Mickey felt almost as much a prisoner as Roy and Lucius. He had no idea what Billy was going to do next nor did he feel in control of his own actions; he felt merely the recipient of their consequences. Roy, for his part, was evaluating the deteriorating relationship between Billy and Mickey with the thought of breaking away with Lucius. Lucius, the switchblade pressed so tightly against his neck that it drew blood, was paralyzed with fear.

It was about eleven thirty p.m. on July 13, 1959 as Mickey pulled the DeSoto off the road next to a dilapidated white wooden farm house, stopped the car, and turned off the engine.

Billy turned to Roy and turned the knife so it glistened against the light of the full moon.

"Okay boy. We gonna let you go home to get some more money, say twenty-five. Now we don't care how you get it, but you be back here in an hour with the money or your friend is dead. Get goin'!"

Roy Amery threw open the door and jumped out of the car. He raced down the road. The sound of his feet hitting the crunching gravel seemed louder than thunder. His only thoughts were to get away, reach town and get help. As Roy disappeared in the shadows he could hear the chilling laughter of Billy Sprouse.

"Hoo boy, Mick! Look at that nigger go, just like a scalded cat at midnight. Hey, you know, I'll bet he's back here before midnight with that money."

Then, as his thoughts shifted, he continued. "Okay, let's get this colored boy into that house and tie him up." Billy opened the back door of the DeSoto and shoved Lucius out before him.

Mickey opened his door and fell in line behind Billy and his captive. All three headed up the steps and through the porch door of the abandoned house.

What's happening here? thought Mickey. *What am I doing in a kidnapping rap, and being run around by Billy? I knew he was a little slow and a little crazy, but I always had control. Now I've lost the handle, and he's gone completely out of his head. I've gotta get out of here!*

"Okay, Mick. Go in the kitchen and you'll find some rope. This is an old hangout of mine. I'll meet you with the boy right up there." Billy pointed out a wooden slide ladder to a loft above them.

Mickey drifted into the kitchen. He thought about escaping out the back door and running away, but he didn't. His eyes roamed mechanically in search of the rope. He found it under some RC Cola crates that had served as seating around the kitchen table, an empty whiskey barrel.

He carried the rope up the ladder to the loft and handed it to Billy. "Okay, now watch, Mick. This is how you truss a cow doggy." Quickly and efficiently Billy tied Lucius' legs to his hands, then around his neck, and finally the rope was attached to a center post.

"There, see Mick, he's all fixed up." Billy stood back to admire his work. "He can crawl around a little, but if he moves too much he'll choke hisself." And to Lucius he said, "You understan' that, boy? Okay, let's go downstairs, Mick. I got a little surprise for you while we're waitin' on the party money."

Billy led the way down the ladder, through the kitchen, and out the back door to an old woodshed in the backyard. He reached in and laughed as he pulled out a dusty, half-empty bottle of Thunderbird wine. "Yep, still here. This is my emergency supply for when the ol' lady kicks me out of the house. Sit down, Mick. It's cooler out here, and we might as well finish this off while we're waiting for that other nigger to come back with the money."

Mickey did as he was told again, marveling to himself that somehow he and Billy had changed places. Now Billy was the talkative one, the one in control, while he, brash Mickey Courage, was the silent mechanical one. He kept telling himself that the whole night of car stealing, glue sniffing and kidnapping was just a bad dream from which he would soon awaken, but he knew it wasn't. He also knew that Billy would hunt him down with the same knife that threatened Roy and Lucius if he tried to run away now.

Billy passed him the bottle of wine as the two

squatted with backs against the woodshed. Both were silent as they traded gulps of wine in the darkness. They had been outside for about fifteen minutes when Billy decided they should go back into the house and check on their prisoner.

They walked through the back door and both Billy and Mickey stopped cold as they looked through the kitchen to the main room and the loft above. There, swinging like a large clock pendulum and making big shadows on the walls, hung Lucius.

Suddenly galvanized, Billy raced through the kitchen to the rope and cut Lucius' body down.

"He's dead. The dumb nigger must have fallen off the loft edge while we was outside," Billy said. "Aw, shit. Well, I guess we can't wait for the money. We better skedaddle."

Mickey's legs went rubbery. He grabbed his head with both hands, and exhaled deeply. They had just killed someone—a real, live person—and all Billy thought about was not getting the party money. It was no use explaining to Billy that they now were part of a murder, too.

Mickey stood where he was in the kitchen. He watched Billy go through Lucius' pants pocket.

"Well, he wasn't holding no more money. But I guess I can use this pocketknife," said Billy, grinning as he carried it back to show Mickey, still standing in the kitchen.

"Now look, here's what we do. Leave the car here and get on home. Make sure you sneak in. Now when that other nigger comes back and finds his friend, he'll probably be too scared to say anything about us. He'll figure it might happen to him, too. But if he does talk, I'll get Johnny Shiflett at the Blue Moon Billiards to say we was there until eleven thirty before we went home. An' nobody gonna take the word of a nigger over us. Right?"

Mickey nodded listlessly. "Billy," he said, pointing to Lucius' crumpled body. "We better stay away from each other until all this blows over."

Billy said nothing, only grinned at Mickey once more as they walked out of the house and down the porch steps. Then he turned and took off in a trot, leaving Mickey alone to find his own way home.

At first, Mickey walked slowly towards the little houses with neatly mown lawns where everyone knew each other. He was heading toward the seeming safety of his neighborhood. He turned around and looked once more at the yellow DeSoto and the tattered white clapboard house beyond. What had happened that night? When did the lark, the joyride, become a kidnapping, a death ride? It was all too late now. He sensed his life would never be the same. And he would never get over the sight of Lucius Johnson's bulging eyes as he hung from the rafters of that house.

Mickey turned again toward town and began running toward the safety of his home.

Chapter 4: Arrest of Mickey Courage

Commonwealth's attorney Jack Forester sat in his car outside the tumbled-down cottage on the edge of town. He could already feel the heat on the back of his neck from the hot July sun. He watched as the body of Lucius Johnson was brought out and deposited in the shiny white Cadillac ambulance. Forester smiled inwardly as the ambulance driver pulled away with his cargo. The university hospital had had that car on order for six months now, and it just came in yesterday.

There's nothing that driver would like better than to really lay rubber with that brand new toy, thought Jack. *But he hasn't got a reason; that black boy he's carrying has been dead for over twelve hours.* This last thought brought the case back to Jack once again as he struggled to make sense of the facts he had gathered so far.

About one thirty that morning a young black boy had burst into the police station, where he found Sergeant Joe Carter on duty. The boy had been near hysteria, providing a good deal of humor to the assorted prisoners whose cells ringed three sides of the Sergeant's desk. Then both the truth and the gravity of his story began to sink in. Apparently he and his friend Lucius had been kidnapped at knifepoint by two drunken white boys and taken to an abandoned house. The boy, Roy Amery, was freed to bring back more money while his friend was held for that ransom. When he returned an hour later with money he had borrowed from his girlfriend, he found his friend "hanging like a rag doll," he explained. "They tied his hands and feet, and they must' a hung him 'til he died! They kilt him! They murdered him!"

Things moved pretty fast from that point, thought Jack. Sergeant Carter and one of his men drove Roy Amery out to the site he described and found the crumpled body of Lucius Johnson. They called into town and were told to cordon off the area and make sure the body was not moved until both the homicide department and the coroner's office had done their jobs.

While waiting for the others to arrive, Sergeant Carter continued to question Amery as the sun began to filter through the scrub pine surrounding the house where the killing took place. Sergeant Carter had learned from Roy the first names of the boys who had kidnapped him and Lucius: Mick or Mickey, and

Billy, the "the meaner one." Roy figured they were about seventeen or eighteen years old. He described Mickey as likely having red hair-- "It was hard to see in the night light"--, about six feet tall and weighing about one sixty-five. Billy, he thought, had black hair, was stocky, about five feet nine and one hundred sixty with his two front teeth broken off.

From as little information as that in a town where everyone knew everyone, Sergeant Carter was able to put a fix on Mickey Courage and Billy Sprouse. They fit the descriptions, and had been pegged as young toughs and troublemakers, but the most they had been brought in for before was assault and battery and shoplifting. No real violence was found in either of their records, although Billy had been described as potentially dangerous. Then the fingerprints on the stolen DeSoto, two positives on the steering wheel, and at the scene of the killing, matched to Mickey Courage, and several latent prints in the back seat placed Billy Sprouse in the car too.

Immediately the sergeant had a warrant issued for the arrest of Courage and Sprouse. Mickey was picked up easily at his home. He was found sitting on his door stoop, hands in his pockets, staring into the distance. The police had been unable to locate Sprouse at his family's house, a run-down shotgun shack complete with eight caged and underfed hunting dogs housed in the back yard. Billy was nowhere to be found. An all-points bulletin was issued for his apprehension and arrest while Mickey was taken in alone.

Mickey Courage cracked pretty quickly under police interrogation. Even a streetwise kid like Courage would break under the Sergeant's tactics: the threat of the billy club, the use of blinding lights, and the veiled promise of agonizing death in the gas chamber if there was no cooperation could be pretty persuasive.

Mickey explained to the cops that he and Billy were just out to have a good time, drinking a little wine, when Billy went crazy. "I think it was the glue sniffing that did it," he explained. He went on to say how Billy had stolen the DeSoto and that he only went along because he was afraid not to do so. From then on, Mickey said, it was like a nightmare he could not wake up from, beginning with the kidnapping of the black boys. "I thought we was just going to spook 'em at first in that old white house, hold one for ransom while the other was freed to get-- We just wanted some booze money," he said.

Finally he explained about Lucius, how Billy had tied him up so if he moved too far the rope would choke him at the neck, how they had gone outside for a drink of Billy's secret stash, and how, after they returned to the house, they found that Lucius had fallen off the rafters and hung himself.

"But good Lord, it was an accident!" Mickey pleaded. "We didn't mean to kill anybody. God, why did I ever go along with it?" The boy collapsed in sobs as he was taken from the room and led to a holding cell.

When Billy Sprouse is picked up, thought Jack Forester, *the ball is in my court. Here we are, in 1959, and the Governor's about to close schools to prevent integration. This case has got more racial overtones than the Civil War, and as commonwealth's attorney, I'm in the middle. And it's more than getting fundamental justice for the victims. If I don't handle this case just right, it could break this town apart.*

* * * * * * * * * *

Jack Forester was considered a product of Charlottesville's wealthy transplant class. He had lived most of his life in Charlottesville and was the son of a well respected banker. He'd been to all the right schools, gotten good grades, and been told on more than one occasion that he resembled Tab Hunter, one of the better-looking Hollywood leading men of the time. For his part, Jack had steadily climbed the social and political ladder. At age thirty-six, one of the youngest commonwealth's attorney Charlottesville had ever known, he was facing a crisis that could destroy not only his future, but even what he had now.

Jack backed up his old Chrysler Convertible, turned it around, and headed down the rock-and clay-filled gully that served as a driveway to the house where Lucius Johnson was killed. He turned left and headed slowly back toward Charlottesville, to Court Square and his office. Jack was still trying to put the case into perspective on its own merits and to decide what it meant to him as the commonwealth's attorney who must prosecute it.

On the surface, the events leading up to the killing were pretty clear. Two stoned and drunken white boys stole a car and kidnapped two black boys. One of the black boys was tied up while the other was let go to collect money to ransom his friend. In trying to get away, the trussed black boy inadvertently hung himself.

"What it amounts to on the surface is grand theft auto, kidnapping, and second- degree murder," Jack muttered to himself. *Two white boys who let their fun get out of hand would be one defense,* he mused. *They didn't mean to steal that DeSoto, only take a little joyride in it. They did not really mean to kidnap those black boys, only scare 'em a little. They shouldn't have had a knife, of course, but Billy would never have used it—after all, his people and their kind were the most frightened by this desegregation business. That and the wine and glue fumes clouded what little judgment those white boys had. As for the killing, well, obviously that was an accident. They could never have guessed that Lucius would crawl over to the edge of the loft and fall off.* Jack could almost hear this refrain, which would be coming not only from the disparate neighborhoods of Billy and Mickey, but from a large segment of the white community as a whole.

There were other factors to consider. While Billy

Sprouse was eighteen, Mickey Courage was still seventeen and could be tried as a juvenile. Mickey confessed to everything, while Billy was still on the lam. If Mickey turned state's evidence when Billy was apprehended, booked, and formally charged, Mickey, technically still a juvenile and an unwilling accessory to an adult, could get off with as little as three to five years, with three-and-a-half years of it on probation. What effect would that have on Charlottesville as a whole, and, in turn, on Jack's own career?

Black society, some levels of it at least, would see the injustice of the white man's legal system. That can't be helped, thought Jack. *Still it would be a fair measure of justice, given the circumstances.* As DA, Jack wanted to represent fairly all of Charlottesville, but voter turn-out was never as high in the primarily black Burley area as in Mickey Courage's neighborhood. *Hard-working blue-collar types, the lesser merchants, they vote heavily*, thought Jack, *and besides, they need someone to stand up for their interests. Why, the blacks have all of the North and the Supreme Court—even our president—to represent them. Yes, that's it. If I give Mickey Courage a break for cooperation and go for twenty years to life for that young animal Billy Sprouse, justice will be served. And I will have protected my interests as well— if I can pull it off.*

Jack turned off Park Street into Court Square. He passed the statue of Robert E. Lee sitting on his horse, Traveller, and reflected that Lee, not Lincoln, was still the South's spiritual father and leader.

As Jack pulled over and parked his car, he took one last look at the courthouse across from his office. It was so tranquil in the early morning with its thirty-foot American boxwoods out front masking its Corinthian columns. He knew he had to somehow separate this case from the desegregation business. He had to keep it a case of cause and effect. *If it becomes a white-over-black issue, I'll have lost for my community and for myself.* Jack looked at the largest of the spreading oaks that bordered the grounds around the courthouse. *That tree was alive when the Civil War began*, he thought. *I hope it's not here to see it happen again.* His earlier enthusiasm now subdued, Jack got out of his car and headed for the gaggle of reporters waiting outside of his office.

* * * * * * * * * *

When Jack Forester had been a school boy, and to a certain extent while he was a college student at the University of Virginia, he was considered quite an athlete. 'Crazy Legs Forester' was one nickname, and, with his blond hair and blue eyes, 'Stepping out with Jack' was regularly thrown around to recall his prowess from his fraternity days to the society cocktail circuit he had cultivated in the years since college. The urge to turn on his heels and dodge the hungry reporters' questions reminded Jack of the days when, with a forearm shiver and a fake to the left, he could escape his would-be tacklers on the way to the goal line.

"Hello, Jack," said Ralph Townsend. "We want to ask you about this here colored boy killing." The other reporters stood back, pads at the ready, as they watched Ralph do his work. At forty-five, Ralph Townsend was as round as he was porcine, the perfect example of too much Jack Daniels and too little exercise. In his perpetual white denim suit, broad-brimmed planter's hat and blue and white polka-dot tie, he could have passed for an extra from *Gone with the Wind*. Nobody knew whether Ralph dressed for effect or just didn't care. What they did know was that he was an excellent reporter who did his homework and feared no one. His interrogation methods were considered classics as far away as Richmond. He had established on more than one occasion, that when he was after something, when he smelled blood, he could be blunt to the point of ruthlessness. Some who had undergone his more brutal interrogations, followed by his write-up and telling summation in the paper, called him vicious and underhanded. To Ralph, seemingly oblivious to praise and criticism alike, the only thing of consequence was the story, all of it, no matter where it led or whom it hurt. "Let somebody else heal the wounds," he used to say at a little pub called The Press Box. "Our job is to show the wounds, all of them, and then watch them fester."

"Well now, Jack. You got yourself a real humdinger this time, don't you? How you gonna go after this one? Two young white boys who let their fun with two black bucks get out of hand? Are kidnapping and murder to be prosecuted to the fullest extent?"

"Now Ralph, you know I never talk about what I'm going to do until I'm before the grand jury for indictments. I'll only speak about the facts and evidence as I know they exist." Jack hoped to elude any further questions until he had had a chance to collect his thoughts. He moved through the crowd of reporters, still smiling in response to Ralph's wink, but blocking the door like a determined sentry at parade rest stood Jerry Parker. Weasel, as he was known to all for his physical and mental characteristics, had, as evidenced by his Hank Williams boots with the three-inch heels, never gotten over his lack of stature. Even wearing the boots, he stood no taller than five foot five. By way of compensation, Jack perceived, Weasel tried to bring everyone down to his level through carefully disguised double-edged questions that lent themselves well to his innuendoed reporting.

"Mr. Forester," began Weasel, his eyes subtly playing off the reporters behind Jack and then nervously returning to the six-foot-two figure whose way he was blocking. "Are you going to stand up for our people, or are you gonna cater to those Commie pinkos in Washington who're trying to push us out of our schools and neighborhoods with this integration thing? Why, if you go too hard on these ol' white boys, the NAACP is gonna win and this whole town is gonna just cave in to their demands.

"Another thing, you're young and ambitious. Everybody's watching you. You've done pretty well too, except for defending those two colored boys who robbed Gentry's Market a few years ago. You should never have gotten 'em off—made the whole black community a little bit uppity. But anyway, you're on the way up unless you blow this case. You are planning to come down on the right side of the fence, aren't you Forester?"

"That's a real nice speech, Weasel," smiled Jack as he reached in and grabbed the little man under either shoulder, lifted him off the ground and redeposited him in the midst of his amused colleagues.

"I really don't have anything solid to give you boys that you don't already know. As soon as I evaluate all the evidence, I'll let you know what we're going to go for. That should be at least another day or so." Once again his eyes met Ralph's as Jack opened the office door and escaped inside.

Chapter 5: Phone Call with the Governor

"Good morning, Alice. Some ruckus outside, huh?" Jack grinned at the woman who had been his secretary, his protector, his consultant and his friend for more than ten years. She had been with him since he graduated from the UVA's law school and elected to hang out his own shingle rather than join one of the prestigious law firms that had beckoned to him.

"Oh, Mr. Forester, am I glad to see you!" Alice responded. "I can deal with those nosy old fools out there alright, but the phone has been ringing off the hook. And you won't believe who's been trying to reach you. Not just the usual riffraff like the mayor, the sheriff and a few concerned citizens. Oh yes, and Mickey Courage Sr. called. But guess who else called? You won't believe it. This very Wednesday morning."

Jack looked at Alice with keen interest. She was

in a rare state of mixed excitement and agitation. Her petite, pleasantly plump figure was shaking like Napoleon at Waterloo. The usually immaculate dark beehive hairdo had tumbled down around her shoulders and her steel gray eyes showed a fire he had rarely seen before. "Okay Alice, who *did* call besides the usual riffraff?"

"Well, you'll never guess, so I might as well tell you. The governor himself called just a few minutes ago. Not one of his aides. I mean Governor Cartridge himself called, and he wants to get together with you in Richmond as soon as possible. He wants you to call him this morning to set up the appointment. And he told me to tell you that if you handled this case properly he would personally and publicly endorse your candidacy for the tenth congressional district set up for election next fall. How 'bout them apples, congressman?"

"Well, I guess I better not keep the governor waiting, Alice. I'll call him from my office to set up the appointment. You better hold all my calls until I'm through with this one."

Jack shut the door to his private office, something he rarely did unless he was with a client. Today he needed that privacy, even from Alice, to work out the Sprouse/Courage case in his own mind. And what did the governor want in exchange for his support? Is this the time he would compromise his career to further it, or would he stand firm on his sense of integrity, and perhaps blow his future? There was only one way to find out.

Jack began dialing the number Alice had given him, the special direct line to the Governor's office. He recalled what he knew of Governor Samuel S. Cartridge as he was waiting for the call to go through. Samuel S. Cartridge Jr., the Pale Quail as his detractors referred to him, had come up through the political ranks the easy way: he started at the top. His father, a general, had roots in Virginia going back to the original House of Burgesses. Samuel Cartridge Sr. married late in life, after an army career, Miss Lulubelle Austin of Waco, Texas, and became an instant oil millionaire. With his newfound millions, the General acquired a great deal of land in the Blue Ridge Mountains. He acquired considerable power through financial backing of favored young Democrats, and, of course, he acquired his only child, Sam Jr.

Jack knew that Sam had never quite measured up in the General's eyes. He had been second string on the prep-school football team, (and that only because of his father's influence, while the General had been an all-prep fullback for two years running. Unfortunately, Sam Jr.'s meager showing in academia failed to compensate for his inability to excel on the playing field. "You've got the mental acumen of that frog you're attempting to dissect," his biology teacher had once told Sam. He was, however, a plugger, and the General was a determined pusher. Between the two of them, Sam had gotten into and out of the University of Virginia with a BA and without flunking a single course. He had served in the Second World War with no noticeable distinction, but had seen some action in the Ardennes Campaign in 1945. It was during this time that, while running from an enemy mortar attack, Sam dove into what he thought was his own foxhole. It was instead a 30-foot ravine; as he tumbled to the bottom, he managed to wound himself in the leg with his bayonet. For this he received the Purple Heart, and when Sam S. Cartridge returned to Charlottesville, the General saw to it that a hero's welcome greeted him.

From there it was law school, required by the General, followed by three years with the law firm of Battle, Battle and Osbourne. During this time the General ordered Sam to join every civic club available. In 1956, the General called in all his markers, and from nowhere, appeared Sam S. Cartridge Jr.: lawyer, war hero, first family of Virginia, and the 1956 Democratic Convention's compromise nominee for lieutenant governor.

In Virginia, as in most states, the office of lieutenant governor was largely superfluous. The secondary representative of the governor, the LG was sent to places the governor could not or would not go, yet the lieutenant governor, for all his powerlessness, remained first in line to succeed the governor should he die.

In December 1958, Governor J. Ray Milligen died of a massive coronary, and Samuel S. Cartridge Jr. was governor of the Commonwealth of Virginia.

Jack Forester knew Sam Cartridge's complete history. He had grown up with him. He knew about the entourage of experts selected by Sam's father who had been with Sam Jr. since law school days. Governor Cartridge had done nothing wrong in his first six months in office. At his father's instruction, he had done nothing but let the administration float along. The strategy was to take credit for all the Milligen policies that succeeded, while divorcing himself from those that failed, thus setting himself up for the November 1959 gubernatorial election.

So what do he and the General want out of the Sprouse/Courage case? Jack Forester mused as the Governor's secretary answered his call.

"Governor Cartridge's office, Miss Johnson speaking. How may I help you?" Sophie Johnson was known for the help she could give or withhold when it came to access to the governor. At the ripe old age of thirty-two, with an Elizabeth Taylor face and a Jayne Mansfield figure, Sophie had learned as much in bed about politics as many learn in a lifetime. She had become the new governor's personal secretary soon after the office fell upon him, and, immediately afterward she made herself his mistress. Many of the governor's supporters felt that he was too much under the spell of this woman. It wasn't that she was his mistress—it was quite acceptable in upper Charlottesville society for a gentleman to enjoy discreetly the favors of a mistress—but when that mistress began to control the decisions he made, she became both unacceptable and someone to be feared. Such was the lot of Sophie Johnson.

"Hello, Sophie. Jack Forester here. I'm returning the governor's call."

"Well hello, Mr. Forester. It is so good to heah your voice. Why Ah haven't seen much of you since you got divorced." Jack had had a brief, disentangled affair with Sophie some years before. He had learned more than he had imagined possible from Sophie about Virginia politics, especially those closed-door secrets that could provide powerful ammunition on demand. And she had enjoyed him: tit for tat, simple and direct.

"Oh, yes. Governor Cartridge is just dying to talk to you about that Sprouse/Courage murder case. He thinks you can help him in his election campaign if you handle the case right. But Ah tell you true, Jack, Ah think he can help you right into the tenth district congressional seat in return. Don't give without getting, Honey."

"You're really something else, Sophie. Thanks. Listen, is he available now?" Jack asked.

"He shoah is, sweetie. Why he told me to break into whatever he was doing as soon as you called back. But Ah'm not to tell you that, Sophie giggled. "See, ol' Sammy doesn't want you to know just how important he thinks you are to him. He's afraid you might ask for a big favor in return. Hold on, honey. Ah'll get him for you."

"Hello, Jack. It's been too long," Governor Samuel

S. Cartridge boomed out. "Must be beautiful there in Charlottesville. With all that rain you've been having, the grain fields must be positively lush. It will make great hay for the cattle. And those hills, those rolling foothills into the Blue Ridge Mountains. God, how I miss them here in the dull flatlands of Richmond. I can hardly wait for the assembly's recess to get back to my farm up your way. You're a lucky man, Jack, to wake up in Blue Ridge country every day."

As usual with Sam Cartridge, Jack was left with a multitude of diverse questions and statements to respond to. This was always his technique, as Jack knew, when he had yet to show his true interest.

"Well, let's see, Governor," began Jack. "It is beautiful in Charlottesville, the grass is green and the hay is the best it's been in five years and the hills still roll. Now, what's on your mind, sir?" Even with the title it was hard to take S.S. Cartridge Jr. seriously sometimes, and Jack wondered who was pulling his strings on this particular call.

Cartridge laughed. "You've always been straight to the point, haven't you Jack? Might even say blunt. But you're a good man on the rise and we might be of use to each other. Did you know, Jack, I've always felt I was in your shadow when I wasn't in my father's? I remember when we were at Episcopal High School you starred as the football team's fullback for three seasons, while I barely got my letter my senior year. You captained the wrestling team while I stayed on the second team. You stayed on honor roll while I almost flunked out twice—and I was trying. Everyone said I was stupid. You remember, Jack?"

"Yes, I remember," said Jack. *And you were stupid,* thought Jack.

The rambling mélange of failure by comparison continued. "I guess we both did all right in college. Then in the war I got wounded in action," Jack chuckled to himself at this, "and came home with a Purple Heart, only to find out you'd come home with two bronze stars and a congressional citation for shooting down seven Fokkers as a flyboy."

"Oh, well," the Governor continued. "And then in law school I got a little jump on you by joining Battle, Battle and Osbourne. I never could figure out why you hung out your own shingle" —*a little independence,* thought Jack—but look at us now, Jack. You're one of the youngest commonwealth's attorneys to serve in Charlottesville, and me, I'm the youngest Virginia governor this century. You might even say you're in *my* shadow now, eh?"

"Sammy, will you please get to the point?"

"Hmmm? Oh, yes." Cartridge was still mulling over the results of his previous monologue, which had placed his career head and shoulders over Jack's. He was on top now. There was only his father's shadow to overcome. "Yes Jack, we're having a little political shindig at the family farm this weekend. We've decided that you could be important to the party's success in the fall election, and we need to have you there. If you're thinking about the tenth congressional seat, you're going to need our help too. The gathering is from four to midnight this Saturday in the main house. Will you be there?"

Jack knew he had no choice. These sometimes boring political get-togethers were essential if one was to be elected congressman from the tenth District in 1960. And he thought he did want that. But why was the party, and why, especially, were Sam Cartridge's people, so interested in him? What could he do? How could the way he handled the Sprouse/Courage trial affect so dramatically Cartridge's election bid? It was apparent to Jack that the suddenness with which the weekend's party was announced meant that it must center on his case. It was going to be an interesting weekend.

Jack thanked the Governor for his invitation and casually accepted. He quickly rang off, making a mental note to call Sophie back before Saturday and find out what the Pale Quail really wanted from him.

Chapter 6:
Capture and Interrogation of Billy Sprouse

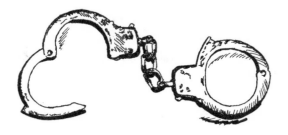

It was twelve thirty p.m. on Friday, July 17th, 1959, three days since the arrest of Mickey Courage on the Johnson/Amery murder/kidnapping case. Jack Forester leaned far back in his chair as he threw his legs up on the desk and closed his eyes. He felt the left knee click and lock as it occasionally did ever since the injury in the '43 UVA/Harvard game. Somehow he had kept the knee a secret from the Air Corps in '44 and had gotten his wings, but when he was tired, the knee would lock on him and begin to ache as it did now. Jack had told Alice to hold all but emergency calls for an hour with the hope of catching a nap.

At twelve thirty-five Jack dropped into a deep sleep. Five minutes later the buzzer woke him with a start. He glanced at the clock and cursed as he picked up the phone, and pressed the intercom button.

"This had better be good, Alice. I was having the

best rest I've had in weeks."

"I wouldn't have woken you for the world, Mr. Forester, except possibly for the capture of Billy Sprouse. They got him. Sheriff Bredlo is just busting a gut to tell you about it. He's on line two. I thought in this case you'd want to talk to him."

"Yeah, of course you're right. I'd better hear what the old redneck has to say before I hear it from the press."

Jack depressed line two as he prepared himself for Bredlo's onslaught.

"Hello, Barry. I understand you picked up Billy Sprouse. Good work."

"Well now, Jack. We didn't 'zactly pick him up," Bredlo responded. "We had to chase him over three counties. Why, the dogs lost the scent two days in a row. Lord, he was slippery. We finally got him holed up in a hollow in Greene County and he backed off in an old squatter's shack. Well, Ah had the boys surround the place and I walked clear in front of the cabin and told him to come out. Told him I'd come in myself and drag him out by the hair if he didn't come out right then with his hands on his head. Well, the son of a bitch shot at me!" Jack chuckled at the vision of fat old Barry, cigar in mouth, diving for cover in front of all his deputies. So Ah told the boys to open up. We must'a broke every windowpane in that old shack. Then Ah asked Mister Billy Sprouse if he might like to reconsidah. The little scumbag came crawling out on his belly; we got 'em twice in the leg.

And Ah personally handcuffed him."

"Well that's fine, Sheriff. But just save the heroics for the press. Is he all right?"

"Who, Sprouse? Oh, hell yes. One of the boys made him a splint and a tourniquet, and the doctor looked at him as soon as we got him back. Yeah, he's fine. Mean little son of a bitch, though. Says he won't say nothing. He just stares straight ahead and says he's gonna kill Mickey Courage if he squealed."

"Hold it right there, Barry! Don't do anything else until I get there. Just hold him. I'll take care of the questioning when I get there in about twenty minutes. Got it?"

* * * * * * * * *

Jack stood behind the one-way glass window that allowed a person to view unobserved the interrogation of a suspect. At the moment, the window revealed Billy Sprouse scowling and drumming his fingers on the scarred steel table behind which he sat waiting in the empty room. Two empty chairs, and a high-intensity lamp completed the view. The one-way window was Sheriff Bredlo's latest acquisition, and he was proud of it.

"Well, Jack, like I told you, this one's an ornery bastard. Won't say nothing 'cept that he's gonna kill squealers. Ah believe he would, too. Almost killed me before me and the boys rousted him out. That Mickey Courage boy says the Lucius Johnson thing was all

Sprouse's doing. Ah believe him now. This guy's a real killer." Barry Bredlo leaned back against the window as he sucked on his stogie and let out his belt a notch on an ever-expanding stomach.

"Right, Barry. Well, leave him alone for now. We don't want to lose the case before he has a lawyer. Let's wait for the court to appoint one on Monday. Meanwhile, please get me a full written report by five this afternoon. I'm going to need all the information I can gather for the meetings I have this weekend."

"Yeah, sure," Bredlo said. "The word is you're meeting with Governor Cartridge at his family estate. That right? Is it about this case? What's it all prove, Jack? Ain't this just a case of another nigger gettin' lynched?"

Jack smiled sardonically as he dodged the questions. "Just have that report to me by 5 o'clock sharp today, Barry. It's important that you do your job by the book. A lot of people will be watching very closely."

"Right, I got yuh, Jack." Bredlo chuckled. "No rubber hoses at midnight, right? Okay. All this fuss over a little ol' colored boy. And Ah'll get that report to you for sure. Listen, put in a good word for me with the gov'ner, will yuh?"

Jack nodded to Barry Bredlo as he took one last look at Billy Sprouse. He was reminded of Injun Joe in *Huckleberry Finn*, determined to kill Huck for squealing. He thought of Mickey Courage in the role of Huck Finn, while Billy Sprouse would play the role of the murderous Injun Joe. Then he looked at the beefy bigot Barry Bredlo again, keeper of them both and probably as much of a racist as Billy. Bredlo would bear close watching.

Jack nodded goodbye to the sheriff, then escaped to the fresh air outside.

Chapter 7: Meeting with Junius T. Jones

Jack walked three blocks to his office and picked up his messages from his secretary. He went into his office and sat down at his desk. He needed time to make order out of the chaos that had destroyed his regimen, the chaos that began with the killing of Lucius Johnson. *The hell with it*, he thought. *All this can wait until Monday. Before I meet with Governor Cartridge and his cronies tomorrow, I'm going down to the river and fish— fish and think. And if I'm lucky, I'll get to talk with Junius T. Jones; might help my head a little. Yes, that's where I'm going now.* Jack told his plan to the bemused Alice, who said she would handle the calls and manage the office.

Winding up Route 53, past Thomas Jefferson's home at Monticello and James Monroe's Ash Lawn, Jack headed for the James River. He turned off Route 53 onto Route 15 South and turned off again at Bremo Bluff. Driving slowly over the Southern Railway tracks, he parked his car just behind the levee that led down to the James River. Jack walked over the levee and saw the river swirling with eddies carrying the Virginia clay, tree limbs, and parts of old rafts and other debris. It had rained heavily the night before, and, as Jack moved to the old fishing landing, he thought that this was the time he loved the old river best: to sit and fish and watch what appeared from upstream, to see visions in the whirlpools to catch a fish or two, and maybe to see the old river philosopher, Junius T. Jones.

There, under the ancient willow where he had appeared so many times before, sat old Junius, perched on a decrepit old Royal Crown Cola crate. He had three fishing poles planted in the mud and was skinning an eel he had already caught. He was dressed in an old army fatigue jacket, World War II combat boots, bib overalls, and an engineer hat. It was his uniform of the day. When he looked into Junius' crinkled face, with its coal black eyes twinkling as he smiled with somebody else's teeth, Jack saw a man of sixty-seven going on twenty-five.

"Hello, Junius, having any luck?" Jack called out as he eased up behind the wise man from Fluvanna County.

"Well bless my soul, if it ain't Jackie Forester! You look like you've got the troubles of the world on your shoulders, boy. Come on down heah, and have a seat. We'll see if we can't catch you a fish."

Jack moved over to the smoothed off piece of limestone he had used as his fishing perch so many times before. "I don't know what it is Junius, but you can always read my mind. Hey, you still using those Champion spark plugs for weights?"

Junius chortled softly. "What do you care, boy? You didn't come heah to fish. You came to get that weight off your soul. But yeah, Ah gots a Champion on this line, AC on this one, and—Ah not partial, you know— an old horse clinch on this one. And all Ah've got is this ol' eel, which Ah gonna use for bait. Them fishes don't seem to take to my night crawlers today." Junius paused as his finger nimbly finished the skinning and vivisection of the unfortunate eel. "Now tell ol' Junius what it is got you slumping like a hound dog out of season."

Jack recounted the Lucius Johnson/Roy Amery murder/kidnapping case and the political stakes that had grown around it. He told Junius about his conversation with Sam Cartridge Jr. and about the upcoming strategy meeting at General Cartridge's estate.

"Yes, Ah already heard about that case, Jackie. Drizzle told me about it. You remember him, he's the younger brother of Rainhat Jefferson, my cousin. Anyway, he was fishing down here just the other day. Well, he read about it in the *Daily Progress*, plus his cousin is married to Lucius Johnson's aunt. You don't got to read about it to know about it."

Jack chuckled. Old Junius probably knew more

about the case through his gossip lines than anybody who had read the *Progress* or any of the national papers. Rainhat Jefferson was the shoeshine boy at the Courthouse Barbershop in Charlottesville, and he had been since 1941. He heard everything and had an uncanny ability to predict both weather and people. He had gotten the name 'Rainhat' because he always wore one when he thought it was going to rain. Rainhat was so accurate that some customers had been known to go home for their umbrellas when they saw him with his head covered. Drizzle, Rainhat's younger brother, who also worked at the barbershop, had acquired his nickname for obvious reasons: he never wore a rainhat and often got wet. Between his two sources, Rainhat and Drizzle, Junius had an inexhaustible, and largely accurate, record of the local news.

"Well Junius, since you probably know more about the case than I do, what do you think will happen when I meet with the Governor and the boys tomorrow? Personally, I just don't like the smell of his invite," Jack explained.

"Now Jack, don't go leading with your chin again. Don't you remember what happened to you at Gentry's Market with Toby Morris?"

"Good Lord, Junius. That little fight happened more than twenty years ago! What in the world does that have to do with this thing?"

"Oh, Jackie. Ah can see Ah still got to school you. Yes, it was just a little fight. Ah don't think you got but one punch in. And it happened a long time ago. But didn't you learn something from how you got beat up? Don' you 'member the lesson of eight?"

"Yes, I remember everything about it, Junius, especially the pounding I took," Jack retorted. He thought about how he had run into Toby Morris outside of Gentry's Market so long ago. As usual, Toby, a muscular, slope-headed member of the Cheeko gang was bullying some smaller kid about being on his turf. Usually Jack would have ignored the typical after-school scene, but somehow, on that day, everything Jack hated, everything that frustrated him, was projected onto the pimple-laden face of Toby Morris. Without realizing consciously what he was doing, he whirled around to face Toby and followed through with a left hook that came almost from the ground and smashed into Toby's cheekbone.

Toby fell to the ground and got slowly up. He was stunned, not only from the physical attack, but also from the shock of being challenged. But he was recovering rapidly.

"What fo' you do that, Jack Forester? Now I'm gonner kill you, boy," he stammered.

"Hold it right there, Toby," young Jack shot back. "I know karate and I could kill you with one blow." Jack tried hard to recall the Classic Comic book article on the ancient fighting art he'd read. "I'm going to count to ten, and if you're not gone by then I'll have to use it. One, two, three—"

Jack blinked in the midst of remembering and

refocused on Junius. "Yeah, I remember it well."

"Well Jackie, you should'a figured the cards you held. You surprised him with that left hook. You had him buffaloed with that karate stuff. But when he didn't leave at eight, *you* should have."

"Well, maybe Junius, but—"

"Hold on, Jackie. Don't run away from the point. At eight he was still there. That meant he probably wasn't gonna be bluffed. That meant you should've got the hell out. Cuz at nine he wasn't gonna wait for you to hit him at ten! Not Toby Morris! And he didn't. That's when he started to beat you like a drum. Lord, if old man Gentry hadn't broken it up, Toby Morris could'a broken every bone in your face, Jack."

"This isn't exactly my favorite story, Junius. I sure hope it's worth hearing again."

"Course it is, Jack! It's learning the value of the number eight. Ah hope you get it this time. Look heah, Ah know your heart. You wanna tell that Governor and the whole world that you're gonna prosecute these white boys what killed Lucius Johnson to the fullest extent of the law. Now you also know that the Governah is up for reelection this fall, and if he can become a hero to his redneck supporters, that would help him immensely. That could be accomplished by an arrangement whereby the white boys, or one of 'em, gets off the murder charge. The Governor can somehow present that as a victory for states' rights and segregation ovah the Supreme Court and integration."

"Yeah, but Junius, you know me. I'm not just going to fall in cahoots with Sammy Cartridge."

"Now Jackie, Ah know that and you know that, but do they have to know that? Don't count past eight for them, Jack. Stand on your principles. Don't agree to nothing, but don't completely shut them out. You need the room to maneuver. You need to know what they're really planning on this weekend, without letting them know what you're gonna do.

"Why, if they knew that you weren't gonna deal with 'em at all, Jack, weren't gonna play political ball, so to speak, they would bury your political career in a beggar's grave. So when yuh count to ten tomorrow, remembah to stop at eight, give both you and them a chance to back out gracefully. If you count to ten there won't be any out. And somebody will have to pull the Cartridges off your political carcass."

"Boy, you are a sly dog, Junius. If I ever run for president I want you for my campaign manager."

"Probably wouldn't work in the north," chuckled Junius.

"Probably not, but listen, Junius. What's the difference between not telling the Governor's boys now how I plan to prosecute or waiting until I'm in court? They're gonna try to bury me politically anyway."

"No Jack, that's the difference between stopping at eight and going on to ten. If you wait until court to reveal your strategy, it will be too late for them. That's when you count to nine and ten. As Ah know you can, you blow the lid completely off what those white boys did to Lucius Johnson and his friend. It'll be too late for S.S. Cartridge and company. By then you'll have the whole county, and most of the community, black *and* white, behind you. You'll be the hero, and Governor Cartridge will do anything for you to share some of that limelight."

"Junius, I swear, sometimes you're the smartest person I ever met."

Junius looked at Jack long and hard and smiled. "Sometimes Ah think Ah is too, boy. But you is one of the best, black or white, and Ah got to do what Ah can to guide you right. Now get along home. You didn't come heah to fish. Ah did, and Ah ain't caught nothing since you showed up. Get outta heah, boy. But remembah what Ah told you when you're with the Governah tomorrow. Remembah the story of the eight."

Jack gave Junius a big bear hug and trotted back to his car. *Somehow*, he thought driving back to Charlottesville, *Junius cleared it all up. It's all coming into focus*—he hoped.

Chapter 8: Visit to Four Oaks Farm

It was Saturday, July 18th, an unusually cool July day, as Jack drove his 1951 black Chrysler convertible along Skyline Drive. He had the top down and, although he was afraid he might never get it up again, the beauty of the treetop greens and crystal blue sky made the risk worthwhile. There was a cool breeze in his face and the most spectacularly clear view of the Shenandoah Valley spread out below him. But this was not an ordinary cruise into the Blue Ridge; Jack was headed to Four Oaks Farm, the General, his son the Governor, and their people. For Jack, it was a kind of rendezvous with destiny: *like Gary Cooper in High Noon*, he thought, as he tried to remember how *High Noon* turned out.

He turned off Skyline Drive onto county road 648, drove for two miles, and there it was: Four Oaks, quite possibly the most beautiful country estate in the Shenandoah Valley. Four Oaks was not a farm. Yes, there were riding horses, brood mares, the odd yearling, several two-year-olds, and a stallion. There were four hundred Black Angus cattle, a full-time farm manager, and lots of working tenants in residence. But it was all for looks. It was whatever the General's wife's money could buy to make Four Oaks the picture-perfect country manor retreat. The intent was to impress, to persuade, and, if necessary, to intimidate the designated guest.

Jack drove slowly down the long drive that led to the main house. It reminded him of those tree-lined avenues of Brussels Paris that he'd seen during the war. He glanced at the endless line of Lombardy poplars on either side of him. They seemed to pull him deeper and deeper into the Cartridge sphere of power. Who but General Cartridge would spend $200,000 on transplanting full-grown trees whose total life span was twenty years at most?

Further in the distance Jack could see the white post-and-rail fence that surrounded the estate, a fence that went on literally for miles and required the full-time, year-round services of one worker tenant to keep it that immaculate white.

Finally, he glimpsed the four majestic spreading oaks that had been planted at the four corners of the main house some 150 years ago. The three-story Georgian house itself was dwarfed by the oaks' magnificence.

Jack pulled around the circular driveway to the

steps of the great mansion. There, at the top of the steps and flanked by the Corinthian columns that made the façade complete, stood a smiling Governor Samuel S. Cartridge, dressed in a white linen suit, wearing a white fedora hat, and pointing at him with his gold handled cane.

He looks like the cat about to swallow the canary, Jack thought. *And I think I'm the canary.*

"Why hello, Jack," the Governor said, oozing down the steps. "So glad you could make it. Come on in and I'll introduce you to everyone."

Jack shook the extended hand and steeled himself for what was to come. It was almost like the feeling he used to have before flying his P-38 into another combat mission.

Governor Cartridge escorted Jack up the porch steps through to the great hallway. He had his arm around Jack's shoulder as he guided him past various rooms filled with people and headed toward the back veranda and the 'important' people. Apparently the others were just for show, as Jack noticed here all the members of Sammy Cartridge's brain trust. He noticed that women were excluded from this room, a tribute to the General's chauvinism and an added indication of the kind of meeting going on here.

Grover Alexander, the Governor's press secretary, with his darting ferret-like eyes, was heatedly conferring with the General, his real boss. Grover, was widely described as "that jackal on hind legs," a reference both to his physical and his mental demeanor. When it came to gathering information or disseminating propaganda, however, he was a genius. "I don't like him much," the General was heard to say, "but he's the best since that Nazi Goebbels. He has his uses."

And there, lounging against the porch railing, stood long and lanky Beasly Potter, arch lobbyist and influence peddler. When the General or his son wanted a critical bill passed or vetoed in the legislature, Beasly knew which buttons to push and, if necessary, which skeletons to reveal.

Jack then spotted Alex Ramos, darkly handsome with his coal black eyes and the athletic build of a panther. Ramos was the governor's chauffeur and the General's muscle man. Ever since Ramos had come out of the Special Forces in Korea, disappeared into the mob politics of New Jersey and been reclaimed by General Cartridge, everyone knew what he was: Alex Ramos was a cold-blooded killer. For protection or for sheer informational purposes, as the Cartridges' enemies knew well, Ramos had no equal. He gave Jack an appraising look as the younger Cartridge pushed him toward the General and his circle.

"Well, Mr. Jack Forester, our youthful commonwealth's attorney from Charlottesville. Ah am truly pleased Sammy was able to get you up here," the General called to Jack. "It's been a long time, but Ah've been keeping up with you, boy. Yes sir, you're building yourself a future: just keep making the right moves. You've got a very delicate case to prosecute, this so-called Lucius Johnson murder."

Boy, he's not wasting any time, Jack thought to himself as he was ushered directly into the General's inner circle.

"Now look, Jackie, why don't you have a cool drink?" The General motioned and from nowhere appeared a white-waistcoated servant offering mint juleps, mimosas, and gin and tonics. Jack settled for the gin and tonic. "Alright, make yourself at home and circulate for a few minutes. Lots of real pretty ladies here for an eligible bachelor like yourself. Well, enjoy. And don't forget to say hi to my wife, Lulubelle. She's a real fan of yours. Alex here will come get you when it's time for our meeting, Okay?"

General Cartridge moved off, and his entourage, including his son the Governor, melted away as well. Jack was temporarily alone. He leaned back against the porch railing and observed the assembled guests anew. *My god,* Jack thought. *Here are all the major political powers in Virginia, the king and the king-makers, and they all come running when the General calls.* Jack spotted Lulubelle Cartridge, leather-faced from too much sun, paunchy from too many club lunches, and laden with diamond earrings and necklaces. Her dowry had primed the Cartridge political machine. Now that the General had made many more fortunes with that original one, the slightly countrified Lulubelle drifted around like an aged pompom girl at the ballet. To the General, she was an embarrassment. He suffered her presence only in payment of a debt to the past.

The two Senators from Virginia, Baily and Jackson, were engaged in a heated discussion in the corner. Senator Baily was principally known for his continuous bills and riders submitted in various forms for states' rights, and it was said that Senator Jackson never voted at all before calling the General's office for instructions.

In addition to the assorted congressmen, the party was swollen with artists, the moneyed and the moneymakers, and the first families of Virginia and those clawing to get there. Flowered designer dresses mingled with linen suits and spats, wide-brimmed hats with Southern club ties, and receding hairlines with rouge and mascara.

"Okay, Mr. Forester, the General is ready for you now." Alex Ramos broke Jack's people-watching reverie. "Follow me."

Threading his way through the smiling faces, Jack found himself with Ramos before a door at the end of a narrow hallway. The door opened into a small but lavishly furnished private office. The walls were of wormy chestnut, the oak floors covered with oriental throw rugs, and there was a Louis Quatorze desk flanked by two Tiffany lamps. The wall behind the desk was covered with diplomas, awards, and memorabilia from the General's many years in politics. He was seated at his desk. His son the Governor, stood at the General's side.

"Okay, Jack, come on in and sit down." The

General motioned to a chair. "Alex, close the door after you and stand outside, please: we don't want to be interrupted by anyone."

"Yes sir, General." Ramos walked out and closed the door behind him.

Jack looked across the desk into penetrating grey eyes. For the first time he felt the concentrated power harnessed in that stare for which the General was so well known. Jack grabbed an elephant-shaped paperweight in front of the General and spun it around towards him.

"All right, General," said Jack. "Now Sammy here invited me up here for this little party, and I'm grateful to be included. But let's get to the point. What do you want from me? What can I do for you?"

"Oh no, Jack, it's what we can do for each other. I know you're headstrong and dedicated and all that, and you should have a hell of a future, but help me out. I'm going to make you a proposition that may not sound entirely ethical to you at first inspection, but I want you to think pragmatically. I want you to think of the superior importance of the ends as opposed to the methods of reaching them, okay?"

Jack thought of Junius T. Jones and the lesson of eight as he nodded to the General. "I'm certainly willing to hear you out," he said.

"Before you make any judgment?"

"Yes, sir."

"Good. Now Sammy," said the General, nodding briefly at his son. "Sit down and don't say anything.

I want you to be here because what happens here can greatly affect your reelection campaign. But keep your mouth shut til we're through, okay?"

Governor S.S. Cartridge Jr. nodded meekly and sat down in an overstuffed armchair. He looked out the lone window in the room as if detaching himself from the proceedings.

Chapter 9: Showdown with General Cartridge

The General turned back toward Jack and began his peroration. "Jack, Ah want you to understand why this case is so important. It's not just a white-over-black kidnapping/murder case. And it's not just about integration. It's about war—an ongoing war. And an ongoing conspiracy to bring down the South and all it stands for."

General Cartridge looked deep into Jack's eyes as he continued. "Now hear me out. You know, Jack, it didn't begin with the War Between the States, the conspiracy against the South," the General began. "No, that was just a war of competing economic interests. The slavery issue was thrown in by the North for morality and international opinion. Christ, Lincoln only freed the Negroes in the conquered South in his Emancipation Proclamation of 1863, nowhere else. Reconstruction was a nasty period for the South, but no worse than any conquered territory sees immediately following a war. Hell, we got rid of the carpetbaggers and the low-life scallywags quick enough, and we put the emancipated voting Negro back in his place.

"The 1880s and '90s were tough on the South only because the old agricultural dependence on cotton and tobacco was dying. And it took time to adjust to the new industrialized economy of cotton mills and woolen mills. It was a painful adjustment, but, combined with the comeback of tobacco and the return of cotton to prominence, the twentieth century saw the slow rise of Dixie again. Teddy Roosevelt openly admired the individualistic spirit of the South and the quality of the fighting man that came from there. Woodrow Wilson himself was born and raised in the South.

"In the early 1900s, the South regained its clout in Congress. The Byrd machine in Virginia, Strom Thurmond in South Carolina, and Huey Long in Louisiana—all were potent forces. While not all were palatable to me, they spoke for the South, and they fought for her because they loved her.

"No, the real conspiracy to kill the South as we know it came not from Lincoln, but from Franklin Delano Roosevelt. That crippled Communist hated states' rights and everything they stand for. Roosevelt's New Deal was nothing more than a package to strip the South of all control within the boundaries of their states. Sure, he and his federal cronies subsidized schools and housing and provided soup kitchen affairs, but at what cost?"

"He held our hard-earned tax dollars as an axe over our heads. All our elections were monitored by the feds, with the threat that we wouldn't get our share of federal welfare unless we met certain electoral standards. What standards were they talking about? The Roosevelt Congresses were probably the most corrupt and buyable since reconstruction and the days of that drunk, U.S. Grant. Roosevelt himself threatened to stack the Supreme Court if they refused to reach the decision he desired, and they did. They prostituted themselves to Roosevelt, supposedly to save the court."

"Yes, Jack, the Roosevelt administration sought to wrest or overturn every last vestige of states' rights, and, in the process, threatened to destroy democracy itself.

"And what was his vehicle, his symbol, the sanctified flag in which he could wrap his every malicious objective? You guessed it: the poor ol' colored boy who was being so badly treated in the South. Even in 1935 our beloved F.D.R. told us how badly we were treating the colored, and how it was time to improve their lot. Oh yes, our knowledgeable president, who may have had a black nanny, went to Groton Prep School, that haven for WASPs in the North, and finally to that cathedral for Communists, Harvard. Why, I bet the closest he's been to a colored person beyond his nanny is his valet and shoeshine boy, but he was gonna tell us how to run our colored, see. And you know why? Forget all those platitudes about equal rights and emancipation. Bullshit. Roosevelt just wanted a tool through which to consolidate and centralize power in the federal government." General Cartridge twisted the elephant paperweight so that it pointed directly at Jack. Then he continued.

"Well, for the better part of his three-plus terms, almost fourteen years of purgatory for the South, he succeeded. The South was in shambles, nearly stripped from the control of her true leaders. The combination of the Depression and Roosevelt's leadership wreaked havoc on our political systems. Little scallywag demagogues like Huey Long were voted into power by ignorant redneck whites and Negroes who couldn't write, but were paid to place their X in the right column. The finest of our youth were leaving their native states in disgust.

"Only the second World War was able to save us from our Rooseveltian agony. As regiments were formed and strengthened and sent overseas, once again we tasted the glory and the pride that was the real South. You remember, Jack, it was the heroism of southern pilots like you that gave us the renewed strength to fight the cancer of Roosevelt and federalism.

"And things began to change for our friend Roosevelt. In 1945 the war was going well despite him. Even though he tried to give away most of Europe and Asia to Stalin and Russia at Yalta, America, with her technology, her vast resources and her heart, remained the supreme power in the world. And she was tired of Roosevelt. A great movement was afoot against allowing three consecutive presidential terms, much less four. Even some of his staunchest allies felt that twelve years were enough for any president. Another term would make the presidency resemble Roosevelt's personal dictatorship.

"When he died in '46, I thought the South's long nightmare was over. The abruptly elevated Harry Truman was a good old boy from Missouri, a former haberdasher made good. We expected so much from him, but outside of executive swearing and playing poker in the White House, he was a disaster. He continued to push black voting rights down our throats, again with the threat of cutting off federal aid, which they had already stolen from us to begin with.

"And then Eisenhower was elected in 1952: midwestern origins, West Pointer, great war general in the European theater of World War II. He was a champion of individual rights and of states' rights, or so we thought. That's why we overwhelmingly supported him in the South in '52."

"And what does he do? Appoints that chameleon Communist liberal Earl Warren to the vacancy as chief justice of the Supreme Court. And what does Warren do? He tries to destroy the South with *Brown v. Board of Education*. Believe it or not, DA Jack Forester, that is what our meeting today is all about, fighting back from that abominable decision."

General Cartridge pushed his chair back and gazed out the window for a moment. Then he turned abruptly back toward Jack.

"That cowardly decision of 1954 marked a funny kind of watershed for the South. Once again the federal government, in the form of the Supreme Court, oozed into the purview of the states and their inalienable rights. Those Communist baboons and their head jackal, Earl Warren, created the final law of anathema when they told us states how to run our own schools, how we've got to integrate them: according to their standards, or else. The 'or else,' we've since been told, is the withholding of federal funds, and even the National Guard has been mobilized to force their wonderful emancipating integration on us, Jack!"

Jack sat impassively, silently, awaiting the General's challenge to him. *But how much more of this hackneyed history lesson do I have to listen to?*

"Once again it's the poor ol' Negroes that they're using as a vehicle to keep the South down," said General Cartridge. "You know it's true, Jack. Those northern liberals don't give a damn about the Negro. The Negroes up north are all hidden in city ghettos, while those creeps in Washington try to force integration on us and our children as they move out to all-white neighborhoods or send their children to private schools. They are moral hypocrites. Yes sir, they're going to see the Negros' rights taken care of down here. They'd probably like to set up the Negroes in government down here just like in Reconstruction days. Meanwhile, they have their colored neatly locked away in concrete jungles, starving in summer, freezing in winter, with no real education at all. But they're invisible and so not subject to the world's judgment. Those hypocritical bastards.

"But this time, Jack, they've gone too far. This time we'll stand and fight, and win, by God. I said that *Brown v. Board of Education* marks a watershed in the life of the South, and indeed it does. In the days of Reconstruction, the North and its scallywags tore at the vitals of the South, and we did nothing because we had nothing. Our rich farmlands were barren from five years of fighting, the heart of our courageous youth scattered in a thousand graveyards. That was 1865.

"This is 1959. We've struggled and sometimes stumbled, but by God we *have* risen again. We've beaten the droughts, and we've beaten the boll weevil, and until Roosevelt we were regaining our strength and our power over internal state's affairs. We are strong today, where the South was barely alive in 1865. Our youth is strong and proud once again. We proved in World War II and the Korean conflict that the fighting men of the South are the best anywhere. Our economy is as strong as it's ever been. Tobacco from Virginia and the Carolinas, soybeans and sugar cane, the return of cotton in the deep South; it's all coming together. And, oh yes, all those sanctimonious northern industrialists have relocated their woolen mills and textile plants to our states because the labor is cheaper and works harder. All of that has made our economy strong. The heart of our people, the courage of our young and the strength of our economy will not let them do to us now what they did in Reconstruction days. We will stand and we will fight. And we will win.

"We will not be forcibly integrated. We will protect our neighborhood schools. We will defend our poor whites and our middle-class whites who fought and struggled to build their neighborhoods and their way of life. We will fight for their rights and they will support us in the upcoming gubernatorial campaign and in your congressional race. We will bring these besieged people of the lower middle class back into the southern Democratic Party. And with this new base, our kind of people will win locally, statewide, at the congressional level, and, ultimately, we will win the presidency."

General Cartridge paused briefly and then continued. "Now here's where you come in, Jack. You have the unique opportunity to send our message first to Charlottesville, to whites and blacks alike. That message will spread like the expanding front of a hurricane, and your prosecutorial tone will be the eye of that hurricane."

"As you know, Jack, this white-over-black murder/kidnapping is getting local, state and national exposure. Why? Because those socialist northern liberals want to see to it that our dirty rotten rednecks get the maximum penalty for kidnapping two Negroes and killing one of them. If we do what's right with a little pressure from them, they figure they can pretty well dictate when and how we integrate.

"But we're not going to knuckle under, Jack. And we're not going to take their interference anymore. We're strong and we're mad. Now the way you prosecute this case will be the first step in delivering our message to the North, their media people and anybody else who needs to know: stay the hell out of our affairs! We'll run our schools and our courts and our neighborhoods the way we see fit. We'll abide by the Constitution, and we'll provide the colored with good schools and neighborhoods, *in their own neighborhoods*. And that's what the Constitution says: 'equal under the law' are all its citizens. Well, okay, they shall be equal, our colored folks, but we're going to live and eat and go to school separately, because that's our right. And we are prepared to fight to protect that right, and to win.

"Now that's the message, Jack. Ah suppose you're still wondering how you fit in." Jack nodded, but he was also wondering if the General, whose face had gone crimson with the effort and intensity of his monologue, would ever get to it.

"Okay, here's my proposal on how to handle the Johnson/Amery kidnapping case fairly, yet still send our message through all the convenient media coverage. As we all know, Billy Sprouse was the ringleader that night. Mickey Courage was bullied into the whole affair. It was Billy Sprouse who tied up Lucius Johnson in such a way that if he moved he would hang himself, and Sprouse has a long record of break-ins, petty larceny, and incidents of violent behavior. Am Ah right?" Jack nodded and even smiled as he realized that the General's private sources had amassed as much privileged information as he had in his capacity as commonwealth's attorney.

"Now, whereas that white trash Billy Sprouse was the instigator of the whole affair, Mickey Courage represents, to an extent, the frustrations of a whole class of people mixed up in this, the hard-working white. Mickey hears his father's harangue about integration and the black threat to their neighborhoods, their schools, their jobs, and their hard-earned way of life. What can be done about it? They don't know. They're scared and they're mad.

"So later on, when he sees a couple of Negro boys almost in their territory, he decides to razz them, that's all: get rid of the frustration and anger built up by his father's speech. It was his companion, that little cutthroat Billy Sprouse, who pushed him unwillingly into kidnapping. And, of course, the so-called murder had nothing to do with Mickey Courage. Are you with me so far?"

"General, let's just say I understand your logic to this point. I don't follow the connection between Mickey Courage and this message you want to send out," Jack said, diplomatically.

"Fine, Jack. If you follow me so far, the rest is easy.

First of all, Ah suggest that you throw Billy Sprouse to the wolves. He's a no-good, he's over eighteen, and he engineered everything that happened that night. Maybe he should get a conviction of first-degree kidnapping and felony murder. He doesn't matter. Just put him out of circulation for twenty to forty years. That'll show those neo-liberal newspaper bastards that our system of justice works just as well for our colored as whites. And that issue won't detract from getting the message out through your description of Mickey Courage or his motives. Through you, Mickey Courage will speak for the anger and frustration of every hard-working white from lower to upper-middle class, and through him, you will show the strength and determination of southern Americans to fight for the right of neighborhood autonomy.

"First Ah suggest you persuade Mickey Courage to turn state's evidence. He's already been more than cooperative, and my people tell me his parents are a good and hard-working Christian couple who would want their son to do so. In return, you plea bargain him to a suspended sentence of five years as an unwilling accessory to manslaughter. Judge Donald Stevens will be the presiding judge. He's a close friend of mine. Ah'm sure he'll go along with your recommendation for leniency in your capacity as DA."

"So, in effect, you throw Billy Sprouse to the wolves where he belongs, and you let Mickey Courage off. You follow?"

Jack looked at the General long and hard. "Yes

sir, I understand the logic of where you're going, and I understand how you would like me to prosecute the case. First of all, let me say I have no current intention of making any such commitment to you, nor do I see how my handling the prosecution in such a fashion would ever lead to getting your message out."

There was silence. The General leaned back in his black leather armchair and rubbed his eyes. He wiped the smear from his face and the back of his neck with a white cotton handkerchief he drew from his breast pocket. He looked to the window and its view of his beloved Lombardy poplars and the mountains beyond, and he looked to the inert figure resting in the armchair next to the window. Then the General returned his gaze to Jack with a renewed vigor. Jack sensed the fire within them, the power of the old man's determination as he prepared himself for what surely must be the climax of his speech.

"You know, it's funny," began the General. "But here we are in the midst of the most important events of this century for our people, for our party, and my son, the governor, sleeps. He has heart, Jack; he wants to do well and he wants to please. But he has no will, and no direction. You have both. Outside of his carefully controlled governorship, Ah could never allow Sammy to advance in national politics. He has no vision and he is weak. In national politics he would be out of my control and he would be manipulated. That could be disastrous to us and to our party, so Ah will never allow it. As much as Ah love him, Ah'd destroy him before Ah'd let him advance beyond the state politics that Ah control.

"You, on the other hand, have it all. You're bright, good looking, young, and hardworking. You come from good stock, and you've proven yourself in war and peace. You're honest, loyal to your friends and good to your family—well, except for those two affairs on the side and a somewhat messy divorce. Oh, don't blush, Jack. My sources don't overlook anything, and we've been following you for a long time, long before this Johnson mess. It simply catapulted you to the front of our search for a new party leader. Ah'm getting too old. There isn't much time to groom a successor. You, Jack, are the right man in the right place, and, yes, at the right time.

"Ah know you are fiercely independent, and Ah won't try to tell you what to do, and Ah never will, no matter what our relationship. Ah promise you that. Ah will suggest and Ah will try to persuade you as Ah am doing now, but you will always make the final decision."

Jack interrupted. "Excuse me, General. I have been patient up to now, sir, and I have listened to you. But now I want you to cut to the chase. Be specific. What is it that you want from me?"

General Cartridge chuckled as he leaned forward in his chair towards Jack. "Cut the crap, eh Jack? Soon you're going to know the importance of this entire prelude. But okay, here's how Ah *suggest* you prosecute this case; then you decide—not now, but after you've had some time to fully consider my suggestions."

"In shorthand, I suggest you prosecute Billy Sprouse to the fullest extent of the law; he's guilty and he's expendable. Also, have Mickey Courage turn state's evidence and accept a plea bargain as an unwilling accessory to kidnapping. Get him a five-year suspended sentence with one year probation.

"You can be the standard bearer, Jack. You bring the message of 'separate but equal' through Mickey Courage in your opening argument and your closing statements. Mickey is a symbol of the white worker's frustration and you tell all those gentlemen of the press that white workers will unite in their resistance to forced integration, that they are strong, and that they will win."

"You hammer that message home, Jack, beginning with your opening arguments in the Charlottesville courthouse next week, and Ah can predict your political future. Would you like to hear it?"

Jack nodded impassively.

"If you follow the broad base of my suggestions, Ah predict you will become a populist hero for the white working masses. With that base in Virginia you can easily win the tenth district congressional seat you're eyeballing for next November. Now, Ah realize you pride yourself on being an independent, but throw your support to Sammy there, and you will assure him reelection to the governorship." Asleep in his chair, the governor snored loudly.

"If those things happen, then Ah will make you a promise. Ah will throw all my support behind your bid for US Congress in 1960. By 1964, with my help, you will have solidified the leadership of the state's Democratic Party, which I assume you will join once you make congressman this fall. By then we will have extended our coalition throughout the South, Midwest and West. That, Jack, may be enough to support a run for US Senate in 1964, and to win. How do you like that scenario?"

"General, that is an absolutely stunning series of political predictions which rests on far too many variables," Jack said evenly. "I really can't respond."

"Whoa, Jack. Ah don't want you to make any decision right now," the General countered. "Ah've put far too much on your plate for you to make any snap decisions. And Ah really don't want you to. Ah'll know what your considered judgments are next week in court. Your opening statement in that arena will tell me everything Ah need to know. Ah'll wait until then."

The General rose from behind his desk and Jack stood up in front of him. Their eyes met.

"There is one last thing, Jack,"

"What's that, General?"

"You give 'em the message—you make Mickey Courage the symbol for resistance to forced integration—and Ah'll do everything in my power to make you the most popular politician since George Washington."

"And if I try the case another way?"

"Ah'll see to it you never get farther than one term as Charlottesville commonwealth's attorney."

Smiling, the General came around the desk and shook Jack's hand. He put his hand on Jack's shoulder, led him to the office door, and knocked twice. Alex opened the door.

"Alex, take Mr. Forester back to the party, please," ordered the General, and to Jack he added, "See you in court, counselor."

Chapter 10: Visitors at the City Jail

It was a hot Wednesday morning, July 22nd. Mickey Courage sat in the corner of his cell at the Charlottesville City Jail. His was the closest to the sheriff's office, the back door of which opened to the city's eight holding cells. Six of the other seven cells were occupied, one of them by Billy Sprouse. The cell next to Mickey's was empty. There was a reason for that.

Commonwealth's attorney Jack Forester had requested that Mickey be isolated from all of the other prisoners until the Billy Sprouse trial was over. As the commonwealth's star witness against Billy Sprouse now that Mickey had confessed and turned state's evidence, it was understood that Mickey Courage needed to be shielded from outside intervention or witness tampering that Billy Sprouse's people might attempt.

And so, during that first week, Mickey lived in total isolation. A deputy walked him to the latrine; a deputy slid his meals through the horizontal slit across the metal bars he stared through every day. For reading he had *Gideon's Bible,* which awaited every prisoner upon entering his cell.

God, thought Mickey, as his latest lunch was passed through the bars. *Chicken and biscuits in the morning, a chicken sandwich for lunch, chicken and split pea soup for dinner, chicken every day except Sunday, when I get turkey. And no one to talk with.* There was indeed no one to talk with. Even the deputies wouldn't talk with Mickey Courage, apparently on Sheriff's Bredlo's orders.

As he sat in his cell, Mickey sometimes had second thoughts about testifying against Billy Sprouse. Although Mickey was isolated from the other prisoners, he knew from the cellblock chatter that Billy was only a few cells away. The scuttlebutt was that Billy didn't talk to anyone, just glared through the bars all day long, and this frightened Mickey.

But hell, he thought, *I'm only going to tell the truth, like that commonwealth's attorney guy told me to do in return for a significantly reduced sentence.* That was powerful persuasion; even so, Mickey feared the vengeance of Billy Sprouse and his kinfolk.

I'm ready to get out of this town anyway, Mickey thought. *If I can just get through this trial and survive a year or two in county jail lock-up, I'll make it. And that's the most I'll serve according to the DA.*

Then maybe I'll go down to Richmond or even up to Warrenton. I've got kin up there. They'll help me get on my feet. That's it; I'll go to Warrenton as soon as I get out.

Okay, he convinced himself, *Now I've got a plan. I know I can make it through this trial now.*

"Hey Mickey, quit your daydreaming, boy. You've got a visitor." It was Sheriff Bredlo himself. "Yeah, ol' Jack Forester, our esteemed commonwealth's attorney, told me to keep you in total isolation, no visitors, until after the trial of your partner in crime. But hell, I ain't gonna deny you a little chat with your daddy. That is, if you want to see him. Apparently he wants to see you 'cuz he's standing right here behind me in my office." Sheriff Bredlo continued his monologue with a slight smirk on his jowly face. "Apparently he *really* wants to see *you*. Looks to me like he's about to bust a gut to get in here to talk to his son. Looks like he's really got a head of steam up about something, Mickey. Geez, I hope it's not about the trial, 'cuz Mr. Forester would be real mad if he knew you were about to talk about the trial." Sheriff Bredlo made an exaggerated wink in Mickey's direction. "But whatever happens between a father and son, it's up to them, right Mickey? So here's the question: You do want to see your daddy, don't you boy?"

Mickey's thoughts were racing. He feared his father's upcoming tirade. He knew from past experience that it would entail yelling, finger-pointing, and threatening of dire consequences if he didn't do as he was told. Mickey knew his father would try to unhinge his resolve to go through with his testimony against Billy Sprouse. He felt it in his bones as he sensed his father's presence. Mickey loved his father but he didn't want to see him at this moment in his life. Still, he knew he had no choice.

"Well," thundered Sheriff Bredlo, "do you want to see your daddy or not? Hurry up. Time's a-wastin'. I got other things to be doin', boy."

"Yes," said Mickey quietly. "Of course I want to see my father."

"Good boy." Sheriff Bredlo practically crowed with delight, knowing the kind of chaos he might be bringing to Jack Forester's case against Billy Sprouse. He did not like Billy Sprouse or the white trash he represented, but something had to be done to keep the colored in their place; that much the General had explained to him. Imagine. General Cartridge himself had asked the sheriff to help him out by letting Mickey's father talk to his son despite Forester's 'no visitor' mandate. *Jiminy, I would have done that myself*, thought Barry Bredlo, *but this is better for me, doing a favor for a man like General Cartridge*. Sheriff Bredlo winked again at Mickey Courage, and then his corpulence disappeared behind the door that separated the cells from his office.

In a moment the door reopened. A guard appeared. Behind him stood Michael Courage, Mickey's father. He was sweating profusely, as Mickey knew he did whenever he was excited or upset or bothered, but there was a coldness in him that Mickey had not seen before.

"Guard, could you open the cell door and leave me alone with my boy? Now?" It was almost a command.

"I can let you in the cell, Mr. Courage, but I was told to stand right outside. Sheriff B. told me himself."

"Oh, go on down and check on Joe Carlson in cell seven," said Sheriff Bredlo, leaning through the half-open door leading to his office. "Joe will want to tell you all about the brawl he got in over at the Court Square Tavern last night. Go on down there, now!" Guard Fred Dudley was happy to comply and to hear about the latest drunken fisticuffs of the man best known as 'The Charlottesville Brawler.'

"That's good," said Sheriff Bredlo as his eyes followed Fred Dudley down the corridor. "Okay, Mr. Courage," said the sheriff, stepping aside, "you have a nice little heart-to-heart with young Mickey. I'll have someone let you out in, let's say twenty-five minutes." He smiled as Michael Courage entered his son's cell and slammed the cell door shut. Sheriff Bredlo disappeared again through the outer door leading to his office.

Mr. Michael Courage stood framed by the closed cell door. He stared down at his son, still sitting in the corner of his cell. Mickey did not know whether or not to get up and embrace his father, so he just looked at the floor.

* * * * * * * * * *

Jack Forester had parked on West Main Street next to the Rotunda of the University of Virginia, about a mile away from the city jail. He was walking there to meet first with Sheriff Bredlo and then Mickey Courage. He was walking because he needed the time to think and to channel his anger before confronting Sheriff Bredlo.

Only thirty minutes before, Joe Smiley had telephoned Jack and announced that, in addition to representing Billy Sprouse, he now represented Mickey Courage and that Mickey Courage had recanted all previous testimony. "It is our position, Mr. Forester, that my client was pressured, intimidated, and generally coerced into saying things he did not do, say, or mean on the night of the incident. Further, his testimony was totally manipulated, scripted, or manufactured by the police in the interrogation room. In any event, he will not be a willing witness against Billy Sprouse. My client, Mr. Forester, will plead 'not guilty' to kidnapping or murder. Our position is that it was all a harmless prank until that colored boy managed to find a way to hang himself."

As Jack Forester was digesting the outrage of this last statement, he asked Joe Smiley one question: "What was it that prompted your client to have this remarkable change of heart?" Jack heard a quiet chuckle on the other end of the line, then Smiley replied, "I can't really say, Jack; may I call you Jack?"

Another chuckle, then, "But I think it may have had something to do with the visit his father paid him yesterday afternoon."

"I see," Jack countered, trying not to reveal his surprise or anger at Sheriff Bredlo's betrayal. "And how did Mickey Courage come to employ your services?"

"I thought you would know, Jack," Smiley answered. "General Cartridge called me to say he felt young Mickey needed better representation than what the city's poor old court-appointed lawyer could do, and, in the interest of justice, he requested that I offer my services to Mickey Courage and his father at the General's expense. You follow me, Jack?"

"Oh, yeah, I follow you, Mr. Smiley. You'll be hearing back from me—very soon, I suspect."

"Well, I look forward to that Jack. I truly do," Joe Smiley said.

Jack quickened his pace as he thought back on this conversation. He knew that the murder/kidnapping case against Billy Sprouse was in real jeopardy. He also knew that the tranquility of Charlottesville could be destroyed as a result of this trial. And then there was his career.

Jack walked past the Vinegar Hill neighborhood, just to his left as he passed the Albemarle Hotel on Main Street. Most of the colored people who lived there viewed it as their special territory, an area the whites left alone unless they were collecting rent. For the whites, it was a slum. For the Negro, it was home, and Jack knew that the non-resident property owners, almost all white, had big development plans for Vinegar Hill. Jack wondered if these plans would create as much unrest amongst the colored as he feared the trial of Billy Sprouse might do.

As he passed the all-black Vinegar Hill Barber Shop, the proprietor tipped his hat to him. Jack passed the Black Dog Bar next, then The Grill, where two suspicious black faces peered out at him.

At the foot of Vinegar Hill began the all-white downtown Main Street. Jack walked past Mr. Bibb's Fish Market, a place you could smell before you saw it. Mr. Bibb himself leaned in his store's doorway, his bald cherubic face clouded by the smoke of his stub cigar sticking out of the corner of his mouth. A heavily stained white apron was wrapped around his corpulence.

"Hey Mr. Forester, I got some mighty good trout just came in this morning."

"Not today, Mr. Bibb. I'm in a bit of a hurry," Jack replied, as hequickened his stride away from Mr. Bibb and toward the city jail only four blocks away.

"Hey Jack," Jonah Bibb yelled after him. "Don't be too hard on that Billy Sprouse and Mickey Courage. They was just foolin' around with them Negroes and they ran into some bad luck, know what I mean?"

Jack waved a hand in dismissal. *Is that really what most white people were thinking?* he wondered. *Kidnap two Negro teenagers, and one of them gets killed. Are the vast majority of whites going to look on it as high jinx and bad luck for the two white perpetrators? Well it was a little bit more than bad luck for the terrified and hog-tied Lucius Johnson, who hung himself trying to get away.* Jack could only imagine Lucius Johnson's unspeakable fear as he tried to escape from the drunken death-threatening white kids.

Well those white kids will be held accountable for what they did. It goes beyond white/black issues or pecking order or even redneck high jinx gone awry. It's about simple justice. That's the very least I can provide the soul of Lucius Johnson and his people. I'm going to see it through, regardless of personal consequences. As Junius P. Jones would say, "Do the right thing and let the chips fall where they may."

Since the General had hired a high-priced lawyer from Washington, DC to represent both Billy and Mickey, without notifying Jack, it was obvious that he could not be trusted on any level.

Accordingly, Jack knew what he must do today: convince Mickey Courage once again that he should testify against Billy Sprouse, that he must tell the *whole* truth, and that the alternative was reindictment on charges of kidnapping and accessory to felony murder.

Jack passed the Victory Shoe Store, so named at the beginning of World War II, and then the Brass Rail, where the daily pool-playing beer-drinking crowd was already gathering. Jack smiled to himself and turned left on Second Street. He crossed Market

Street, walked past Lee Park, crossed Jefferson Street, and finally got to High Street, where he turned right and walked the two final blocks to the sheriff's office and the city jail attached to its rear.

Jack walked up the steps, pushed open the screen door, and walked straight to the sheriff's desk.

"Good morning, Sheriff Bredlo. We need to talk *right now*. And then I need to talk to Mickey Courage. You got me?!"

Bredlo looked up, obviously startled. His face flushed crimson as he gathered himself and struggled to his feet.

"Now see here, Jack. I'm in charge here. You show me a little respect, barging in here and giving me orders and all."

It was clear to Jack that Bredlo was flustered and that the best time to get what he needed was right now, in the flush of Bredlo's panic, before he had a chance to recover. "Sit down, Sheriff, and hear me out," ordered Jack, "or I'll help you out of your job quicker than you can say Jackie Robinson." It was obvious to Jack that the sheriff was frightened of something he might know.

Commonwealth's attorney Jack Forester stared down at Sheriff Barry Bredlo across the gnarly wooden and metal desk from which Bredlo did his work. The desk was full of black marks from cigar ashes that had dropped from his chomping cigar and smoldered on pieces of the desk before being snuffed out. There was a half-empty orange Nehi in the corner, a picture of the recently dishonored Senator Joe McCarthy in another corner, and an eight-by-eleven portrait of a porcine middle-aged woman Jack assumed to be Bredlo's wife, but there were no children pictured. There was a framed portrait of Senator Strom Thurmond, formerly a Dixiecrat candidate for president. The smiling Thurmond was waving a Confederate flag and pictured behind him were two leering South Carolina state troopers.

My God, thought Jack. *Why not add an engraved invitation to happy hour with the Ku Klux Klan from the grand wizard himself?* At least Jack knew with whom he was dealing.

Jack Forester leaned all the way across the desk in such a way that Sheriff Bredlo could not avoid making eye contact. In fact, Jack was practically nose to nose with the sheriff as he reached down and grabbed him by his right shoulder epaulette and shook him hard. He could see the terror in Bredlo's eyes.

"Sheriff," said Forester in a low, measured tone, "unless you cooperate with me right now, unless you come clean in the next two minutes, I will see to it that you are stripped of that badge and that you never see the inside of this office again unless you're being led off to jail on fraud and corruption charges."

Jack was bluffing, but he did not think Barry Bredlo knew that. Jack had his face so close to Bredlo's that he could see nose hairs quivering in the sheriff's flaring nostrils and sweat dripping from Bredlo's chubby pock-marked cheeks to his neck and the sweat-stained collar below. It was obvious the sheriff was not certain what Jack knew and that he was terrified of something there was to know—something apparently far more serious than disobeying the commonwealth's attorney's isolation order in favor of granting a request for a favor from the General. There *was* something more, thought Jack: fraud, embezzlement, staff abuse, prisoner abuse. Jack did not know which, but he pressed his advantage against the sheriff's fears.

"You get one shot with me, Barry," said Jack, using the familiar address. "Be quick and be truthful and your career might not be over. Now, who persuaded you to let Mickey Courage see his father?"

"It was General Cartridge," said Sheriff Bredlo in a small voice. "I mean, Jack, you don't know what pressure he put on me. The general convinced me it was the right thing to let Mickey talk with his daddy."

So, thought Jack to himself, no *more surrogates; the General is* directly *inserting himself into the Sprouse/Courage murder/kidnapping case.*

"Okay, Sheriff. Here's where you get to keep your job or go to jail, if you know what I mean. I wager you listened to everything Michael Courage said to his son, didn't you?"

"Jack, you know I don't eavesdrop on my prisoners' private conversations. That would be wrong."

"Bullshit, Barry. This is your last chance. I don't have time for this." Jack grabbed a piece of Bredlo's shirt and pulled him even closer. "What's it gonna be? Or do I just bring charges against you right now?"

"Okay, okay, take it easy," said Bredlo, as Jack released him. The disheveled sheriff pulled back in his chair away from Jack's powerful hands and his unrelenting stare.

"You're right. I do tend to keep my door open, so I can keep an eye on the inmates. And I can hear pretty much everything that goes on in cell one, where Mickey Courage is. I thought I might pick up some valuable information, uh, for the prosecution, of course. So I gotta admit I had my ear to the door pretty good, you know what I mean."

"In other words, you heard pretty much everything, right, sheriff?" Jack was pressing, hard.

"Well, yeah, I guess I did." Bredlo looked up, a small smile on his face. Maybe it was the power of knowing he knew what Jack wanted to know.

"So spit it out. Now."

The sheriff's small smile disappeared.

"All right Jack, I'll tell you everything. I was gonna tell you anyway." Bredlo began recounting for Jack everything he remembered about Mickey Courage's visit with his father. It amazed Jack how much the sheriff recalled, but then, Jack supposed, Bredlo must make a habit of eavesdropping. Jack wondered how often after overhearing just the right conversation, Sheriff Bredlo had used confidential information to blackmail an inmate, his visitor, or both. If Bredlo feared Jack had discovered blackmail, Jack could use that fear to turn the slithery Bredlo away from General Cartridge and back to his side. Jack arrived at this deduction as Sheriff Bredlo, under fear for his career or worse, recounted almost verbatim the conversation between Mickey Courage and his father. It was the information Jack needed to determine how to go forward with the case.

"Well," Sheriff Bredlo began, "I gotta tell you, Michael Courage was at his Irish redneck rabble-rousing best. He preached to his son about standing up for his own people, about the larger cause of protecting his people against these uppity niggers trying to take neighborhoods and jobs from hardworking whites, about how Negros and liberal whites would use this case to catapult their cause onto the front page of every newspaper in this state. Moving up and pushing hardworking whites out, that's how they would use this case," he said.

Sheriff Bredlo smiled at Jack and continued, "Yeah, that's right Jack; I gotta pretty good memory for this particular sermon laid on Mickey Courage by his daddy. Let's see, what else did he say? Oh, yeah. He told Mickey that if he turned on Billy Sprouse, it would be like selling out his own kind in the turf war between the colored and themselves. And, Jack, when Mickey told his daddy he was only going to testify to what actually happened, his daddy jumped in his face. Uh, I was kinda peeking through the door. It was just too good. And anyway, he told Mickey there are different ways of telling the truth while still defending his own class.

"Jack, I'm telling you, Mickey's dad convinced him that it was better to go to prison for twenty years with Billy Sprouse than to play it safe and be a tool for the commonwealth's attorney and the colored cause," Bredlo continued.

"Then, of course, he told him about that high-class lawyer General Cartridge got for him, and that it was likely he'd get him off with little or no prison time and probation. By the way, that lawyer came by here too; thought you'd like to know. Well, between his daddy and that lawyer, they got poor Mickey believing his only chance is to go with Billy Sprouse. He's gonna say you scared his statement out of him. You know, it was the cops and you and nobody from his side. Yeah, he's gonna take it all back. What would you say? Oh yeah, he is recanting it. Well, the last thing I guess you ought to know, Jack, is that he doesn't want to talk with you unless his lawyer is present. So you see, I can't even let you in right now."

Sheriff Bredlo looked up into Jack's angry stare. "Uh, but I'll tell you everything I hear, okay? You look after my little problem and I'll help you with yours, okay partner?" Once again Sheriff Bredlo looked up slyly hoping for some kind of approval.

"I'm not your partner, Sheriff Bredlo, and don't you forget it. You report back to me everything you think might be useful to me in this case, and I'll see what I *don't* have to pursue among your own problems, got it?"

"Yes, sir," said Sheriff Bredlo meekly.

God, what kind of blackmail or fraud scheme is Barry Bredlo into? Jack wondered. *Whatever it is, I'd better find out if I'm going to keep him in my pocket.*

"All right, Sheriff," said Jack, pushing back from the sheriff's desk. "I'm going to walk over to my office to set up a meeting with Mickey Courage and his lawyer. You keep letting me know whatever you think I need to know."

"You can count on me, Jack."

"Yeah, right," said Jack as he pushed open the screen door and stepped out into a hot July morning. He slammed the door behind him.

Chapter 11: Charges Considered and a Solitary Lunch

Jack crossed Jefferson Street and walked quickly down the one remaining block to his office. It was already scorching. He pulled a handkerchief from his breast pocket and wiped the sweat from his brow. He started to look up into the infinite blue of the sky, but the sharp glare from the sun made this almost impossible. Like Icarus flying too close to the sun, Jack wondered if he had bitten off more than he could chew. He knew that he would do the right thing; he wondered if it would cost him his future.

"So be it!" Jack said loudly as he opened the outer door to his office.

"So be what, Mr. Forester?" It was good old Alice, faithful, efficient, and dependable as ever. She gave him a Mona Lisa smile like she already knew what he had been talking about to himself.

"What else, Alice? It's that Mickey Courage/Billy Sprouse affair. Seems like everyone's got a strong opinion on this one, and they don't seem to match up too well."

"Boy, tell me about it," agreed Alice. "Everybody keeps asking me how you're going to prosecute this case. I keep telling 'em it's none of their business, 'cuz it's none of mine. And then I tell 'em I don't know what you're going to do, anyway."

Alice paused and gave Jack a little wink. "So what *are* you going to do, Mr. Forester?" Jack leaned down and gave Alice a peck on the cheek. He grabbed his messages from the in-box. He stood up, and, as he turned to go into his own office, winked in Alice's general direction and said, "I'm having a private séance in my office, Alice, to determine that very thing. Don't let anyone in but God, and check his identification, and if it says General Samuel Cartridge, I don't want to see him right now, even if he says he *is* God." Alice laughed out loud as Jack shut the door behind him.

The office was Jack's inner sanctum, its paintings, photographs, degrees, and trophies all part of who he was. A large, much scratched and polished oak desk dominated the east corner of his office, strategically placed to catch the early morning sunshine through a window that framed the continual business of Court Square. The desk had been with him since law school at the University, and, although many had urged him to upgrade to a modern edition of polished metal and veneer, he had steadfastly rejected their advice.

This was the desk from which he'd prepared for his law exams and for that famous moot court victory over fellow law student Robert Kennedy on the merits of the 1896 Supreme Court decision in *Plessy vs. Ferguson*. It was still his desk when he graduated summa cum laude from the University law school in 1950 and when he'd successfully prepared for the bar. It had been his desk when he had prepared for all his cases in the first years of practicing private law, before he ran for commonwealth's attorney. And that is why Jack had brought the oak desk into his office and had the new one, already in place, removed and given to a member of his staff.

For Jack, the old desk had become a metaphor for what he believed in. *It is more about values than tradition for its own sake*, thought Jack. *Values and justice and not just looking to the past, but to the future that should be, that can be.* Jack settled into his comfortable red leather swivel chair. He started thinking about Mickey Courage and Billy Sprouse and their terrified Negro victims.

A night of youthful redneck high jinx gone bad—true, but so much more. The use of a six-inch knife, a legally lethal weapon used to threaten murder, was felony kidnapping. The fact that poor Lucius Johnson hung himself with the same rope used to tie him, and that the accidental hanging occurred during the commission of a felony, made it felony murder. That's what it was, and there were no redeeming factors to make Jack lessen the charges for Billy Sprouse. As for Mickey Courage, because of his age and because he was not the ringleader, if he cooperated fully with the prosecution, there would be lesser charges as determined by a plea agreement.

Jack looked out his window to Court Square. He could see ripples of heat rising up the trunk and through the leaves of the famous Bagby Oak Tree, said to be over one hundred years old; it had been alive since before The War Between the States.

Well, here we go again, thought Jack. He picked up his phone as he heard the buzzer from Alice, who told him that Joe Smiley was on the line and wanted to have a private meeting.

"Okay, Alice," said Jack. "Tell Mr. Smiley that I can meet him here at 2:00 this afternoon. I need lunch and a good walk to prepare for the likes of him."

"It's eleven thirty now. Do you want me to pick you up some lunch from Timberlakes, or are you going out?"

"Out, I guess. I'll brave the public and go around the corner to the Court Square Tavern. Thanks, and Alice, hold all my calls until after that two o'clock meeting."

Jack rang off and started to put on his jacket, but he remembered it was hot outside and left it off. As he passed Alice in the outer office, he straightened his tie, ran his fingers through his hair, smiled, and said, "The young commonwealth's attorney has got to look dignified at a time like this, Alice."

"Mr. Forester, you're as trim and good looking as the picture of you coming off the football field for UVA years ago. Those reporters can't touch you."

Jack smiled again as he disappeared out the front door into the blazing August heat and walked to the Court Square Tavern two blocks away. As usual at lunch time, the tavern was full of lawyers, businessmen, and, in the corner, a round table was crowded with the reporters Jack had come to know so well, from the *Daily Progress*, the *Richmond Times-Dispatch*, and even the *Washington Post*. They rose as one when they saw Jack. Before they could say a word, Jack was upon them. "I have a meeting with the attorney representing Mickey Courage and Billy Sprouse at two o'clock this afternoon. I will issue a short statement and answer a few questions at three o'clock at my office regarding their case. I will specify the official charges the commonwealth will be bringing. Don't ask me any questions now so I can eat my lunch in peace, okay?"

Jerry Parker of the *Daily Progress* started to speak, but Jack cut him off. "And Jerry, if you don't allow me to have my lunch in peace, I won't be talking to you on any subject anytime." Jerry slouched back into his chair, and Ralph Townsend of the *Richmond Times-Dispatch* smiled, "You got it Jack. Hey, the ham and cheese is terrific today, and that homemade lemon iced tea will cool you down real good. See you at three, Jack."

Jack smiled as he left the reporters. He saw a small table in the corner next to the kitchen and ordered his lunch. He sat uninterrupted as he wolfed down a sandwich, sipped his iced tea, and thought about his upcoming meeting with Joe Smiley.

As he drained the last of his lemon iced tea, Jack popped a cube of the remaining ice in his mouth. He sucked at it and swirled it around the roof of his mouth. *Cooling, and better for you than Red Man Chewing Tobacco*, he thought. Jack stood up, left enough cash to cover his bill, and stepped out the tavern's side door. Again a blast of hot July air enveloped him as the chunk of ice in his mouth melted to nothing. It was one thirty in the afternoon.

Oh, what the hell, thought Jack. *I'll head straight back to the office. Maybe Smiley will be early. I'd like to hear what kind of defense he may have concocted for a case like this. Maybe he'll just try to negotiate a reasonable plea agreement; that would make things a lot easier for all of us. Nah, that would be too easy.* Jack chuckled to himself as he stepped through the door of his office ten minutes after leaving the tavern. He had a little bet with himself that if Smiley were waiting in his outer office it would be about a plea bargain, if late a technical defense, and if on time, Smiley would simply be feeling Jack out, offering little in return for the moment.

Jack slipped past Alice, who was on the phone. She nodded toward the in-box, and Jack took the messages with him into his office. He sat down at his desk, read and discarded two of the messages, and held onto the third one. It was from Joe Smiley to say he was running a little late. He offered his apologies and hoped it did not inconvenience Jack.

"So my question is," said Jack aloud to himself, "will it be a technical defense now that he's chosen to be late, or has he got a hole card he hopes to play to his clients' advantage?" Jack decided to keep his calendar clear until two thirty, after which time, he had instructed Alice, Mr. Smiley would have to make a new appointment for later in the week.

Chapter 12:
Defense Attorney Joe Smiley and the Not Guilty Defense

At two twenty-nine, Alice buzzed Jack that Mr. Smiley had arrived and asked if she should she show him in.

"Wait ten minutes and then let him in, Alice. I can play this game also."

At precisely two thirty-nine, Alice opened Jack's door to reveal the self-importance that was Joe Smiley. At five-feet-five, approximately 150 pounds, he had the predator grin of a Chesire cat.

"Hello, Mr. Smiley. You look just as I pictured you on the phone." Jack pointed to the chair across from his desk as he stood up to shake the extended hand. "Please, have a seat."

"Well, I believe I will, Jack. Thank you. I have some really good news for you about this case." Joe Smiley slid into the red leather cushioned chair across from Jack and made deep eye contact. "Yes, sir, I think this is going to make your day."

Jack paused for a moment, returning the stare without civility. "All right, Mr. Smiley, spit it out. What have you got for me? Make it fast. I've got other appointments backed up."

Smiley shifted back in his chair across from Jack and the old oak desk and then leaned forward to reach up and plant his elbows on its edge. His hands clasped each other to form the church and the steeple Jack had learned to make in Sunday school many years before. Smiley seemed to be nibbling on his steepled fingers. He closed his eyes as if struggling with what he was about to impart, though Jack suspected it was well rehearsed. He found the performance mildly entertaining until Smiley opened his eyes and began to speak.

"Jack, this whole thing is a travesty of justice. After some intense discussion with my young clients, I have determined that, in fact, *they* are the real victims in this sorry affair. I think when you hear what I have to say, you'll agree."

"Mr. Smiley, you can't be serious!" said Jack.

"Oh, but I am, Jack, er, Mr. Forester."

"Mr. Smiley," Jack said in a measured tone, "the solid evidence I have is that these white boys, your clients, kidnapped two young Negro boys, that they used a deadly weapon in the commission of a felony, and that, in the commission of that felony kidnapping, one of these Negro boys was killed.

"Now I'll give you three minutes to show me

how your clients, the perpetrators of this heinous offense, are, in fact, the victims. Remember, you are not grandstanding in front of a jury, so skip the histrionics. Just spit it out."

"Why of course, Jack," Joe Smiley said as he rocked back in the wing chair that seemed to envelop him. "I'll make it simple. Those young Negros are known homosexuals, and they actually were soliciting Mickey Courage and Billy Sprouse on the night in question. Why, when Mickey and Billy realized what was going on, they decided they had to teach them a lesson."

What a smarmy little bastard this guy is, thought Jack, but decided to hold his tongue until he'd heard Smiley's full defense.

"First of all, you should know that those Negro boys got into the car of their own volition. There was no kidnapping. They thought Billy and Mickey were going to take them to the house in question to, you know, fool around, and, you know, do whatever those queers do. My clients were very angry at being solicited, so it was their plan all along to teach those Negros a lesson they wouldn't forget. The plan was only to rough 'em up a little, scare 'em so they wouldn't try to hustle other white folks.

"Well, I guess it got a little out of hand when they tied up one and made the other one go after wine money, but they didn't really want to hurt them. They were just trying to frighten them, teach 'em a good lesson."

Joe Smiley seemed to catch his breath, then dove in again. "If that one Negro boy hadn't tried to jump off the loft to escape, we certainly wouldn't be talking about kidnapping and felony murder. At most it would be assault and battery, maybe false imprisonment. How about one to five, suspend four? Now, that would be a good plea agreement, Jack. Let's see, Billy Sprouse would serve about six months in the state penitentiary in Richmond, and, since Mickey's only seventeen he can serve six months at some juvenile detention center. Put 'em both on probation until they're twenty-one. In this way, Jack, the Negro population gets some of the justice they're crying out for, and you become the champion of hardworking white families. Oh, and by the way, Jack, if we can more or less work out the plea agreement along these lines, I'll withdraw my clients' charges against the Negro boys for soliciting them."

Joe Smiley straightened up in his chair to look Jack square in the eye, "So, what do you say, Jack? Do we have a deal?"

Jack paused for about ten seconds to absorb the full impact of Smiley's strategy to demonize the victims and make the perpetrators the victims. Then he began, "Mr. Smiley, I'll tell you a funny little story about justice as you have presented it.

A white lady from Massachusetts was driving with her husband down a dark country lane in a small southern town about midnight a few years ago. Because her right headlight was not working properly, she did not see the two young black boys walking on the right side of the road. She hit them head on. One boy crashed through the windshield and ended up in the rear seat of her car. The other one was knocked fifty feet down the road. Both were killed instantly. When the deputy sheriff arrived and heard the hysterical woman's explanation of what had happened, that her headlight was out and that she had not seen the boys, the deputy put his arm around her shoulder and said, 'Now don't you worry about a thing, Ma'am. It'll all be taken care of, and I am sorry about the inconvenience. But don't worry anymore. See that dead nigger in your back seat? We're going to get him for breaking and entering. And that one lying dead down the road? Why, we'll charge him with leaving the scene of an accident.'" Jack Forester looked hard at Joe Smiley, who had laughed involuntarily, then shut his mouth as he realized how effectively Jack had ridiculed his defense strategy.

"Your defense produced another emotion in me, Mr. Smiley. It doesn't make me laugh. It makes me want to throw up. Your time is up. Get out of my office." Smiley scurried toward the door as Jack came toward him. "And if you actually use that pitiful defense, I will beat you like a drum in court, and then I will get you disbarred."

Jack watched as Joe Smiley almost trotted out of the outer office and was heard to say, "You're going to be sorry about all of this, Jack Forester."

"I don't think so," Jack yelled after him. Then he looked around the outer office. There were five reporters awaiting the three o'clock interview. "Hmm, where do we begin, boys?"

Chapter 13: Press Conference

"Hey, Jack," yelled Jerry Parker of the Charlottesville *Daily Progress*, slithering off his chair in Jack Forester's reception area. "Wasn't that Joe Smiley you just ran out of here? Isn't he that high-priced lawyer from DC? Boy, I know about him. He could have gotten Jack the Ripper off on grounds his mother didn't like him and he was simply acting out. So, who's he representing, Mickey Courage or Billy Sprouse?"

"Yes, that was Joe Smiley I just ran out of here, Jerry. He says he is now representing both of them," said Jack evenly.

"Um, well now, who is paying his fee, Jack?" asked Ralph Townsend of the *Times-Dispatch*. "His retainer alone has got to be more than those boys' families see in a year. So who's footing the bill?"

"You'd have to ask Joe Smiley about that," said

Jack.

"But you do know, don't you, Jack?" said Townsend.

"Yeah, I think I do know, Ralph, but you boys will have to dig that up on your own. My job is to look at the evidence, make an assessment, and bring charges accordingly. I have made that assessment, and I am ready to certify felony charges in the city municipal court tomorrow morning."

"So what are you really going to charge 'em with?" asked Jerry 'the Weasel' Parker, "integrating their clubhouse under false pretences?" A couple of the reporters guffawed at this attempt at humor, but the rest looked away as if more embarrassed than amused by their colleague.

Jack looked down at Jerry Parker. Was his the voice of the majority of Charlottesville's working class… that it was all just a youthful prank that had gotten out of hand on a hot summer night?

Then Parker spoke again. "Hey Jack, we all know those white boys need to be punished for what they did, but it doesn't seem to be that big a deal to me. If that one Negro boy hadn't gone and hung himself, this whole thing would all be back page news."

"In your mind, perhaps," said Jack evenly. "You'd probably say the Negro boy tried to get away with more rope than he could steal. You're hopeless, Jerry. Let me try and set the rest of you straight on what this case is about.

"We have a young Negro victim, Lucius Johnson,

who died while trying to escape two vicious white punks who had assaulted him, kidnapped him, blindfolded him, and tied him up to extort money from his friend. Now remember this: they promised his friend that they would kill Lucius if he didn't come back with the ransom money. Billy Sprouse confessed as much in his interrogation by Sheriff Bredlo. Now you can imagine how terrified sixteen-year old Lucius Johnson must have been, trussed up like a turkey and not knowing whether his friend would return with the money or whether he would be killed as his captors had promised. So when Lucius Johnson thinks that Mickey Courage and Billy Sprouse have left that old, broken-down, abandoned house, he tries to roll and crawl his way to freedom. What he doesn't know, because he is gagged and blindfolded and trussed up like a cow doggie, is that he is tied to the vertical beam of a second-floor loft. He scrapes and rolls and pushes himself to the edge. What he cannot discern until it is too late, until he feels himself falling off the edge, is that he has moved just far enough for the rope to pull taut against the rafter, and one young terrified kidnap victim is hung to death, his body turning and twisting in the air."

Jack spun around and held the front page of that day's *Daily Progress* in front of the reporters. Abruptly, he pulled it apart and held out its torn fragments.

"I hope I have painted you boys a little clearer picture of what happened that night. That young black boy, sixteen-year old Lucius Johnson, is dead. He has no future, killed through the malicious and felonious actions of two young hoodlums. Now maybe that doesn't mean much to you, Jerry, but it does to me.

"More important is what it means to the commonwealth. Well, here it is: Billy Sprouse and Mickey Courage committed felony assault, kidnapping, extortion, and second-degree felony murder. Those are the charges we will certify tomorrow in corporation court, and those are the charges we will prove. That's it. No more details for now."

Jack started to go back into his office, but turned to face the reporters again. "I tell you what, Jerry. Why don't you scamper on over to the McIntire Building, where I understand Joe Smiley has set up his local office. I'm sure he'll share with you the kind of defense strategy you'd like to hear, unless you're interested in the truth."

"Uh, one last question, Jack." It was Townsend of the *Times-Dispatch* again. "Are you worried that this case could exacerbate racial tensions? I'm already hearing lots of concern and not a little bit of anger about this case, in both the white and the Negro communities."

"Yeah, I know, Ralph. It has been less than a week since this crime occurred and I am aware of the tension, the misinformation, and the anger. That's why we need to get the truth out there about what really happened and assure all our citizens that the commonwealth's office will seek justice, not vengeance and not a cover-up—justice that all of our citizens can live with.

"Now I believe that Mr. Smiley is going to try and besmirch the character of the victims in this case and then play to racial fears and prejudices. I hope that our community will rise above gutter tactics, just as I hope you reporters, as a group, will be objective and thorough, put away your prejudices and tell the truth – the whole truth. Good day for now." Jack eyed Jerry once more, then turned and, slipping into his office, closed the door gently behind him.

Jerry Parker, Ralph Townsend, and the other reporters were left looking at the closed door and then at each other. Almost as one they nodded their goodbyes to Alice, headed out the door into the blistering four o'clock heat and struck out for Joe Smiley's office only three blocks away.

The receptionist at the McIntire Building informed them that, although Mr. Smiley was extremely busy and normally could not be seen without an appointment, he respected the press and the good work they did, and would therefore grant them a short interview to set the record straight on the Billy Sprouse/Michael Courage affair.

The reporters were led into Joe Smiley's large corner office. It had one window overlooking Court Square, and another facing Jackson Park. A royal-blue, deep-pile carpet covered the entire floor, with two oriental throw rugs placed at the entrance to the office and another under a side table. Four high-backed oak chairs faced a giant mahogany desk on which sat a Tiffany lamp, some gold framed pictures, and what looked like an in-box of legal documents. Behind the immense desk, almost consumed by it, sat the diminutive Joe Smiley. Behind him was a life-size portrait of General Thomas 'Stonewall' Jackson in full military regalia and seeming to thrust his sword at some unseen danger.

"Come on in, boys. Glad to see you." Smiley motioned toward the high-backed chairs in front of his desk. As they all sat down, Ralph Townsend looked around in amazement at how quickly Smiley had put together and decorated his temporary office in such grand fashion.

"Yeah, I know," said Smiley, nodding in Townsend's direction. "I'm on the road a lot handling special cases for Stepfoot and Johnson, so I've learned to set up shop pretty quickly when I come to a new venue. Basically, I hire an interior designer when I get into town. Her job is to get me what I want. I do have specific tastes. She finds the appropriate office space and decorates according to my instructions. Since time is usually of the essence, my firm pays 'em pretty well. I had Fanny Brace of Stedman House do this project. I think she did a pretty good job, don't you?"

"I do," said Ralph Townsend, "except that it looks like old Stonewall is about to run you through with his saber." Smiley looked over his shoulder, giggled nervously, and rolled his large leather chair slightly to the left of Jackson's thrust. He gathered himself up and put his elbows down on the desk as widely apart as he could manage so as to project size and strength. Then he began to speak.

"Now I know you've heard the talk about my clients. I can't give you much in the way of specifics until after the pleadings tomorrow, but I will tell you this, and you can mark my words: the only thing my clients are guilty of is overreacting to immoral advances."

Joe Smiley stood to his full height, behind the immense mahogany desk and in front of Stonewall's saber and said, "okay, boys, no questions today. You've got my statement. Put that in your newspapers tonight. Just know that my clients are not guilty of any unprovoked kidnapping or assault. I will give you the full particulars tomorrow after the pleadings in corporation court."

As Smiley ushered out the reporters, he did respond to one query. "That's right, er, Mr. Townsend, is it? We are not contesting what happened that night, but, as you will see, it is *how* it happened and *why* it happened that will be our focus. You will see that, in many ways, my clients were the initial victims that night. They certainly are not guilty of any unmitigated assault, kidnapping, or murder charges. That's right, boys, my clients were victims of immoral advances. Make sure you write that down."

Joe Smiley closed his office door on the reporters

who were still shouting their follow-up questions: "And what do you mean by 'immoral advances'? Do you mean these colored boys were coming on to them?"

Smiley chuckled out loud as he walked back to his desk, turned his back on Stonewall, and sat down. *That ought to get the rumor mills going,* he thought. *We'll see how hot we can make it for commonwealth's attorney Jack Forester. Let's see if I can get to that self-righteous paragon of virtue who ran me out of his office. Let's see if I can run* him *right out of town. Wouldn't General Cartridge be pleased with that?* Smiley chuckled again as he grabbed his favorite writing instrument, a Parker T-Ball Jotter, and proceeded to write up his defense draft. A script is what it was, for once completed, he would have to convince Mickey Courage and Billy Sprouse that the young Negroes could have been homosexuals, that they may have intended to make immoral advances, and that their own motive in beating up the Negroes and messing with their heads was simply anger that these perverts might actually think that two young white studs such as themselves would actually enjoy being propositioned by homosexuals.

Woulda, shoulda, coulda, thought Joe Smiley. *In the world of defense strategy, you have to grab onto the best tactics, even if they do stretch the truth a little bit. Since the facts of the case are largely indisputable,* thought Smiley, *I have to get into the heads of my clients as well as the alleged victims. If I can prove to the satisfaction of an all-white jury— and I will make sure of that jury make-up—that there is even the possibility that a homosexual come-on preceded the alleged assault, kidnapping, and murder, then I can make my all-white jury want to acquit on the theory of outrageous provocation. In this town, where there is a growing fear and dislike of forced integration, a verdict of not guilty would send a message to the Negro community at large: Don't push too hard. Stay in your place and stay in your neighborhood.*

I am going to provide this jury with the opportunity to send that message. I am going to provide them with the "immoral advance" defense, and that's all they will need to acquit my clients. I am going to win this for General Cartridge, and he is going to require my services a lot more often, chuckled Joe Smiley.

As for that Negro boy who died, thought Joe Smiley, *I do feel a little sorry for his family and for the sorrow this defense may cause them, but it's up to Jack Forester to protect the Negro boys, not me. My job is to give my clients the best defense I can under the circumstances. I don't have to prove them innocent, just not guilty of the charges as presented.*

"Oh, and I will," said Joe Smiley out loud. "And when those twelve good white jurors come down with a verdict of 'not guilty,' it will be all over for Jack Forester, too."

Chapter 14:
Thursday Indictments in Corporation Court

The presiding judge, Judge Donald Stevens, looked down from the bench at Billy Sprouse and Mickey Courage. Sprouse was short but muscular. He was wearing the same clothes in which he'd been arrested six days before. The grungy white T-shirt and crumpled blue jeans he'd probably washed in the basin in his cell, and he was wearing the same scuffed-up black work boots. He appeared excited, even arrogant, unlike his slightly taller companion, who was subdued and seemed to be staring at his own feet.

Jack Forester watched as Billy Sprouse stared at the judge defiantly, often turning to grin at family and friends in the packed courtroom. He could see that Sprouse was almost proud of the actions that led to this courtroom drama.

All of this was not lost on Judge Stevens. He banged

his gavel. He had seen, read, and heard enough. When the bailiff called for silence, he leaned down from his bench in the general direction of Billy Sprouse and Mickey Courage and addressed them, "Mr. Sprouse and Mr. Courage, I have read the particulars of your arrests just last week. I won't comment on the facts of the case at this time, though I find the evidence compelling. To the matter at hand, I order you both held without bond for our corporation grand jury, which will meet tomorrow morning at nine o'clock. You are currently being charged with felony assault and kidnapping with the intent to extort, and second-degree felony murder, an act arising during the course of a felony. If any or all of these charges are certified by the grand jury tomorrow morning, your trial will start as soon as a jury has been impaneled. It is my opinion that we should be able to commence your trial as early as nine a.m. Monday."

A look of shock registered on the face of Mickey Courage as he heard again the gravity of the charges against him. Billy Sprouse continued to stare at the judge defiantly. This was the most attention focused on him in his life, and he was relishing it.

Judge Stevens continued, "I see you boys are represented by an attorney. A bail request may be made at tomorrow's hearing. In the meantime, you are remanded to the city jail where you are to be held without bond. This hearing is adjourned."

As the boys were led out of the courtroom, handcuffed together, Mickey Courage looked into the 'congregation': about 80 percent white, mostly male, a few smiling encouragement. There was his father, giving him the thumbs-up, but many were just standing there staring, as if to say, "How could these boys do such a thing— no matter whether the victims were Negro boys?" Meanwhile, there was Billy, handcuffed to Mickey, smiling and waving with his free hand as best he could, as if he had done something special for white folks everywhere by showing those uppity Niggers a thing or two.

At the back of Judge Stevens' courtroom stood about twenty Negro adults, most of whom had taken off work to see if justice would actually be served in a white on black crime in which one of their own had been caused to hang himself. It was too much like the Negro lynchings of the not-too-distant past, and they wanted to see if it was all starting again. They did not smile as the two white boys were led past them. Mickey Courage could feel their cold stare. They seemed to look right through him.

"Hey, buck up Mick," crowed Billy. "We're going to be heroes by the time this is all over. Why, Mr. Smiley says he's designed a surefire defense for us that's gonna beat all the charges. He's gonna tell us about it this afternoon." Billy Sprouse smiled again as the deputies wedged a path for their prisoners through a small crowd that had formed outside the courthouse.

"Yes sir, Mick, this is going to be a ball. Hell, I can't wait to get to court."

Mickey said nothing. He wondered what possible

defense that slick Washington lawyer could have come up with that would allow them to get off scot-free.

Jack Forester walked down the steps of the courthouse not far behind the spectacle of Billy Sprouse and Mickey Courage being led back to the city jail only two blocks away. He wondered at the makeup of the waiting crowd and what they really thought about these two, the victims, and what it all meant in their own lives. The twenty or so Negros, were silent, but he could see the anger in their eyes. The rest were mostly anti-integration merchants and blue-collar types, Jack surmised, who couldn't decide whether to treat the perpetrators as heroes to their class or as hooligans who had disgraced their people. *Perhaps the verdict is still out*, thought Jack.

In the crowd there were few, if any, representatives of the upper classes: the *nouveau riche*, the wealthy transplants, and the old-Liners. Integration was no immediate threat to those who could afford to send their children to private school or to boarding school and who could always be insulated in the confines of their private country clubs: Farmington if you were lucky enough to be accepted as a member, Fry Springs for second-tier people.

Of course, there were also the myriad all-male service clubs for the merchant class and blue-collar workers. They were apprehensive about integration of the Negro. They felt that women's search for equality in a man's world was a novelty to be dealt with gently but firmly. Most married men in 1959 felt confident that they could keep their women in line; they weren't so sure about the Negroes, and so those most directly threatened by integration were here watching, waiting, angry, and frightened. Black or white, what would this trial mean to them?

At this moment Jack realized he must speak to Mickey Courage's father, then to Mickey and his lawyer. He must offer him a way out, a chance at the future, and at the same time ensure conviction of Billy Sprouse. In this way, Jack thought, maybe, just maybe, he could get justice for the Negro victims while preventing simmering racial conflict from exploding into a full-scale riot. Jack knew that, if the Joe Smiley team were successful in floating the immoral advances defense, the outrage of the murdered boys' families could easily erupt into violence in the streets, their own mini race riot. *Under those circumstances, who could blame them, thought Jack.*

I have got to squash Smiley's defense strategy before its ugliness penetrates the courtroom. I now know I need Mickey's testimony to counter whatever slime Smiley can concoct, and that means I must offer a plea bargain that Mickey Courage's family can't refuse.

Jack walked quickly, nodding at the reporters and other interested citizens who were vying for his attention. "Hey, Jack, you really going for a murder conviction?" "Hey, Jack, you really think you can win this one?" "Are you really sure you *want* to win this one?" Jack turned abruptly at this last question to find its voice. It was Alex Ramos, General Cartridge's security assistant, driver, and bodyguard—his man for all reasons.

"Yeah, I'm sure I want to win this one, Alex. Tell the General this case is about justice, not power and privilege." Then, before anyone could do a follow-up, Jack strode away, his right arm in the air as if to signal that he did not wish the reporters to follow. They did not.

Lord, thought Jack, as he reached his office and picked up his messages from Alice, *this is going to be a very long day*. He turned to Alice and smiled wanly, "Alice, I need some time to think. Meanwhile, will you call Michael Courage? Ask him if he is aware of Joe Smiley's defense strategy. Tell him the commonwealth's attorney wants to know if he is really happy with that characterization of his son. If not, tell him I would like a meeting with him and his son at his earliest convenience, say tomorrow afternoon. Of course, as long as he is representing his son, Mr. Smiley would need to be there, but if, upon reflection on the nature of the current defense strategy, Mr. Courage chooses to dispense with Mr. Smiley and his services, then it would be just us three. We leave that up to Mr. Courage, Alice, and we pray he does the right thing. Then call Joe Smiley and tell him we have requested this meeting and that we are still prepared to talk about a plea bargain. That ought to cover Lawyer/Client issues as well as stir the pot nicely."

Alice smiled broadly as she wrote down this last instruction. Jack Forester winked at her. Then he became serious again and continued, "Lastly, can you get me a meeting with the family of Lucius Johnson? I'd like to pay a visit to them, in their home, and sooner rather than later. I want them to understand how this case is going to be played out. I want them to know that, while it may get a little rough in the courtroom, I will win for their son. His memory will be vindicated, and justice will be served. I want them to know that the vast majority of this community will be behind them and will want the same justice that they seek, once all of the facts come out." Jack looked up at Alice and asked, "Do you think you can set up those meetings, Alice?"

"You know I will, Mr. Forester."

"And do you think it will all work out?"

"Honestly, I don't know, Mr. Forester. One thing I do know: it's the right thing to do, and if anybody can pull it off, you can."

"I hope you're right," said Jack. "Once the jury is impaneled, and we'll probably finish with that today, we'll go to trial and there'll be no more time to prevent this trial from being taken over by the bigots and the fearmongers."

"All right, Mr. Forester, I'll go make those calls. I guess you need to work on your opening statement. By the way, you probably haven't had time to look at today's *Richmond Times-Dispatch*," said Alice.

"Anything important?"

"Here," said Alice, as she handed Jack the paper with a front page headline which read, "Will racial tensions explode in Charlottesville?" The sub headlines read, "Two white boys accused of felony murder of two colored boys. Whites claim homosexual defense."

My God, thought Jack, *Smiley had already leaked his slimeball defense to someone in the press, even before he pretended to negotiate with me.*

Chapter 15:
Friday Drinks at the Farmington Tap Room

The news was out all across the many layered social strata of Charlottesville. The two white boys were to be tried on charges of kidnapping, extortion, and felony murder. A grand jury had certified the charges and a jury had been selected. Judge Donald Stevens had set the trial to begin at eleven o'clock on the following Monday.

It was expected to last no longer than two days. Such was the normal procedure in Charlottesville in those days. The right to a speedy trial was strictly observed. The nature of the justice meted out was open to debate. Too often justice was tempered by a man's class, social standing, or race.

At Farmington, it was the Friday cocktail hour in the cavernous tap room where golfers and tennis players gathered to discuss the winners, the losers, and the events of the week in a town they largely controlled.

J.T. Dixley motioned to a black waiter, "Another Cutty on the rocks, Skippy, and don't overdo the rocks." The two other men sitting at his table laughed agreeably as they, too, ordered refills. It had been a long week, what with those redneck hooligans bringing primal fear and loathing to the surface. J.T. didn't like it for business reasons. He had over fifty Negroes working in his textile plant, in an industry that was falling apart. It was all he could do to keep the white workers confident that they would maintain their place in the pecking order. In fact, without the cheap Negro labor, *they* would be out of work.

J.T. Dixley reached out for the Cutty Sark refill that Skippy had just placed before him. He picked it up and looked through the prism of the glass. He looked through its distorted view of his own knotty pine table, past which he could see his drinking companions across the polished black flagstone floor, and the other pine tables packed with leaders and leader-makers of Charlottesville society. Farmington, whose manor house was designed by Thomas Jefferson himself in 1820 and established as Farmington in 1927, was rapidly became the epicenter of Charlottesville politics, breeding and money.

J.T. Dixley, owner of the Dixley Textile Mills, president of Dixley Brick and Block, and Vice Chairman of the Board of People's National Bank, held control of that epicenter. He and fellow Farmington member General Samuel S. Cartridge were considered the two most powerful members of the club and probably of Charlottesville society. J.T. Dixley swallowed his second scotch on the rocks, he felt anger bubbling up within him, anger about that whole stupid redneck assault on those two Negro boys. It wasn't so much the immorality of it all, or even its inherent injustice; it was about money, money that the stupidity of two redneck teenagers could cost him and his businesses. J.T. Dixley had little tolerance for stupidity, especially when it cost him money.

One of his tablemates interrupted his musing, "You know, J.T., that Mickey Courage/Billy Sprouse thing has been blown totally out of proportion. Hell, you know what it's like for a young buck on a hot summer night with nothing to do. Those boys were just out to have a little fun. I admit it got a little out of hand. I don't deny that. And they should be held accountable. And yes, I'm sorry one of those Negro boys accidentally went and hung himself, but that was all unintended. I say send Mickey Courage and Billy Sprouse to reform school for six months and put 'em on probation for a year after that. But that's enough. And I'll tell you why, J.T. Convicting those boys of kidnapping or second-degree homicide or any such foolishness will make the Negro community think we're rolling over, that we are kowtowing to 'em. We can't have that. All this integration bull put on us from that Commie court that Eisenhower has put together. First the school integration, now they want to eat with us in our restaurants. Hell, next thing you know they'll want to go to our movie theatres. Then they'll think they have the right to join Farmington Country Club. We just can't have it. We've got to send a message through this trial that they've got to stop pushing. We've got to keep 'em in their place. We didn't have any of this trouble before forced integration. And I think the colored people were happier too. So I say let's stop all of this foolishness right now, before it's too late. We've got to look after the whites—yes, I mean our rednecks—if we're going to keep it all together. Don't you agree, J.T.?"

J.T. Dixley looked at the long angular face of Bill Barton, a trust fund baby who had earned his money the old-fashioned way: he had inherited it. Barton spent most of his productive day on the golf course or in the tap room gossiping. Dixley stared hard at Barton and said, "What you just said was about as stupid and shortsighted as what those boys did, and it's that stupidity that could blow up your precious society right in your smug face. Do you know why?"

A chastened and slightly embarrassed Bill Barton said nothing, preferring to look down at his shiny lace-up cordovans.

The third person at J.T. Dixley's table was Justin Logan, a thirty-something up and-coming land speculator whose family had moved to Charlottesville in the late 1940s. Logan was undeterred by J.T.'s harsh words for Barton. He leaned his short wiry frame toward Dixley, his blue eyes twinkling, and, with a voice and a face said to charm ladies over and under fifty, responded, "So, J.T., tell me, if we're all so stupid, am I to presume you're not?" He chuckled, as, self-consciously, did Barton. Logan sat back in his chair for the next move. When there was only a cold silence and a steady stare from Dixley, Logan restated his case. "So J.T., will you share your godly wisdom with us poor incoherent Blue Bloods?"

Logan laughed again, but Bill Barton did not join him. All the tables around him had gone quiet as well. Dixley stood up as if to address the whole crowd. They all wondered if the great J.T. Dixley was about to speak to them or, as Bill Barton feared, to leave the room in disgust. Many of those at surrounding tables had overheard the thrust of Logan's petulant questions. Everyone knew that J.T. was not a man to take even the mildest of insults lightly.

Dixley's voice pierced the cacophony of the Farmington Country Club. "Before I leave tonight," he said, "I have a few parting words for you self-righteous so-called patricians of the south. Those of you who can trace your roots back more than three or four generations will find, for the most part, the Irish underbelly, the Italian WOP, the English working class, or the Welch coal miner, as I do. We came here for freedom and opportunity and to have a better life than that which we left behind."

He continued, "We created our own new pecking order – do you think our reborn culture will free you from what you left behind? I think not. We have already freed the black sweat laborers. We cannot do without them. And mark my words, Gentlemen, separate but equal is not the reward they will accept for their toil. Full assimilation is what they will have. If you want to fight it in your mills and your banks, your manufacturing plants, fine. Not me. I'm a realist, not an idealist, and not a bigot.

"I believe they work better for me when I let them *have* their share, their integrated place in my mills. Fight it if you will, make jokes and snide remarks about your nobility and the inferiority of your colored neighbor. I say your plants will flounder with black worker infighting, picketing, layoffs, and the like. Meanwhile, mine will thrive. I will embrace the chance because I know it is inevitable. I will make money on it and one day soon I will be pleased to sit right here with you and with my black superintendent as the new member of good old Farmington Country Club."

J.T. Dixley tapped the empty chair next to Barry Van Supleworth III, "Right next to you, Barry. Soon my black superintendent will be your newest club member. And he'll be sitting right next to you, drinking his gin martini." With a short staccato laugh, J.T. Dixley walked out of the Farmington Country Club, leaving those behind him to contemplate his words.

"I'll tell you one thing Harvey." said Charles Van Horn Jr. to his golfing partner sitting next to him, "those niggers can work in my mill, but they'll never go to school with my son at Episcopal High School, even if they have pushed their way into our public schools. And they sure as hell are not going to join me at Farmington Country Club unless they want to be a cook in the kitchen or a waiter on the floor or a caddy on the golf course. Right, Harvey?"

Harvey Weinstein, in fact the newest member of Farmington and president of Citizen's Bank, which held loans for many of the members of Farmington, paused for a moment and said with a twinkle in his eye, "I don't know, Charlie. We let you in. I would have preferred another pal from the synagogue instead of just one more white anglo-saxon protestant."

There was silence followed by nervous laughter as the assembled members of Farmington Country Club grasped the irony of this last remark.

"Yea, why did we let Charlie in?" asked Joe Pace from table three.

More laughter, except for Charlie, who remained silent. With this last humorous remark, they felt they could all leave, honor still intact.

Chapter 16: Friday Night at the Riverside Grill

Meanwhile, at the Riverside Grill, cement truck drivers and finish carpenters, brick masons and mill workers, house painters and plumbers all stood elbow to arm pit at the long U-shaped bar. They, too, were celebrating the end of a long work week on this crowded Friday night. They were drinking their longneck Budweiser or Pabst Blue Ribbon, the occasional boiler maker and Ballantine Ale. There were even a few Pepsi drinkers, for Charlottesville was a Pepsi town, but not usually on a Friday night. If the Farmington crowd were the makers and shakers in Charlottesville, then these men were the fuel that drove its work engine. In this little bar tavern overlooking the Rivanna River at the dividing point of city and county, the grill was never cleaned—only scraped in order to preserve a unique flavor where the flames enveloped the hot dogs and hamburgers alike, a flavor that was a mix of the past and the present. When your hamburger arrived, charred on the outside, rare on the inside, on a paper plate with home-grown tomato slices and onions and crowded with a mess of French fries, with ketchup, mustard, and mayonnaise on the side, you knew you were a part of the Riverside experience on a Friday night.

Friday was also payday, a time when this hardworking, hard-living crowd was at its loudest, rowdiest, and most jovial. Tonight, though, there was a somber, even sullen mood in this all-white, all-male working class establishment. The Billy Sprouse/ Mickey Courage mess bothered them. No Negro had ever tried to be served here, and that's the way they liked it. After all, everyone had his own place. This is how they thought at the Riverside. The Negroes had Vinegar Hill in town and Brenwanna just on the edge of town near the Twin Lakes. There they could party and dance and drink as much as they wanted. Just do it at their places, like we do at ours. This white working class was okay with separate but equal. Many of them worked with the Negroes during the day, and for the most part everybody got along fine as long as everyone stayed with his own kind at night. The Riverside crowd didn't much like the forced school integration that had started just a few years before; in fact, they had resisted it with basement schools and private white schools if they could afford it. They had, however, eventually accepted the bitter inevitability of public school integration and had become almost comfortable with the reality. Some of the Negroes they knew from work were good people, and some of their kids were very good athletes. Integration had produced a better football team. Charlottesville only had one previously all-white high school, and nothing brought the town together like a good football team.

The Riverside crowd had come to grudging terms with school integration. Some even embraced it, but few wanted to share their after-work watering holes, the last bastion against disapproving wives and the Negro who threatened to push by them in the pecking order of life.

Standing at the bar, Joe Dykstra, a plumber, turned to his friend, Bill Fallow, and observed, "You know, Bill, those guys at Farmington, mostly our bosses, don't give a damn what the niggers do as long as they keep working and don't riot. Well I don't care either, as long as they don't push into our neighborhoods, our pools, and our bars. They got their own, for God's sake."

Chapter 17: Saturday before Trial: A Tennis Morning

It was about seven forty-five Saturday morning, July 25th, 1959, as Jack slowly drove his black 1951 Chrysler convertible down Farmington Drive. The white canvas top was down and the southwesterly breeze was still agreeable. The heat of the day had not yet arrived, and Jack hoped for a break from the murder-kidnapping case which had suddenly dominated his every waking moment.

Jack patted the red leather back of his forward passenger seat: "Come on, Jack. Time to do your duty."

First coal black eyes appeared, then a large, mostly black, mostly Labrador retriever leapt from the back into the front passenger seat. His tail wagged fiercely against the armrest, as he leaned over to give his master a big lick.

"All right, stop it, Jack. It's bad enough we have

to share the same name. Oh, all right." Jack the man received a few more wet licks as he reached out and scratched the dog behind the ears. Then Jack pulled back his hand and turned down Tennis Lane. Jack the dog barked as if in recognition that the pleasantries were over and now began the serious business of guarding the car while his master was off hitting a rubber ball with a wooden stick with a rounded head and a net in the middle of it. No doubt the game would have been better without the stick or the net. Still, Jack the dog understood that this was what men did. It was a mystery, but it seemed to give his master pleasure so the dog was okay with it.

"All right, Jack," said Jack, getting out of the car. "Here's our special shady spot. You guard the car. It's okay to nap occasionally. I'll be back in about an hour and a half." Jack the dog locked his eyes on his master to acknowledge that he understood his job.

Meanwhile, Jack the man walked away through the giant box hedges towards the fifth of Farmington's famous red-clay courts, acknowledging to himself that he had a better understanding and warmer relationship with Jack the dog than with anyone else.—certainly more so than with his ex-wife of five years, who had given him the dog after the first four years of marriage. "I've named him Jack to remind me of your better nature—you know, loving, feeling, and amusing—so even when I have to put up with serious preoccupied Mr. Lawyer, I am reminded of your better side."

"What about the kids," Jack had reacted. "Won't they be a little confused about the name?"

"Oh no, darling. Both Henry and Julia know the difference between Jack the daddy and Jack the dog. Jack's all play and no work. Daddy's all work and no play."

God, thought Jack, as he nodded at his early morning doubles partner. Six years later and five years divorced, he wondered if his ex had been right. *Henry's eleven and Julia's nine. I get to see them once a week and two weeks in the summer if it doesn't conflict with their mother's schedule or mine. I hardly know them. All I know is Jack the dog.*

"Hey, Jack, wake up, boy. We've got a tough match this morning." It was Jay Cutler, Jack's weekly doubles partner. They had known each other since the University of Virginia Law School, where they had won the prestigious moot court trial award. Jay had gone on to private practice, with a specialty in real estate law. His principal client, the I. M. Knot Hurt Company, had made him a millionaire.

Jay Cutler seemed to have it all, and sometimes Jack wondered if he himself had made the right choice in the service of the people. He felt tired this morning, and though he kept fit with his daily run and workout schedule, Jack felt every one of his thirty-six years. Jay, looking both fit and relaxed, seemed full of energy.

"Come on, Jack," said Jay, as he repeatedly tapped the tennis ball in the air with his racket. "We need to get these guys early today. They're about ten years younger than us thirty-something geezers. They think we're over the hill. Get that weary DA look off your face. We are better than these guys. They're young and I think they're in better shape. We've got to demoralize them early, make 'em think they just can't beat us. You know, like you do in court. If it goes to a third set, they *will* beat us, cuz ole buddy, by then we *will* be out of gas. But they can't know that."

After a pause, Jay continued, "So here's the plan. We come at 'em fast and hard, never let up, just like we did in Moot Court, eh Jack?"

Jay slapped Jack on the back and they both laughed at his pep talk. They walked out to the tennis pavilion to introduce themselves to their younger opponents.

Jay was a shifty lefty and Jack was known for his powerful forehand from the right. This immediately and temporarily confused their younger opponents. Jay and Jack won the first two games.

In the third game, Jack served a hard topspinner to the deuce court and Fred Unger and his partner, Bill Carter, stood frozen in place as Jay blasted the weak return shot into the open court. On the next point Bill Carter whipped a second serve down the line and Jack, with a lunge to his right, stopped the ball in mid-air and dropped it over the net—perhaps with a little luck, but it was a phenomenal shot. Jay Cutler chuckled and whispered to Jack loudly enough for the others to hear, "You sure have that drop shot working today, Jack." Smiling, Jack turned his back to the net and walked down to the deuce court.

With the score thirty-love, Jack rocketed an ace down the T of the deuce service line. Forty-love and a second serve with a high topspin caught Fred Unger off-guard again. Jay intercepted his weak return at the net and again slammed into the open court: third game to Jay and Jack. It was 3-0 in the first set. More impressive, the young guns hadn't won a single point. They had a 'Who are these guys?' look on their faces.

"A couple more games like this, and these guys are going to fold," Jay said to Jack, again loud enough for their opponents to hear. "Let's turn it on."

Fred Unger slammed his first serve to Jack. Jack caught up to the speeding ball as it spun wide to his right and was just able to flick it down the line. He caught an embarrassed Bill Carter going the other way: love-fifteen. Then, Fred Unger missed his first serve to Jay by going for too much. Jay lined up the weaker second serve and slammed it at the feet of the onrushing Fred Unger just as he was reaching mid-court. The ball spun off Fred's racket and dribbled off towards the tennis pavilion, where the Saturday morning crowd was beginning to sense something special was happening on court five. Love-thirty.

A double fault to Jack made it love-forty. A lefty forehand return from Jay caught the youngsters off-guard yet again. Another game to Jack and Jay, and still their opponents had yet to score a single point. This fact was not lost on them, nor was a gathering crowd of spectators in the pavilion about to let it go.

"Hey, have you kids won a single point against these old men? It looks like they've got a choke hold on you." The crowd laughed good-naturedly, because all tennis is supposed to be a good-natured, good-sportsmanlike game. It was apparent to Jack that he and Jay had gotten into the heads of their opponents. Jack overheard Fred Unger whisper to Bill Carter, "I can't believe this crap. We should be killin' these guys." But they did not appear to believe it themselves. The exuberant weekend crowd of spectators loved the early morning drama unfolding. It was as good as a Bloody Mary pick-me-up.

For Jack and Jay it was one of those magical tennis days when they could do no wrong. They moved in unspoken synchronicity, as one unit, from side to side, smothering the net and making difficult, even seemingly impossible, shots. Of course, a faster, younger team like Fred Unger and Bill Carter couldn't be held scoreless forever, and as they began recovering some of their lost confidence, their youth and speed began to catch up with Jack and Jay. Almost imperceptibly, the momentum and the games seemed to move away from Jack and Jay.

It was 4-5 in Jack and Jay's favor with Fred Unger serving at thirty-forty to Jay. If Jack and Jay won this point, they won the set and could regain the momentum. If they lost, the game would go to deuce, and, with the onrushing younger opponents beginning to turn it on, the point might prove a turning point of the match. The four players on the court knew it and certainly the crowd of spectators sensed it.

Jay received a hard flat serve to his lefty forehand and chipped a screamer down the center between the other guys. Both he and Jack, sensing their tactical advantage, rushed the net as Fred Unger scrambled in retreat to catch up to the ball. He was just able to reach it, and with the racket fully extended and with a perfect flick of the racket, he lobbed it over the rushing Jack. Fred relaxed visibly as he watched his lob soar over Jack's head and deep into the baseline, where it appeared Jack could not get to it in time. Fred watched with amusement from the baseline as Jack raced to catch up with what was obviously a topspin lob winner.

But then, as if in slow motion, Jack did reach the ball still going away from the net. He knew he would have to hit it really high if he was to have a chance to reverse its arc and send it back across the net. He did. Jack's return sailed so high that all four players waited together to see where it would land. The ball was momentarily impossible hard to see, lost in the morning sun. Exasperated, Fred Unger shielded his eyes with his left hand. Suddenly, he saw the ball drop out of the sunlight onto the baseline tape just next to him and bounce up again in a lazy arc towards the giant hedges which framed the court. Fred raced back to the hedges, desperately reaching up for the ball with his racket, much like a center fielder might reach up to rob a hitter of his home run. To no avail. As Fred slammed into the hedges, he could only look up to see the ball land softly on the very top of the hedges, as if nesting.

The point was over. The game was over. And the first set belonged to Jack Forester and Jay Cutler. The players and spectators looked in amazement at the ball, still nestled, for all to see, atop the hedges. There were the usual comments from the fans: "That was a hell of a shot, Jack." "I've never seen anything quite like it." There was a smattering of applause, and then another voice from the crowd said, "Well, Fred, I think you boys are going to get schooled today. Might as well just lay back and take your medicine." The crowd laughed good-naturedly, but Fred turned in the direction of the voice and said, "Screw you, Rogers." This outburst was understandable, given the way the last point had played out, but the crowd did not like it.

"Oh, it looks like Martha put a little too much starch in Fred's shorts last night," continued Joe Rogers. "Well, I figure they'll hang pretty loose once this match is over." The crowd laughed again, as everyone thought this last comment was pretty amusing everyone except Fred and his partner.

As they prepared to begin the second set, Unger whispered to his partner, "Okay, let's quit screwing around and put these guys back where they belong – in their middle ages." Unfortunately for Fred, Joe Rogers, who had moved his lawn chair to the very edge of the pavilion and practically onto the court, overheard this last remark and loosely and loudly paraphrased it, "Hey Jack, Fred says you guys are too fat and too old to beat them a second set."

"Hey, that's not what I said, Rogers," yelled Fred from the court.

But it was already too late. Fred had taken the bait, and Jack capitalized on the moment, "Well, Fred, we've still got a little left in the tank for two old and fat guys." He stared down at Fred in mock anger.

"Jack, I didn't say that." Fred was practically whining in his exasperation, but Jack, with a wink to Jay Cutler, turned back in Fred's direction of Fred and continued, "Okay, Fred, that's it. Let's just see what you can show us. Talk is cheap."

"Yeah," Joe Rogers agreed from the sidelines. "Let's see what you've got, Fred."

"Shut up, Joe," said Fred, pointing his racket at his own personal heckler.

The whole pavilion was in an amused uproar. They knew now that Joe had gotten Fred's goat, and sensed that Fred had lost his composure and was about to lose his temper.

"So," said Jack, "it's your serve, Fred. Any other gratuitous remarks, or can we continue? Jay and I would like to get going if you guys have caught your breath." There was more appreciative laughter from the pavilion as Fred practically ran back to the service line.

Fred wound up—"This one's for you, Jack!"— and blasted his first serve into the deuce court. Jack could not even get his racket on the ball, but it did not matter.

"Just wide, Fred," he said.

"Are you sure?" Fred was glaring across the net.

"It was wide," Bill Carter confirmed. "Come on, Fred. Second serve." Fred hit another blistering serve, harder than the first but six inches too long.

"Double fault, Fred. Love-fifteen." Jay Cutler got into the act.

"I know the score, Jay," said Fred, as he proceeded to blast two more errant serves in the general direction of the ad court. It was love-thirty to Jack and Jay.

Fred pushed his next serve into the deuce court and Jack drove it behind Bill Carter at the net and down the line, a clean winner. At love-forty, Fred hit a sharply angled topspinner to Jay's backhand, or so he thought. He had momentarily forgotten that Jay was a lefty, who consequently was able to get around the offering with a hard forehand topspin which took the serve on the rise and drove it past the startled Bill Carter at net and just out of the reach of the hard-charging Fred Unger. First game of the second set at love to Jack and Jay. Not even close. Fred had lost his serve, his biggest weapon, at love. It was more than a game to him now.

Fred was embarrassed. His inner anger turned on his racket. He flung it at the hedges, surrounding the courts and drove the handle deep into the bush, so that only the head stuck out. The gathered crowd went silent at this outburst. A little ribbing, a little gamesmanship, and trading little sarcasms, good-natured and not, were all considered part of the mental game. Throwing your racket, as Fred had just done, was considered over the line, juvenile, and not acceptable in the unwritten tennis etiquette rules. Everyone knew this at Farmington, including Fred Unger.

Slowly he walked over, pulled his racket out of the hedges, and turned to the others on the court. "Sorry, fellas. I guess it just slipped out of my hand."

At 1-0, he and Bill Carter crossed over to the other side. Everyone waited for another riposte from Joe Rogers, but there was none. It would have been too easy. Unger was already a broken man and had embarrassed his partner by his actions.

There were a few good rallies in the second set, but it appeared that Fred and Bill were just going through the motions, as if they couldn't wait to get off the court and away from this match, this crowd, and the embarrassment of it all.

The second set was over in thirty minutes, 6-2 for Jack and Jay. Fred and Bill walked slowly to the net, shook hands, and offered their congratulations. Then they practically raced off the court to avoid the good natured catcalls. They must have overheard one in particular, "Old guys win—again!" It was Joe Rogers, who came out onto the court, turned to Jay Cutler, and said, "Well, how'd I do, Jay?"

Jay and Joe roared with laughter.

"Joe," Jay said, "that was the best bit of heckling I've seen."

"So, do I trophy?" said Joe.

"Yes, absolutely. You've earned that six-pack of Bud. Hell, I'll even drink it with you." Jay turned to Jack. "Yep, Joe was our secret weapon, Jack. I couldn't tell you about it, or you wouldn't have let me do it. Worked great, didn't it? The only thing worse for Fred Unger than losing so badly and then losing his temper would be to tell him that we set him up. He'd probably commit suicide in angst if we told him. So we better let sleeping dogs lie, eh Jack? Fred will get over it. Might even make him a better man for the lesson. So will you join us in a celebratory beer?"

"No," said Jack with a level gaze at his erstwhile partner. "You two rogues, er, should I say partners in crime, go enjoy the tainted victory." Jack chuckled as he turned to Jay again. "You know, Jay, I think we could have beaten them without Joe's antics. Now we'll never know. Joke's on us."

"Oh, come on, Jack. I was just looking for a little extra fun."

"And a little insurance," said Jack.

"Maybe. Hey, you on for next Saturday, same time? We're on a roll now, you and I."

"You and Joe are on a roll, not me. I'll pass on next week."

"Oh, c'mon Jack, don't be such a straight arrow."

"I guess we all have our true natures, Jay. Maybe that's why I work for the commonwealth and you make all that money in real estate development." Jay stood speechless at this retort.

"See you later, Jay." Jack strode away to the comfort of his car and the better company he now sought, Jack the dog. People were such a disappointment after you got to know a good dog.

* * * * * * * * *

Jack found Jack the dog curled up in the driver's seat. The sun had shifted with the day. Its warm rays had pierced the previous shade and were providing Jack the dog an excellent sun bath. He was quite obviously asleep on the job.

"Oh, Jack," whispered his master as he approached the car. Jack the dog bolted upright in his master's seat, turning his head from side to side to show he had been guarding the car all along.

"Easy, boy," said Jack, opening the door and accepting a lick to the accompaniment of the tomtom pounding of dog tail on the leather seat. "Okay, move on over to your side. It may be Saturday, but we've got a lot of work to do before the weekend's over."

In total understanding, Jack the dog eased over to the passenger seat, his tail still wagging at the return of his master. As they drove off down Tennis Lane, turned right onto Farmington Drive, and headed back to town, wind blowing in their hair, Jack reached over to scratch his dog behind the ears. He smiled as Jack the dog turned to show his teeth. It was a joyful smile, as if they shared the mutual thought, "It doesn't get any better than this."

Chapter 18: Walking to the City Jail

Jack had left his car at home on Rugby Avenue. Jack the dog was looking after it from the relative shade of the fenced-in backyard. Once again, Jack had decided to walk to his office and then to the city jail for the meeting that Alice had set up with Mickey Courage, Billy Sprouse, and their lawyer, Joe Smiley. Jack hoped that Mickey's father would be there, too, but did not know if he would appear.

Jack had reluctantly concluded that the only way to reach a workable plea agreement with Smiley was to include Billy Sprouse. If the meeting, distasteful but necessary, went as Jack hoped, he would persuade Smiley and the boys to take a plea. Billy Sprouse would get less than he deserved, but Charlottesville would be spared the angst and expense of an ugly trial and the possibility of riots that might come of it. That was the nature of a good pretrial agreement.

Hopefully, Jack could put a good face on it all so that the blacks would accept a lesser measure of justice and the whites, especially the working-class whites, would accept what they knew against all prejudice was a fair punishment for the crimes committed by two of their own.

Hell, thought Jack, *at least there'll be no riots from either side, and maybe even some newfound mutual respect between the two races would come from it all. Wouldn't that be something?*

Jack climbed to the top of Rugby Avenue, turned left onto Rugby Road, and kept walking down the hill at Preston Avenue, where Rugby Road forked to the right. Jack looked to his left, between two brick ranch houses, and saw his old sledding hill, where white boys from Rugby Road and black boys from below Washington Park would converge on a snowy day and race their Flexible Flyers, their Silver Saucers, and their flattened corrugated cardboard boxes down suicide hill past evergreen trees, past hedges, and, heads held just above the ground, fly under the barbwire fence finish line.

There would be races and laughter, falling down in the snow, and perhaps a spontaneous snowball fight with seamlessly integrated teams. At the end of the day, everyone would wave and say "see you" before going to their separate but equal houses. It was a moment of true equality, a fraternity, a snow memory.

Well, thought Jack, *perhaps it can be a little more*

like that in this case. Still, we adults are not yet ready for the total mutual acceptance given by the very young.

Jack passed Washington Park, designed and built for a neighborhood that was ninety-five percent black. Jack looked over at a baseball game as the pitcher threw a hard slider. "Strike three," said the umpire, as the ball slammed into the catcher's mitt.

Boy, thought Jack, *we could have used him at Episcopal High School in the prep championships against Woodberry Forest in 1939. I bet Coach Brinser would have fought hard for an 'academic' scholarship to get him on the team. But he's black. It would never have happened then. It might today. Perhaps one day soon the combination of sports, talent, and general enlightenment will overcome our casual prejudices.* It was a thought.

Jack walked up the hill and looked to his left at the Washington Park pool. It was the first pool built with this Negro neighborhood in mind, and the City Council was proud of itself for what it had done for its Negroes. Washington Park was an example of how 'separate but equal' could work. While the city's other four pools were for whites only, this pool was packed with Negro swimmers and splashing Negro children in the adjoining wading pool. The pool was surrounded by picnic tables laden with apples and bananas, all manner of sandwiches, bowls of salad, and various cooling drinks. It was a clear, hot, Saturday afternoon in late July. What better way to spend it than at a picnic at your own neighborhood pool?

People just being people, thought Jack, *except that they are all black—separate but equal.* Jack knew that one mile to the south of Washington Park one could find the all-white Belmont Pool, where kids would be splashing in the pool and others playing softball in the field to the right. There it would be all white and happy. Well, weren't they happy here at Washington Park too?

Jack wondered if forced school integration really was the right way to achieve equality between the races. Gradually, naturally, segregation might dissolve of its own irrelevance, except that it might take another fifty years of flickering bigotry and race abuse for it to happen. Sometimes you had to jump-start the system. One could not afford to wait to appeal to everyone's better nature. In Charlottesville, forced school integration had worked better than most had imagined. There had been no major disruption of life, no fiery riots or Negro bashing—yet.

In the spirit of peaceful mass resistance, some neighborhoods had started all-white basement schools, there were a plethora of all white private day schools, and, of course, there were always the elite white prep schools like St. Christopher's in Richmond, Woodberry Forest north of Orange, and Jack's own Episcopal High School in Northern Virginia. These were boarding schools, restricted only to those who could provide both pedigree and wherewithal.

The prep schools to the north—St. Paul's,

Groton, Exeter, Lawrenceville, The Hill School, Taft, Hotchkiss, and others—were for the sons of Charlottesville's more liberal blue bloods, who philosophically agreed with the concept of integration and racial equality, but, as practicing elitists, felt compelled to send their sons to the institutions that would best nurture their destiny to be the true leaders of all races in the coming years.

This left Charlottesville's merchant man and the blue-collared class below him to bear the actual brunt of integration. Initially they were more than a little resentful. Over time, however, forced integration had broken down much prejudice and misunderstanding and ameliorated the fear that the Negro threatened their living and working environment.

As Jack walked past Lane High School on his left, he proceeded to climb the hill which gave the street its name, High Street.

Two blocks from the city jail, Jack stopped his integration reverie and refocused on the task at hand. He decided to walk straight to the city jail for his meeting with Joe Smiley and his clients, Mickey Courage and Billy Sprouse. He knew that, if he stopped by his own office, even on a Saturday, there would be messages left for him by Alice, who always came in on Saturday morning to catch up. She, too, would need questions answered, and today Jack did not want to be distracted, even by the very worthy Alice.

Chapter 19: Jailhouse Plea Bargain

Jack carried only his appointment book and a yellow legal pad on which he had scribbled some notes early this morning. As he opened the door to the sheriff's office, he found Sheriff Bredlo himself smiling at him from behind the scarred and memorabilia-cluttered pine-wood desk.

"Why hello, Jack Forester. I was waiting on you," gushed Sheriff Bredlo. "I got the word from that Joe Smiley that you was going to meet with him and the boys, so naturally I just wanted to be around and see if I could help out. You know General Cartridge has called me a couple of time to see how this thing is going, but I didn't help him much, 'cuz I want to do right by *you*. You're still going to look after *me*, right?"

Jack still wondered what specific impropriety Sheriff Bredlo had committed that he believed

Jack knew about, and decided again to keep that misperception as his ace in the hole. A sheriff can be helpful or not in procedure and protocol in small but important areas that can affect witnesses, perpetrators and juries alike, and Jack intended to keep Sheriff Bredlo in his vest pocket for as long as he could.

"I told you before, Barry, you just continue to do your job right by me. That's what I want, that's what I expect, and that's what I will appreciate. Do we understand each other?"

Sheriff Bredlo's smile revealed twenty-five years of bad dentistry. It was as if he thought they had some secret pact, and that was fine by Jack.

"Well, that's great. Hey, listen, they're all here already chattering away in the conference room: that lawyer Smiley, Courage, and Sprouse of course, and, oh yeah, Mickey Courage's father showed up, too. I think it sort of took that Smiley by surprise, 'cuz they're going at it like a couple of junkyard dogs. I got Jones and Franklin, two of my best deputies, looking after 'em. And hey, I got Mickey and Billy shackled hand and foot just to let 'em know not to get smart with anybody."

After a pause, the sheriff continued, "They're waiting for you, Jack. You want to make 'em wait a little longer, or shall I walk you on down there?"

"No, that's fine, Barry. Let's go," said Jack.

A private hallway led to the interrogation room, which also served as a conference room. It could be reached in two ways: from a door in the sheriff's office and down a narrow corridor, for lawyers, visitors and officers, or from a separate passageway leading directly from the jail cells themselves. In this way, Sheriff Bredlo could control, from his desk, access to the interrogation room at any time.

It was rumored that he had this conference/interrogation room bugged in order to violate attorney-client privacy rights whenever he thought it might provide some advantage to himself. Since this illegal wiretapping, if detected, could be grounds for censure, immediate dismissal, and possibly felony charges, Jack suspected that this rumor was true and that this was the secret that Sheriff Bredlo thought Jack had proof of. Accordingly, Bredlo was hoping he could render favors in return for which Jack would continue to look the other way.

"Yeah, Jack," said Barry Bredlo, opening the door to the dank, dirty and dimly lit grey cement passageway. "I kinda overheard Michael Courage telling that slick DC lawyer he wasn't gonna let any son of his get involved in some homo defense, so I think you got some real leverage here. Why if I was you—"

"You're not me, Barry, and I don't want to know how you overheard privileged communication between a lawyer and his client. Do you understand me?"

"Uh, sure, Jack, anything you say. I was just trying to help," said a chastened Barry Bredlo.

"Just walk me in there, Sheriff. We've done this a

few times before."

"Right, I got you, Jack." Sheriff Bredlo led the way to the end of the corridor, inserted a key, and opened the door. Billy Sprouse sat at one end of a scarred metal table, his hands and feet shackled. A deputy stood directly behind him. Billy stared straight ahead, as if all alone in the room. In a sense he was, just as he had been most of his life.

At the other end of the long, narrow, table sat Mickey Courage—shackled, but wearing a clean dress shirt and khaki pants his mother had brought him the day before. She had also delivered some homemade fried chicken and apple pie. As was the custom, these had been shared with the deputy on duty, who was subsequently more inclined to look favorably on Mickey's needs and requests and to grant such privileges as an extra phone call to his father.

Still, Mickey looked glum as he stared across the table at his father, who was attempting, as was his habit, to take over the discussion, in this case with Mickey's lawyer. "Hey, you can say that Billy was sucked in by the colored boys' homo advances and that's why he got mad and did stupid things. Yeah, go ahead if Billy don't care; that's his right. But my son's still got a future and I'm not gonna have it screwed up by having him branded a queer for the rest of his life."

About this time Sheriff Bredlo opened the door behind Michael to reveal himself and Jack Forester.

"Well, hello, boys. Sounds like a big ruckus going

on in here. Good thing our district attorney, Mr. Jack Forester, has, umm, come to your rescue." Bredlo turned and bowed in Jack's general direction.

"Y'all pay attention and I'll bet he'll straighten out this whole mess." Bredlo turned again to Jack and continued, "I'll leave 'em to you, Jack. Any problems, the deputies and I will take care of them. Meantime, I'll be in my office if you need me."

Yeah and I'll bet you'll be listening to every word, thought Jack.

Sheriff Bredlo backed his corpulence through the doors and disappeared as he pulled it shut.

"All right, let's get down to business, Mr. Smiley. I'm prepared to offer your clients considerable leniency if they plead guilty to the charges against them. Listen carefully, because I'm only putting this offer on the table for a very short time. It's better than your clients deserve, but, in the interest of sparing the community the divisiveness of a racially charged trial and acknowledging your clients' relative youth, I'm offering them a break—Mickey Courage particularly, but you must take it or leave it—right now."

Joe Smiley had listened carefully. He dropped all pretense of being the dapper little DC lawyer looking for the proper stage on which to showcase his skills. Cold coal-black eyes met Jack's across the table. It was now all about the business at hand; no more dancing around the core of the matter.

"Mr. Forester, it is my belief that you fear that an open trial of my clients would quite possibly incite the working class of this town, white and colored alike, to some kind of violent confrontation. A trial, you fear, could produce racial turmoil in Charlottesville for years to come, do you not?"

After a pause and no response, Smiley continued, "As I understand it, Charlottesville has been spared interracial unpleasantness by and large, while proceeding with desegregation in its own special way. Unfortunately for you, this trial could change all that."

"And your point is?" intoned Jack.

"Well, my point is this, Mr. Forester. Before you make your final offer to my clients, I suggest you make sure it truly *is* your best offer. Consider all the consequences if we do not reach agreement. What I'm saying, Mr. Forester, is that it is not just the fate of these two boys you hold in your hands; it may also be the fate of your whole community. If you overreach yourself now, you stand to lose not only the trial and the support of the community at large, you also could destroy your own political future.

"So my point is that perhaps you'd like to reconsider your best plea offer *before* you put it on the table. I think you understand me now, Mr. Forester."

"Are you through, Mr. Smiley?"

"For the moment, Mr. Forester."

Jack looked around at his audience. Billy Sprouse, with a tight smile, looked in the direction of his lawyer. In his street-smart wisdom he understood exactly what was being negotiated. The fact that he might have a part in keeping those niggers in their place made Billy feel good.

Jack observed that Mickey Courage was looking miserable, as if wondering how he ever got into this mess. He was sitting in a corner, avoiding his father's glare and possibly wondering if he was ever going to get out from under his father's shadow.

Meanwhile, Billy Sprouse, as well as the two deputies, and quite possibly Sheriff Bredlo by way of the bug, were waiting for the next shoe to drop.

The silence was deafening. Jack kept staring, and Joe Smiley took his continued lack of response as indecision. Finally, Smiley could not contain himself any longer. "So what's it going to be, Mr. Forester? Are you going to work with us and this community? Let's hear it," he said, holding his arms out wide in an expansive gesture. "What have you got for us?"

Jack walked to the head of the table and sat down. This meant that Joe Smiley, in the middle of the table, Mickey Courage and his father across from Smiley and away from Billy Sprouse sitting in the far corner, all had to turn their head towards Jack as he dropped his legal pad on the table.

At this moment, Jack held the power, symbolic and actual, and he intended to keep it, just as he intended to convince this lawyer and the defendants alike of the tenuousness of their own position. First, he turned to the bombastic little lawyer from Washington and said, "As the commonwealth attorney of Charlottesville, I am responsible to represent the legal interests of all the people of Charlottesville. And yes, Mr. Smiley, I do feel a larger responsibility to the general welfare of the citizens of my community and must consider how this trial might affect them. While I agree with very little of what you say, I accept your premise that this trial could enflame and further arouse the current anger and mistrust between our white and colored communities.

"A plea agreement acceptable to all sides could maintain the peace, and perhaps even begin rebuilding mutual trust. On the other hand, this town can handle this trial if need be. We will confront the issues at hand and produce a successful prosecution of your clients without bringing racial chaos to the community. Frankly, I think the white and colored alike around here are more upset about what these boys did than with each other. It was senseless and cruel and stupid. Not much sympathy for your boys, even from the working class white, Mr. Smiley.

"Still, offering your clients a plea agreement may be the most painless way out for all concerned. It may even be the easy way out; I don't know. In any event, I'm willing to offer it right here, right now, no negotiations, to get this mess behind us."

Jack heard a loud theatrical guffaw coming from the general direction of Joe Smiley, who fluttered his eyes and spoke. "Mr. Forester, does your speech go on much longer or do we get to hear your offer sometime today? My clients would probably like to get back to their cells before dinner is served."

Billy Sprouse laughed out loud and said, "Yeah, Mr. Forester, I'm getting pretty hungry for some of that jailhouse chow."

Michael Courage said nothing, but his son Mickey said quietly, "I'd like to hear your offer, Mr. Forester. I want to get this thing behind me too."

"Shut up," said Billy.

"Let me do the talking, son," Smiley quickly interjected.

Jack saw his opportunity. "Right, Billy, I know you're anxious to get back to your cell, and you, Mr. Smiley, probably can't wait to take your fee and get back to DC, so I'll lay it out for you—one time—no negotiation—the best and only offer you are going to get."

"Billy Sprouse, you are currently charged with kidnapping with intent to extort money. You also are charged with felony murder. If convicted, you could be sentenced to up to twenty years for kidnapping and fifteen years to life for felony murder. In exchange for a plea agreement, I am willing to reduce the kidnapping charge to false imprisonment and the felony murder charge to involuntary manslaughter: three to five years on the first charge, and seven to ten on the second." Jack continued, "You could be out in ten years on good behavior. You will serve your sentence at the state penitentiary in Richmond.

"Mickey, for your cooperation, I'm offering you the same deal on the first charge of false imprisonment and will drop the second charge. Since you are only seventeen, you will be allowed to serve your term in a juvenile detention center in Goochland County. At age twenty, you will be eligible for release for good behavior. If not released at that time, you will serve the rest of your term in the state pen with Billy Sprouse."

Jack stood up and put his finger to his mouth to silence Joe Smiley. "If we proceed to trial, you both could be facing thirty-five years or more in prison. Now talk it over with your lawyer, but not until I leave."

Jack walked to the side door leading to the corridor, which, in turn, led to the sheriff's office. As he backed out the door, he looked at Mickey and said, "It may be better than you both deserve, but it is your chance for a future. I suggest you take it. It's a little bit before two o'clock. Let my office know by four thirty or the deal is off the table and we go to trial."

"We need to talk, Mr. Forester. You know you can do better than that," started Joe Smiley.

"I'm done talking Mr. Smiley. Let me know by four thirty; no later."

Jack closed the door behind him, walked down the hall, and opened the door on Sheriff Bredlo, who smiled and asked, "How'd it go, Jack."

"You act as if you don't already know, Barry," said Jack, opening the screen door to the ninety-degree heat that awaited him outside. He turned back to Sheriff Bredlo and said, "I'll be in my office until five o'clock. Would you make sure that, if either Mickey Courage or Billy Sprouse wants to call me, you get him to a phone."

Sheriff Bredlo kept nodding and smiling as Jack stepped out into the heat. What was it that Shakespeare had said in one of his plays? "Strange bedfellows we keep?"

As Jack walked out of the city jail, he hoped his high-stakes plea negotiation would play out as planned: that Mickey and his father would take what they knew was a good deal vs. having to present an odious defense and that Billy and his lawyer Smiley would reject the stiffer agreement and use the same defense as previously presented. Jack felt confident that, with Mickey's cooperation he could send Billy to jail for a far longer time than what was offered today while Mickey, as the less culpable of the two, would have the opportunity to rebuild his life after only three years in jail with three years' probation.

Chapter 20: Saturday Afternoon Office Visitor

It was now two o'clock on a hot Saturday afternoon with the temperature in the high nineties. *I don't even want to know about the humidity*, thought Jack, as he completed the three-block walk to his office and unlocked the door. He silently thanked Alice for leaving the air-conditioning on when she had left earlier that day. He grabbed the three messages she had taken for him that morning and moved into his office, closing the door behind him. Sitting at his old maple desk, he began making notes on Monday's upcoming trial. He began with his statement of charges and his opening statement, all the while wondering if Mickey Courage would break away from Joe Smiley's grip and agree to his terms for the plea bargain. Jack already knew that Smiley would push his clients to go to trial by convincing them that he could defeat all charges the state had put against them. Would

Mickey and his father break from Smiley's grasp and take the plea? Would Billy refuse the plea and roll the dice? Somewhere during these musings, Jack put his head down on his desk to rest *just for a moment.*

He was awakened by a loud knocking on the front door. He sat up, looked at his watch, and noticed he had been asleep for nearly two hours. It was four o'clock.

Jack quickly got up, went through his door and past Alice's desk, and opened the outside. A frail looking back man of about forty-five with salt-and-pepper curly hair and a small goatee, was staring up at him. The man was leaning on a cane and holding what looked to be an old Bill Hogan golf cap.

"Are you Mr. Jack Forester?" he said in a raspy baritone voice unlikely to come from such a small frame.

"Yes, I am," said Jack softly.

"Well, I am Joseph L. Johnson. I'd like to talk to you about my boy. Will you hear me?"

It was a kind of proud pleading, and Jack could see Mr. Johnson's eyes start to glisten.

"Of course," said Jack. "I know you made a four o'clock appointment through my secretary. Please step into my office and we'll talk." Jack ushered Mr. Johnson back into his office and sat him down across from his desk. Jack could see the sweat pushing through the fiber of the blue T-shirt with two crossed clubs and 'Farmington Country Club' embroidered on a pocket.

"Mr. Johnson, it's a hot day and all I have in my refrigerator is water and beer. May I offer you something?"

Mr. Johnson looked up from his chair where he had crooked his cane on one arm and settled his flat hat on top of the cane. He leaned on the arm of the chair as if to catch his breath.

"What are you having, Mr. Forester?"

"Why I believe I'll have a beer," said Jack, walking to the small executive refrigerator that was sitting on a table behind his desk. He opened the door. "How about you, Mr. Johnson?"

There was a silence followed by the same slightly raspy rich baritone voice, "Well, my wife Jessie would want me to have water, but she's not here and I don't want our district attorney to drink alone, it being Saturday and all. Why, I believe I'll have a beer too."

Both men laughed a little as Jack brought Mr. Johnson his beer and sat down behind his desk with his own. Jack felt some of the tension leave the man's face as he saluted Jack with the beer and proceeded to take a long swig. He put the beer down on the right arm of his chair and looked up at Jack. "You know, Mr. Forester, I haven't had a drink in five years—doctor's orders. Jessie's, too. Ever since I got emphysema. But I don't seem to care so much about living anymore. My only son Lucius got killed last week. He was a fine boy. Only sixteen. Do you know, Mr. Forester, he was a starting junior varsity halfback at Burley High School? Oh, he was fast, and he was smart, too.

Almost straight A's. We hoped he might go to college, first ever in our family. He was such a good boy. He loved everybody. He didn't have nothing against those white boys. Why'd they have to hurt him like that?"

After a pause, he continued, "Mr. Forester, this is a small town and even the walls have ears. God knows the city jail does. I hear they're going to try and make my son out to be a homosexual who was trying to come on to those white boys and that's why they did those things to him. Well, if he had been, I would have still loved him just the same. But I know he wasn't no male prostitute. He was always crazy about girls. His friend and Cousin Roy Amery had been going steady with Charlene Morris for three years. I think Roy still plans to marry her when he graduates from high school, but my only son Lucius isn't going to graduate or marry or have children."

Johnson changed his tone. "Mr. Forester, I want to know, are you going to let those white punks who killed my son...Are you going to let them slander his memory and walk away free, or will you get justice for me and his family and for his soul?"

"I'm gonna get you justice, Mr. Johnson," said Jack.

"White men's justice?"

"All men's justice," said Jack.

Johnson took another long swig of his beer and stood up. "Well, I'd better get home. Jessie and my girls will be wondering where I went."

"Mr. Johnson, may I offer you a ride home?" Jack

knew he could borrow Sheriff Bredlo's jeep, and he wanted to offer something more to the proud man standing in front of him.

"No thank you," said Joe Johnson as Jack walked him to the door. "If I can still lug around a white man's golf clubs, I can walk me home. But there is one thing you can do."

"What's that?" asked Jack.

"You can speak to my people at Ebenezer Baptist Church tomorrow. Tell 'em you really do represent all the people. Tell 'em you're going to get justice for my son."

"What time do you want me to be there?" asked Jack.

"I'll tell Reverend Turner you'll be there to speak at ten thirty."

"I'll be there."

Joe Johnson shook Jack's outstretched hand, tipped his hat, and walked out the door. He turned around one more time. "Don't let us down, Mr. Forester. We're mighty tired of disappointment."

Chapter 21: Waiting for a Call

It was five o'clock and no call had come from the city jail. Jack gathered his notes on yellow pads in preparation for Monday's opening statement. He dropped them into the old leather briefcase he and Jay Cutler had won at the moot court championship at UVA law school against Robert Kennedy and John Tunney many years before and prepared to walk home. He was not surprised that Joe Smiley had not called back. The little Bantam rooster from DC would want to showcase his talents in the open arena of trial warfare. He might run the risk of extending his clients' jail time against the long shot of getting them off entirely, or at least making a grand statement at their expense.

Jack knew that only Mickey Courage's voluntary eyewitness testimony could crystallize the events of that night in such a way that the healing process between black and white could begin and the community could avoid being rent asunder by the effects of Joe Smiley's strategy. General Cartridge, Jack now knew, wanted to send a message, to put integration back in the bottle and the Negro back in his place. This trial was a vehicle and Joe Smiley his catalyst. Jack knew what he was up against.

Still, there was no phone call, and Jack realized that malicious intent would be especially hard to prove without Mickey's cooperation, while Joe Smiley's strategy of claiming homosexual advances made on his client would bring additional insult to the family of Lucius Johnson.

As Jack stepped out into Court Square and turned to lock the outer office door, he heard the phone ring inside. It was ten minutes past five o'clock.

Jack unlocked the door, walked back inside, and picked up the phone at Alice's desk. He leaned on the edge of her desk and, looking out the window towards the courthouse across the street, he spoke. "Hello, Jack Forester here."

"Mr. Forester, it's Mickey Courage. Sheriff Bredlo said I could call you if I wanted, now that I have my father's okay."

"So, why are you calling me, Mickey?"

"My father agreed that I should take the plea agreement because, more than anything, he hates that homo defense and doesn't want to be a part of it. For me, I just want to tell the truth. I feel bad about the colored boy who died, even if it was an accident. I'm not going to lie to make him look even worse. Hell, we did it, Mr. Forester. We grabbed them, kicked them around, and held one while Billy made the other one go get party money. We were just plannin' on scarin' the hell out of them and then lettin' them go, but we screwed up and that one just hung himself trying to get away. But we did it. I feel really bad for that boy and his family. I just want to tell the truth. I don't want to hurt his family anymore."

"Will you tell exactly what happened in court?" asked Jack.

"Yes, sir."

"All right then, the plea agreement I offered you earlier stands. I don't need Billy Sprouse, and I suppose he is taking his chances with Joe Smiley. Now, I'm going to put you up in a hotel in Orange over the weekend. Call it protective custody. There'll be people wanting to get at you until this thing is over. I'll make all the arrangements with Sheriff Bredlo. You hang tough and you'll be okay. Can you do that?"

"Yes Sir," Mickey Courage answered slowly.

"If you do your part, tell the truth and don't back down against a defense that will try to break you any way it can, if you can do your part, I'll do mine. And you'll have that future once you've finished your sentence. Agreed?"

"Yes, sir."

"Okay. Stay right where you are and put Sheriff Bredlo on. I'll get you squared away."

"Hallo, Jack. We gonna get the boy to talk for us?"

"I believe so, Sheriff, and I thank you for your interest," said Jack, feeding Bredlo's ego, "but I need your help right now to make it all work."

"Say the word, Jack," gushed Sheriff Bredlo.

Jack and Sheriff Bredlo agreed that Mickey Courage should be moved that night to a safe house in Orange, a little farm town about twenty-five miles north of Charlottesville.

This precaution was necessary. It was remarkable how efficient jailhouse communication was, and once word got out that Mickey had turned state's evidence, both Jack and the sheriff knew that there would be immediate attempts to get back at the snitch.

"Don't worry, Jack," said Sheriff Bredlo. "Deputy Bryson will walk Mickey back to his cell and wait for him while he gathers up his things. Then we'll transport him on over to Orange immediately. Billy Sprouse and his people won't have a chance to get at him."

"I appreciate your good work, Sheriff," said Jack.

"And I appreciate your looking after me, Jack," said Bredlo.

Still wondering at the sheriff's obsequiousness, Jack also wondered how much of this latest development would get back to General Cartridge. *A servant with two masters is not all that reliable*, thought Jack, as he closed the door to his office and began the twenty-five minute walk home. Bredlo feared the incriminating information he believed Jack had on him; maybe that would be enough to keep him in line for now.

Chapter 22: Walking Home to Jack the Dog

Jack walked past the courthouse, where he would present his case on Monday. He wanted to get lost in his surroundings. He walked down High Street onto Preston Avenue and past Lane High School, where the football team, coached by the great Tommy Theodose, had recently won the district football championship. Four blocks up, Jack decided to cross over on Rose Hill Drive, which intersected Rugby Avenue, where he lived. He passed Jackson P. Burley High, an all-black high school and home of the Burley Bears, who were to send several football players on to the National Football League. Coach Theodose of the all-white Lane high school had said to his own team, "Hey, you guys think you're good, you wouldn't last two quarters with those colored kids at Burley. But don't feel bad. This year's University of Virginia football team couldn't go one quarter with 'em."

Jack chuckled at this irony as he passed the Burley football field and the colored neighborhood that surrounded it. Then, as if the area were divided by some invisible mandate, he passed into an all-white neighborhood, and there was WCHV, the headquarters and home of Charlottesville's first radio station, where the very exciting radio program "Name that Tune", was hosted.

Jack turned left on Rugby Avenue as he contemplated his plans for the evening with Jack the dog, preparing for his talk at Ebenezer Church—a nice evening, he hoped. Proceeding up Rugby Avenue the last three blocks to his home, Jack passed the little road to Mrs. Davis's Play School, down which he had walked to school with his cocker spaniel many years before. He had walked because, if you were five years old in the mid-fifties, your mother could pack your lunch, and you could walk a half-mile to school relatively safely. Bringing your dog was optional, as Mrs. Davis often explained.

Jack walked on past Sara Eager's house. When Jack was six, Sara had been his first true love, not unlike Victor Mature and Dorothy Lamour in *Winged Warrior* which he had recently seen with his parents at the Ridge Drive-In. Unfortunately for Jack's feelings, Sara's parents saw it all as puppy love. He was the pup, and Sara had neither love nor basic interest in him. *My first unrequited love*, smiled Jack to himself as he turned into his own driveway.

He could see Jack the dog on the front porch of the

white clapboard Cape Cod cottage. The dog watched him carefully, probably had smelled him coming for blocks, but did not move; he merely sat on his haunches and stared directly at Jack. Jack stared back.

The dog's tail, as if unattached, commenced its steady tomtom pounding, beating the wooden porch deck ever louder as Jack approached. Save for that tail and the eyes that followed Jack's progress up the driveway and then up the steps to his front gate, the dog remained motionless. Jack entered the yard and closed the gate behind him. His master's escape rendered finally impossible, Jack the dog leapt from the porch and hit the ground running. He brushed by Jack's left side and kept going for ten yards, then screeched to a halt, pirouetted, raced ten yards past Jack's right side, turned, stopped, and waited. Jack the man dropped to his knees and waited. Man and dog faced one another like two gun slingers squaring off.

Suddenly, the dog raced at Jack and, in two bounds, had him covered in wet, sloppy kisses, pushing and growling all the time. Then Jack the dog fell on his left side in expectation of his daily rubdown and scratch behind the ear that only Jack the man could administer. There was a full rubdown ritual, after which, as if by some unseen, unheard signal, man and dog jumped up as one and headed into their house.

"Let's get something to eat, boy," said Jack the man, as the two of them disappeared through the screen door.

Chapter 23: Showdown on the Gordonsville Road

Jack the dog lay in the corner of the living room hallway quietly watching his master prepare a canine meal in the yellow Pullman kitchen. The dog could smell the rich aroma of canned Pard dog food being mixed with kibble in his very special dinner bowl. Jack Forester was thinking about his own dinner and the evening work to come afterwards as he placed the bowl before his grateful tail-pounding dog.

Jack returned to the kitchen to prepare his own dinner, homemade spaghetti carbonara. As the spaghetti boiled for seven and a half minutes, he gathered his utensils together with a bowl and a plate and sliced up a tomato, which he added to the prepackaged meat sauce. Two minutes before harvesting the pasta, Jack pulled cucumbers, lettuce and an onion from his icebox and quickly made a salad. He then tasted the steaming pasta straight from the pot. It was cooked just right: not too chewy and not too brittle. He added the sauce and some parmesan cheese, three strips of pre-cooked bacon, and his dinner was made.

Jack the dog had long since finished his own meal and had eased into the Pullman kitchen in the hope of helping his master eat his. Jack Forester smiled as he sat down at the kitchen table for his dinner. He gave the dog a pat on the head, but no food. The wall phone rang, and Jack dropped his fork as he reached to answer it. It was Deputy Bill Bryson, a man who had risen from the hollows of Greene County, adjoining Albemarle County. Jack had grown to like and respect Deputy Bryson in their years of working together. Bill's manner was curt and direct, as was his way.

"Jack, I don't like to gossip, but I thought you should know about this stuff. Sheriff Bredlo just got off the phone with General Cartridge. I know it was him 'cuz I answered the phone. They talked for about twenty minutes. In fact, as soon as the sheriff got off the phone, he went and got Mickey, had him handcuffed and all, and went running out the door. He told me to stay put. Now I can't say exactly what all went on in the phone conversation, Jack, but I don't think he's taking Mickey to any old safe house. I think he's gonna take Mickey to meet with the General's people somewhere along the way."
Jack clenched his teeth and involuntarily tightened his

hold on the phone. Despite the incriminating evidence Bredlo feared Jack held on him, he had betrayed Jack to General Cartridge, presumably in expectation of greater reward.

Bill continued, "I don't know what they have in mind, but it don't smell right. That's why I called. That's it." Jack thanked the deputy for his call, told him he'd take care of it, and quickly rang off.

"Damn," exclaimed Jack out loud to no one but his dog. He realized now why the bumbling, obsequious Sheriff Bredlo had been so accommodating. The idea that it was about his 'looking the other way' for the sheriff's bugging offenses was a complete ruse. It was, in fact, to find out what Jack was doing in the Mickey Courage case, what he was planning, even as Bredlo seemed to be helping him in the execution of his plan.

What if Barry Bredlo had reported back to General Cartridge about Mickey Courage and the safe house in Orange? Probably he had done so. And what if General Cartridge had decided that Mickey Courage must not testify in any case, that in the name of preventing a black over white victory symbolic of many to come, his testimony must be prevented? With the help of Sheriff Bredlo, Mickey could be kidnapped and secreted for the duration of the trial, or, if necessary, even eliminated—whatever the General thought necessary to preserve Charlottesville society as it was now. *Mickey Courage was simply an expendable pawn in his game of social strata chess, as I am*, thought Jack.

My God, thought Jack. *What a fool I've been to think I could keep that weasel Bredlo in line.* He kicked his dog's water bowl across the floor and then quickly apologized to him. "Sorry, Jack," said Jack as the dog looked at him quizzically not particularly cowed, but concerned. Jack laughed as he realized what he must do.

Bredlo's been in Cartridge's pocket all along. I've got to get to Mickey Courage before the Cartridge people do. Although Sheriff Bredlo had left only minutes before with Mickey Courage, Jack probably could not catch him. Jack thought quickly and then made a call to Gordonsville Sheriff A. P. Shotwell.

Sheriff Shotwell had been a friend of Jack's ever since Jack had reduced a criminal trespass charge against the sheriff's son to simple trespassing and, because of his age, had him placed on six months' probation. Jack believed that Sheriff Shotwell would help him if he could.

"So let me get this straight, Jack," said Sheriff Shotwell, responding to Jack's request. "You want me to intercept Bredlo's Jeep on the Gordonsville Road north of Charlottesville when he crosses over into my county and tell him that the witness's cover has been blown and that you have ordered me to take custody. Is that right?"

"That's right, A. P. Will you do it?"

"Hell, yes. I'll take a couple of my deputies with me to make sure that fat ole Bredlo goes along with it and all."

"No questions asked?" said Jack.

"No, sir. You're an officer of the court, and you did me a good turn with my son. By the way, where do you want me to take the Courage boy once I make Bredlo give him up?"

"Will you take him to your home and call me when you get there? I know it's a little unusual, A. P., but I am really worried about that boy's safety."

"Happy to oblige, Jack," responded A. P. Shotwell. "I'll even have the missus cook him up one of her famous homemade lemon meringue pies."

Jack quickly added, "And look, A. P., this may be dangerous. There are a lot of people who really don't want Mickey Courage to testify in this case."

"Thanks for the warning, Jack, but I kinda had that figured out, what with the urgency in your call. Don't worry about us. I'll have plenty of people looking after Mickey and us too. We take care of each other pretty good around here. Any stranger comes around, I'll know early and often, and somebody'll be on 'em like bark on wood. Don't you worry about a thing, Jack."

"I'm mighty grateful, A. P. Do you have any other questions for me right now?"

"No, sir. I've got my orders. We'll find Sheriff Bredlo and his jeep pretty quick. We'll get Mickey and bring him on back to my house. As soon as we have him secured, I'll call you to get your next instructions. How's that sound, commonwealth's attorney Jack Forester?"

"That sounds great, Sheriff. I owe you."

"No, Sir, we're even," said Shotwell. "Besides, we're on the same side."

Jack rang off, believing he may just have saved the outcome of the trial and quite possibly the life of Mickey Courage. He needed to be very careful. He was aware of the far-reaching power of the General and his willingness to use that power even if it meant going outside the law.

Jack pecked at his dinner, already cold, patted Jack the dog on the head, and began preparing his talk for the upcoming Sunday sermon at the Ebenezer Baptist Church. He kept looking at the wall phone and the hanging clock to its left, awaiting the call of A. P. Shotwell.

Ninety minutes later it came.

"Hello, Jack. We had us a time. Yeah, we pulled 'em over about a mile south of the Gordonsville rotary. They said they were on the way to a safe house in Orange and asked why we had stopped them."

A.P. continued, "I told 'em plans had changed, that you had ordered me to take Mickey Courage off their hands. I tell you, Jack, that Sheriff Bredlo was mad as a hornet. It kinda tickled me. But my boys knew what I wanted to do, so while I was gabbing with Bredlo, they just reached in and pulled Mickey out of the back seat. Before Bredlo was aware of what was happening, they had him in one of the patrol cars and sped away towards my house. Man, Bredlo was jumping up and down outside his jeep, screaming at me, but I really didn't pay much attention. I just tipped my hat, got into my vehicle, and drove off."

"Did Sheriff Bredlo ask you where you were taking Mickey?"

"Well sure he asked, Jack, but I told him you wanted it kept confidential, even from him. Now that made him really mad. but I figured it was the right thing to do. So what's next?"

Jack smiled to himself. "A. P., can you hold Mickey until Monday and bring him to me in court about eight thirty that morning?"

"You betcha."

"And can you provide your home as his safe house until after the trial?"

"It would be my pleasure, Jack."

"You're a good man, A. P. I knew I could count on you."

"Look, Jack, I don't know what this is all about, and I don't *want* to know, but I respect the way you run your office and I appreciate what you did for my son. So enough said. You can count on me."

Jack thanked the Louisa County sheriff again and rang off. He breathed a sigh of relief. Now he could see the way through tomorrow and the trial.

For the first time he believed he knew how he could pull it all off.

Chapter 24: Sunday Morning

Jack awoke with a start. It was six a.m.,, but he'd only gone to bed at three, when he finally felt that what he'd written for the congregation of Ebenezer Baptist captured the essence of what he was trying to convey. Now, only three hours later, he was awoken not by his alarm, which he had set for six thirty, but by the insistent ring of his telephone.

"Hello," said Jack, a little groggy as he tried to clear the sleep from his voice.

"Hey, Jack. This is A. P. Shotwell over at Gordonsville. Thought you might like to hear what happened after we got Mickey over to the house last night."

"Is everything all right?" said Jack, now fully awake. He sensed the tension in the voice of the Gordonsville sheriff.

"Oh, hell yes, Jack. I told you us country boys

take care of one another, but we did have us a time. Somebody in that Cartridge camp must've figured we'd be bringing Mickey back to my place, and they sent some people on over to try and grab him up."

Jack cinched up his pajamas and tightened the drawstrings. He began pacing up and down the hallway as far as the telephone cord would allow. He listened intently as Sheriff Shotwell continued his report. His questions could come later.

"Truth is," continued Sheriff Shotwell, "I bet they sent people to several likely places looking for him. As it turns out, they musta figured they got lucky with us. I think they was camped out in the woods all night. They probably spotted Mickey when he was helping the missus bring in some eggs from our laying chickens.

"There was three of 'em, not from around these parts, more like pros, you know—*hitmen*. Anyway, they closed in on Mickey and the missus from three directions, with one keeping an eye out for where I might be.

"What they didn't know was that I had my cousin Leroy sitting up in a turkey shoot roost about twenty feet off the ground in an old locust tree. He was holding a twelve-gauge shotgun. Then my brother Earl actually slept in the henhouse when I told him there might be some prowlers looking for Mickey Courage.

"Well, they both had Mickey and the missus covered at the same time as that threesome was closing in on them. Old Leroy let loose a twelve-gauge buckshot from overtop 'em. Peppered 'em pretty good. Then Earl, looking like a giant two-legged straw-covered chicken, came out of the henhouse and fired on 'em with his twenty-gauge. That threesome musta just turned and ran as I think Earl got 'em pretty good in the backside.

Well, they ran off into the woods and we heard a truck drive off. I can guarantee you this, those boys won't be in any condition to come back anytime soon. They're too full of buckshot." A. P. Shotwell laughed out loud, and Jack couldn't help but join him.

Then Jack spoke, "They may still try again with somebody else, A. P. You think you can handle it?"

"Handle it?" said A. P. "Those boys ain't nothing compared to the firefights I used to be in over in Korea a few years back. As for the missus, she's got her dander up now. She won't give up Mickey to nobody until this whole trial mess is over with. I tell you something, Jack, I'm not afraid of too many men, but I pity anyone who gets on the wrong side of my old lady. Now don't be trying to take Mickey away from us, Jack. We won't let anything happen to him."

"Do you need more people?" said Jack.

"Thanks Jack, but I'll have people from all over the county looking after us once word of this little incident gets out. We don't take kindly to outsiders messing with our people. Any of General Cartridge's group comes into this county looking for Mickey Courage anytime soon, we'll know they're here almost before they do. And I promise you this, Jack, if they do come back, two things will happen. One, they won't get Mickey, and two, bad things will happen to them."

"Say no more, A. P. That's all I need to know. I'll see you and Mickey in my office Monday morning at eight thirty.

"We'll be there, Jack."

"I know you will, A. P. And thanks." Jack rang off and proceeded to shower and get dressed in his Sunday-go-to-meeting suit. Jack the dog, having already let himself out the screen door to do his morning ablutions, was back and circling his food bowl in anticipation of his breakfast.

Sunday is the proverbial day of rest, thought Jack as he leaned over to tie his shoes and then stood up to put on the jacket of his tropical tan suit. *Not today*. He had chosen a white button-down shirt and a narrow red tie which he twisted into a half windsor knot. The idea was to project the authority of the commonwealth's office without appearing like a white plantation owner looking for recruits in a black church.

Showered, shaved, and dressed, Jack walked into the kitchen, where he found Jack the dog looking up at him from his bowlside position, his tail lightly tapping the fake-brick linoleum floor.

"All right, Jack, Pard and kibble for you, burnt toast and a fried egg for me, water all around," Jack filled his dog's water bowl and poured a glass for himself. He pulled the necessities from the refrigerator and got to work. Ten minutes later, the dog was devouring his meal. Jack sat down to a fried egg, toast, orange juice and some instant Nescafe coffee.

Not bad for daily meal #1 at bachelor headquarters, he thought. Five minutes later, the dirty dishes were in the sink to be tended to later, Jack the dog had received his instructions to guard the house, and Jack was walking up the hill on Rugby Avenue. Jack liked to walk whenever he could. It cleared his head, helped him think, and gave him a moving ground-level observation post from which to see what was going on in his community.

Both Jack and his dog understood the work to be done. Today, Jack the dog had the territorial imperative, while commonwealth's attorney Jack Forester had to convince an all-black congregation that his office, an all-white enclave, would do everything it could to secure justice in the kidnapping/murder of Lucius Johnson.

Jack turned left onto Rugby Road and then cut down Preston Avenue past Washington Park. He was not thinking about the gradual black/white societal changes in Charlottesville; he was thinking more about his prosecution of one seemingly insignificant case which, in the larger scope of things, could actually signify whether or not societal progress had been made in providing colored people real equal rights under the law.

The issue is not segregation vs. integration or even

the concept of separate but equal, thought Jack. *This case will test whether Charlottesville justice can be blind to race and class as it has not been in the past. And the central question is whether the colored race or any other minority can get, practically speaking, equal justice under the law. The fact that an all-white jury has been impaneled for this particular case might make this all black congregation suspicious, and I can't blame them,* thought Jack. *If I am to convince them that I can get justice for them even under these circumstances, then perhaps they will believe that our current society's systems of laws will now respect and protect their rights and legal interests as equally as it does those of the white man.*

Jack rehearsed his church presentation, talking to himself and wondering if he could pull it all off. He had better.

"... It may not always have been that way in the past, but I promise you even handed justice, fair and equally administered in this trial," said Jack, practicing out loud. "I will pledge to you that..."

Boy, I've got a lot riding on this, thought Jack, as he picked up his walking pace. Somehow, I've got to win over this constituency and maintain my white supporters while protecting my office from the malice and force of General Cartridge's people.

Jack was nearly there, a block away from Ebenezer Baptist Church. Across from the church on West Main Street, he could see the newly opened Gaslight Restaurant, designed by his cousin John Tuck to be a southern version of New York City's 21 Club. On the restaurant's patio were seated University students and townspeople alike having their Sunday breakfast, some nursing Sunday morning hangovers. From this vantage point, they could hear the beautiful soaring sounds of the black choir and congregation across the street. Perhaps the Gaslight's patrons were hoping for a little Sunday forgiveness for themselves by virtue of proximity. Typically these Sunday brunchers watched as the all-black congregation arrive in their Sunday finery—the women in colorful dresses, high-heeled shoes, straw bonnets and wide-brimmed hats, the men in their best white linen suits, red bow ties and fedoras. Some of the Gaslight Sunday brunchers chuckled at the pageantry, but gradually they found themselves pulled into the majesty of joyous smiles and greetings, the shaking of hands and bear hugs of these people, as the spirit and glory of their beliefs shone forth even across the street to the people at the Gaslight Restaurant.

As the church doors closed behind the worshippers, the brunchers could only hear the rich drone of words in prayer they could neither hear nor understand, but the music, the voices raised in joyful exultation, the blessings of the Gospel, perhaps this is what brought a sense of salvation across the street.

The usual weekly sermon and soulful happening was not to be today, for, marching up and down West Main and Sixth Streets in front of Ebenezer Baptist Church, to the railroad tracks beyond and then back again, marched men dressed in white sheets and others, uncovered, marching with them. They held crosses and sticks above their heads, sticks which could only be described as clubs, and yelled the usual racial epithets in the general direction of Ebenezer Baptist Church and its arriving congregation: "Hey, niggers, don't get uppity! We know where you live!"

And there was Sheriff Bredlo, standing at the intersection of Sixth and West Main Streets, smiling as he directed the marchers. Beside him were the deputies, looking vaguely uncomfortable. It appeared theirs was the duty of keeping this a peaceful demonstration.

Sheriff Bredlo spotted Jack and grinned, "Well, hello, Jack. Guess I forgot to tell you about this here legal march. Yep, they came in and got all their parade permits last Friday. Seems like they knew you were going to be here to speak to your colored friends even then. Well, how about that? Our very own highly esteemed commonwealth's attorney is here at this all-nigger church to apologize for the white race and promise to do better, or something like that. Ain't that right, Jack?" Bredlo raised his arms for effect, a sort of unwritten Halleluiah, and continued, "Anyway Jack, these lawful marchers and members of the local order of the Ku Klux Klan knew you was gonna be here, and they, along with these other townsfolk here, just wanted you to know how they feel about all that."

Jack moved in so close to Barry Bredlo that he violated that unwritten rule of acceptable minimum space between two people talking. Bredlo quickly dropped his arms. Jack gently grasped Sheriff Bredlo's uniform lapel and twisted hard. "Well, you'd better keep it peaceful, Barry, real peaceful. Or I will come down on you harder than you'll ever know for dereliction of duty and for all your other indiscretions." Jack released the sheriff's lapel and the pudgy man, now sweating profusely, jumped back a couple of steps.

For once Bredlo was silent, visibly shaken. Jack pointed at the Sheriff just before crossing the street through the marchers to the entrance of Ebenezer Baptist Church. "If you want to keep your job, you will do your job this morning. Keep it peaceful," Jack repeated.

Barry Bredlo still said nothing, but Jack felt reasonably sure that he had made his point. As he walked across the street, Jack gazed back at this tub-of-guts sheriff, his shirt and belly spilling over his belt, and he knew he could not underestimate his malice or his duplicity.

"I don't have to like 'em, but I will enforce the law," Sheriff Bredlo yelled after Jack. "By the way, General Cartridge sends his regards. And we'd all like to know where you hid that Mickey Courage boy." Sheriff Bredlo laughed a joyless staccato laugh as he moved off to tell a black bystander not to harass these lawful marchers.

Jack arrived at the steps to the entrance of the church and prepared to walk in. "Our commonwealth's attorney is a nigger lover," screamed a marcher cloaked in his raiment of white sheet.

Jack disappeared through the door with these words of hatred ringing in his ears. An usher came to walk him down the aisle to the very first pew, a few steps away from where he would make the most important presentation of his career, and perhaps of his life.

Chapter 25:
Ebenezer Baptist Church: Talking from the Pulpit

Jack looked down from the pulpit of Ebenezer Baptist Church. He had been introduced as the commonwealth's attorney and "the man who says he will get us justice in the Lucius Johnson kidnapping murder case." Jack felt eyes looking back, reflecting a different viewpoint—some encouraging, some curious, and a large number hostile. Jack felt the coldness.

After all, he thought, *these people have experienced a lot of white man's justice in the past, imperfect at best, and in many cases for the colored man there has been precious little justice at all.*

Jack stood still. He looked out on the congregation once more, gazed down at his notes, then cast them aside and looked up. He knew what he wanted to say to these people. He had been thinking about it long before the Lucius Johnson murder/kidnapping affair.

"Thank you for letting me speak to you this morning," Jack began. "I've often heard you singing from across the street, but I take it as a real privilege to hear your voices and see your faces from inside Ebenezer Baptist Church."

There was a murmur of approval and some appreciative smiles at this beginning. Still Jack felt the coldness, suspicion of him and his brand of justice, and who could blame them, what with the Ku Klux Klan marching just outside with the apparent approval of Albemarle County's own Sheriff Barry Bredlo. Jack decided to address that issue head-on.

"What you see outside," said Jack, pointing to the church doors, "odious as it may seem, is freedom of expression. As long as those klanners are orderly and don't interfere with you or your business, and they have secured their marching permit, they have a right to be out there."

The church went quiet. The silence and the hostility were palpable. *Here's where I show the equality and fairness I said I stood for*, thought Jack. He leaned over the pulpit and continued.

"But that's why I'm here, to tell you that if *you* want to march in front of the courthouse tomorrow or every day of the trial, you have that right, too. Some white people might not like it, but it is your right, and I'm here today to tell you that your rights will be respected and they will be protected.

"As for securing justice for Lucius Johnson and his family, we have the evidence and we have the corroboration to prove kidnapping and second-degree homicide. I want you to understand that the defense will raise false issues in order to confuse or even prejudice the jury against the victim. That, too, is their legal right. They will try by any means available, ethical or not, to prove, not that their client is innocent of the charges, for they know they cannot prove that their client is innocent. What they will hope to do instead is to create a cloud around our case in order to prevent us from proving it beyond, and I emphasize *beyond* a reasonable doubt. Their goal is to sufficiently confuse or prejudice the jury so that at least one, if not all, will refuse to find the defendant guilty beyond a reasonable doubt.

"Let me make it clear to you how the court system works," Jack continued. "If one or more jurors refuses to join in a guilty plea, and the deadlock cannot be broken, then we will have what is called a hung jury. If that were to happen, the defense probably thinks we won't pursue it, or that we will accept a plea to a much reduced charge such as simple assault and false imprisonment. I want you to know that it is my firm intent to win this case with the current charges in place. But juries and judges can be unpredictable. I promise you that, if for any reason these charges are dismissed, or in the event we get a hung jury, I will proceed immediately to refile the charges. I will not let Mr. Billy Sprouse escape the justice and the punishment he deserves."

Jack again looked out on the sea of black faces.

He saw consternation and anger. Could the killer of Lucius Johnson really beat these charges in court?

A large middle-aged black man stood up and broke the silence, "Are you telling us that that redneck punk who beat up, kidnapped, and caused the death of Lucius Johnson, are you telling us he might go free? How do we know you're really going to retry him, once your high-powered white friends tell you it wouldn't be in your best interest? Shoot, I bet the only reason you're here today is so you'll look good next week when that cracker gets off. Oh yeah, I can hear it now, 'I did the best I could. Why I even spoke to that colored church to make sure they wouldn't riot when they got an unfortunate verdict.' Hell man, you're just bullshitting us, just like all the other do-gooder honkies before you."

The man sat down and there was an angry buzz around him, and it wasn't because of his slightly inappropriate language uttered in church. Ebenezer Baptist Church, the one relatively safe forum in which the black community could candidly express its views, had heard it all over the years. No, the angry buzz was in agreement with the viewpoint expressed, that perhaps Jack was really just one more white politician *not* looking after the black interest, but rather just trying to keep them in line for what promised to be an unpopular verdict.

The anger in the church was palpable, and Jack felt it. He looked down at the sea of angry faces and continued, "I promise to you that there *will* be justice for Lucius Johnson. We will convict Billy Sprouse of felony kidnapping and second-degree homicide, and I assure you he will go away for a long, long time."

Jack continued, "We will win because we have not only the evidence to convict, but also the confession of the other boy involved, Mickey Courage. Because we know he never wanted to take part in the kidnapping or the homicide that resulted from it, and in exchange for his testimony, we will let him plead to a lesser offense. But make no mistake! Mickey Courage, too, will be held accountable for his actions. He will be incarcerated for a period of time, and then placed on parole for up to three years. For now, we need his testimony to block the defense strategy. Without the testimony of Mickey Courage as to what really did happen that night, we might not win this case, and the justice we all seek might not come about.

"As your commonwealth's attorney, I will not rest until Billy Sprouse is convicted and locked away from society. I know you have not always seen justice in the past. I am here this morning to assure you that in this case you will have justice. Just as you will survive the unpleasantness of those marching outside, and you may have to endure false charges and innuendo made against Lucius Johnson, I promise you here this morning that you will triumph in the end. You will win justice for Lucius Johnson and his family. This I promise you. Why? Because we have the witnesses and we have the evidence and we have a fair judge. Justice will prevail."

Jack started to step down. Then he looked up and out on the congregation once more. "I welcome any of you that can to be present for the trial. It starts tomorrow, Monday, at nine a.m., and will probably last about two days. Then the jury will deliberate. If it goes according to my plan, Mr. Billy Sprouse will be convicted and sentenced before the end of the week.

"I ask for your prayers and support."

Jack smiled, stepped down from the pulpit, and walked down the aisle past watchful eyes. He felt a sense of relief that many in the congregation believed that Jack Forester would do the right thing. As he pushed open the door to the hot July sunshine and the rabble of Klan marchers and their supporters, he felt he had accomplished what he had set out to do at Ebenezer Baptist Church that morning. He had brought a measure of hope and faith that justice would be served. Now he hoped mightily that he could, in fact, deliver that justice.

As the church door closed slowly behind him, he heard Reverend Alvin Edwards' invocation. "Let us pray for Mr. Forester and for the soul of Lucius Johnson, and for justice. Amen."

Chapter 26: Jack Practices his Serve

Jack threw his tennis racket and two cans of balls in the back seat of his convertible. The top was down and the morning sun had made the red leather interior warm to the touch. As he started the engine and began backing down his driveway, Jack could hear insistent barks coming from Jack the dog in the fenced backyard. *Not this time old boy*, thought Jack. *I need some time to myself.*

Jack backed out onto Rugby Avenue and began the drive out to Farmington Country Club. He needed time alone, away from everybody—even Jack the dog. He wanted to reflect on the upcoming week: the trial, the town, Billy Sprouse, Mickey Courage, Barry Bredlo, A. P. Shotwell, General Cartridge, his town, his world—all that would test him.

Jack drove past the Tavern, a popular restaurant and watering hole for University students and townspeople alike. He turned left onto Emmet Street, passed the brand-new Barracks Road Shopping Center on his right, then turned right on University Drive, past the Lady Astor Courts. Two miles west Jack turned right over the railroad tracks and down Farmington Drive, a beautiful country lane shaded by the famous giant cedar trees framing it.

Jack parked his car in the parking lot across from the tennis shop, just as he had the previous day when he and his partner had beaten the young turks in a terrific doubles match. He grabbed his gear, and eased in through the box hedges and trotted down the path towards court number one. It was free, as Jack had expected it would be in the heat of the day. He had avoided Mike Dolan, the tennis pro at the tennis shop. Mike was a wonderful coach and a dear friend, but talkative, and Jack just didn't want to hear another twice-told Mike Dolan story today. Jack opened the gate to number one and threw his canvas bag on the bench. He pulled out his six used tennis balls, positioned four in his left hand and two on his racket, and walked to the deuce baseline on the near side of the tennis court. He began to practice his serve the hard flat first serve, and the looping American twist second serve. First the deuce court, then the ad court, hard first serve followed by the topspin looper. He walked slowly to the other side of the net to pick up the balls, turned, and practiced serving from the other side. Working on his serve, working up a sweat, and getting a physical rhythm going created in Jack a kind of mental rhythm he found helpful.

After about twenty minutes, Jack had worked up a good sweat, but he kept moving. His first serve was really popping and his second serve kicking high and wide. Jack felt good and, for the first time in awhile, relaxed.

He was picking up the six balls for another round when he was interrupted by Sally Fretango, a recent divorcee sometimes referred to as a grass widow.

"Hi there, Jack, you look hot and healthy," she laughed gaily. "Why don't you quit practicing your serve and come have lunch with me."

"Thanks Sally, that's a nice offer, but I've got a big day tomorrow. I need to get home and start preparing."

"Oh, pshaw Jack. I know you. You've been preparing for that silly old trial forever. I know how you work."

"Well I want to practice my serve a little longer, Sally."

"That's fine, Jack. I'll go on down to the Taproom and have Skippy prepare a picnic of fried chicken, cole slaw, sweet ice tea, homemade biscuits, and that great apple pie. Now you know you've got to eat lunch at some point. Why not make it a picnic with me? Can I get an amen, Jack?"

Jack laughed. "Amen, Sally. I surrender." Jack served a bullet first serve to the ad court. "I'm parked behind the tennis shop. I'll meet you there in twenty-five minutes."

"Atta boy, Jack. I'll meet you there with the goods. Let's jump in that beautiful old convertible of yours and take a ride up Afton Mountain."

With picnic and Sally in tow, Jack drove west as instructed, past hay fields which fed black Angus cattle, past beautiful antebellum manor houses with their circular driveways, past Ivy and the little farming town of Crozet. Still on Route 250 West, he began the ascent up Afton Mountain.

"Just keep driving, honey," said Sally gaily when Jack asked where they were picnicking.

Jack looked over at the long flowing brown hair as it blew across Sally Fretango's green eyes, full lips, and perfectly tanned face. *She's quite pretty when she smiles*, Jack thought, *and even when she doesn't. About thirty-five, no children, and recently divorced. That's about all I know about her*, thought Jack, *except that I keep running into her on the tennis courts. And yes, I had noticed that supple figure in the short tennis skirt and her engaging smile, a certain gentle laughter she carries with her in good times and sad.*

As a lawyer, Jack had heard about the bitter divorce proceedings Sally had suffered. Her ex-husband, Bob Barclay, was a very wealthy land speculator who had strayed once too often, and Sally sued for divorce. In an effort to protect his assets, Barclay and his lawyer had tried to brand Sally an adulteress. To their chagrin, they could find nothing, and any effort to manufacture evidence or build innuendo, had been quashed by the court. The result was a large settlement and a sadder but wiser Sally Fretango—independently wealthy, too.

I kinda like her spunk, thought Jack. *It must have taken some courage behind that smooth exterior to ask me out for a picnic. For lots of reasons, I might have politely, but firmly, declined. But for some reason I didn't. And I'm glad, I think.*

"All right, Sally. You're the boss, but I'm getting kinda hungry," Jack said.

"Keep driving, Jack. We're going to the top of Afton Mountain for the best simultaneous view of the Piedmont and the Shenandoah Valley you'll ever see."

"And after we get to the top of the mountain for this fabulous viewing, which, as a local boy, I know pretty well, are we going to picnic on the Shenandoah Parkway?" Jack wanted to know.

"Oh no, Jack," said Sally softly with a Madonna-like smile. "Much more secluded, more spiritually and sensually uplifting."

"You mean Swannanoa?"

"That's right Jack. Swannanoa, home of 'The University of Love.'"

They both laughed at the thought. *Very cool*, thought Jack. *I haven't felt this much at ease with a woman in a long time.* Jack glanced over at Sally again as they passed Royal Orchards and other mountainside retreats and the myriad of roadside stands selling fresh fruits and furniture and various tourist trinkets now made in Japan. Jack focused on Sally, wearing a blue and white seersucker tennis skirt cut well above the knee and a white blouse open to the third button: subtle, but inviting. And then there was the gently irreverent spirit and her quirky sense of humor. There was something about her he found really appealing. They were just two people, in the beauty and freshness of the moment, taking some joy in each other's company, even now in this comfortable silence.

Sally spoke first. "Jack, let's enjoy this afternoon, just for itself. No worries, no guilt, just us in a lovely moment in time."

They arrived at the magnificently mysterious Swannanoa. It had been built in the twenties by a railroad baron for his wife as a cool summer retreat from the sweltering flatland heat that was Richmond in summer. He had brought masses of marble by boat from Italy and had hired Italian stone masons to properly construct an italian palace on Afton Mountain. Beautiful piazzas with elaborate fountains, wide marble steps, and high ionic columns framed the front entrance of the manor house. The door opened onto a twenty-five-foot-wide marble staircase, covered by a red oriental runner, descending from the second floor.

But the wife of the railroad baron died before Swanannoa was completed, and he lost interest. It was only when the famous philosopher, sculptor, painter and self-acknowledged clairvoyant Walter Russell arrived years later, with his equally ethereal wife Lao, to lease the estate, that the palace acquired its lasting identity as the University of Love. For years, Swannanoa was host to gala receptions and visits from the internationally famous. There were mysterious séances and much sculpture created, the most famous of which was the fifty-foot likeness of Christ which became known as Jesus Christ of the Blue Ridge.

But that, too, was long ago. Walter had died and left his widow alone to greet the occasional visitor as she floated down those same marble stairs clad only in a silk dressing gown.

"Welcome to Swannanoa, The University of Love," began the diminutive lady who appeared to be in her late seventies. She peered out at them and smiled. "I'm Lao Russell, widow of the great Walter Russell, with whom I founded the University of Love at Swannanoa." At first Mrs. Russell seemed disappointed when Sally told her they were here for a picnic, not a tour. Almost instantly she regained her composure.

"Ah, what a beautiful day for two young lovers. You must share your picnic with the spirits on the grounds of Swannanoa. Might I suggest the high meadow just beyond the statue of Samuel Clemens? How Walter loved that man. He made a little bronze bust of each of the characters from *Huckleberry Finn*. Walter also carved a beautiful marble bust of Albert Einstein; they were personal friends, you know. Oops, I digress. For two such lovers as you, every moment together is precious. Your picnic awaits you just beyond those bushes in the distance. From there you can see a piece of the valley to the west and one hundred miles to the east; that is, if you're not just looking at each other."

Lao Russell smiled coyly, and, as she turned to go inside the Italian palace that was still her home, she said simply, "Enjoy each other." Then she was gone, disappearing behind the great oak entrance door into the palace and the University of Love within.

Sally erupted into a low giggle as she grabbed Jack by the hand and led him back to the convertible to gather their picnic things, a blanket, the Taproom special luncheon, and two pillows which Jack assumed Sally had transferred from her car back at Farmington.

They walked around the palace to the beautiful garden: the fountain, the reflecting pools, casually strewn lilies and daffodils—all gently neglected, yet seeming magically to take care of themselves. There were magnificent trees: stately oaks, flowering maples, even a seventy-five-foot blue spruce towering into the mountain sky.

Walking through a small grove of giant American boxwoods and up a gentle slope, Jack and Sally found themselves in an open meadow of green grass and mountain flowers, a scene that might have been painted by Matisse. As Lao Russell had described, to the west was a narrow view of the Shenandoah Valley, while to the east they could see nearly the entire Piedmont region into Charlottesville and opening up towards Richmond beyond. It was magical. Jack stood for a moment to take it all in. He noticed that he was still holding Sally's hand in his own. That, too, seemed magical.

He gently pulled away to spread out the picnic blanket while Sally knelt to pull the corners square. Then she laid out the utensils, cups for the iced tea, and plates for the fried chicken, biscuits, cole slaw, and famous Taproom apple pie. Still kneeling, she faced Jack and the view towards the Shenandoah Valley, while Jack sat cross-legged facing Sally and Charlottesville far below. As Lao Russell had predicted earlier, however, they were only looking at each other. Neither one spoke in the comfort of their silence. They shared the moment and became a part of it.

Finally, Sally said, "We'll eat, and then we'll walk, Jack Forester. We'll begin to know each other today."

"Umm, that was wonderful," said Sally, a few minutes later as she finished her last bite of Apple Pie.

"Hey, Jack, you've barely touched your pie."

"After three pieces of chicken and that second three-layer butter biscuit you forced on me, I feel like a stuffed Buddha," Jack said, rubbing his stomach.

"Why, it's true," said Sally laughing. "You do seem to have a case of expanded tummyitis." She reached over to touch Jack on the rise of his belly, and, as if losing her balance, she fell into him, her arms reaching around his waist to catch herself on the ground behind him while her chin came to rest upon his chest. She looked up and kissed Jack lightly. He put his arms around her as if to help her keep her balance. They both were laughing softly as they rolled with the pull of gravity and fell together on the soft grass just to the left of the blanket. Jack felt her warmth beneath him. She clung to him and pressed her cheek to his cheek, her warm breath blowing past his ear. He heard its quiet roar, and felt its heat, then he sensed his own.

It was one of those beautiful days that happen now and then, when two people find in each other something they hadn't known they'd been seeking and come together, like the final two pieces of a puzzle, to reveal something new and warm, a new innocence and joy that might only last a moment. It didn't matter as long as they were in that moment.

They kissed and held each other tight on that Sunday afternoon, the day before the Billy Sprouse trial was to begin. It was a day, not of consummation, but rather of anticipation of things to come. Jack gently rolled over, allowing Sally to sit up, her legs straddling his own. She looked down and said, "Jack, I think I'm going to like you for a long, long time." She knelt down and kissed him gently on the lips, then the tip of his nose, and both cheeks. Then she sat up again, pressed her hands against his shoulders, and said, "How about that walk you promised me? Now get up."

Sally pulled back from Jack as she rose to her feet. Jack was on his knees, his arms wrapped around her waist. He rose almost vertically, his mouth brushing past the rise of her breasts. Standing, Jack looked down at Sally's upturned face. He kissed her firmly and said, "I feel strongly the same way, but I'll have to check with Jack the dog before I can commit to any meaningful relationship." Jack winked as he started to pull away, but not before Sally punched him lightly on the right shoulder.

"Just so you know, Jack Forester, I'm a mean and determined woman. And by the way, who do you think feeds Jack the dog all those club biscuits while he's waiting in the car for you to finish off some unsuspecting, overconfident younger tennis opponent? Sally Fretango, that's who. I liked him before I liked you, or maybe I knew I would like you because I like him. They say a master and his dog are very much alike. So why don't you bark two times for me?"

"Woof, woof, baby," said Jack. They laughed and fell standing into each others' arms once again.

"Oh, God," said Sally softly as she held Jack tightly. "This is the best." In that moment, for them both, it was.

The drive home in the old convertible was a slow breezy blur: a few words, hands entwined, and warmth between them. Jack turned left on Tennis Road off Farmington, and stopped his car next to Sally's Plymouth station wagon. Sally turned, kissed Jack on the cheek, and slipped out of his car.

"Jack," she said pointing at him as she backed up towards her own car. "I will be thinking of you all this week, but your mind will be, and should be, on the Billy Sprouse trial. You know you can call me anytime."

Jack smiled and started to speak but Sally cut him off. "If I don't hear from you by next week, I'll come steal Jack the dog and take him to Swannanoa."

"Could I ransom him, though?"

"Only in person."

"Now, you've got yourself a deal, Ms. Fretango."

"I'm serious, Jack," said Sally as she opened the door and got into her own car.

"So am I," said Jack. He drove slowly back to 1717 Rugby Avenue, to Jack the dog and final preparations for the trial of his life, the big question remained: Was Mickey Courage still safely under the protection of Sheriff A. P. Shotwell?

Chapter 28: The Billy Sprouse Trial

In the 1959 version of social evolution, an impaneled, all-white jury made up of nine men and three women sat in the jury box to hear the Billy Sprouse case. The few members of the black population who were called to appear on the grand jury were denied for cause by the defense.

The jury had not been sequestered and it was a small town; it seemed that everyone knew on Monday morning that Mickey Courage had turned state's evidence in return for a plea agreement. It was therefore assumed by many, both in and out of the jury box, that Billy Sprouse could not deny the assault and battery charges, nor the kidnapping of Lucius Johnson with the intent to extort money, nor the consequent felony murder charges.

Many of the press believed now that, even with his high-priced Washington, DC attorney, Billy Sprouse would plead guilty, perhaps to less severe charges based on extenuating circumstances, whatever they may be. According to this theory, his attorney would plead for leniency for the youthful and obviously white offender. Then the all-white jury, having heard a tearful and remorseful confession from the defendant, would sentence him to eight to ten years in prison with early release available assuming good behavior. Everyone could go home secure in the knowledge that justice had been served while not disrupting the natural order of things. As many members of the legal community would put it, a modicum of justice would have been served up to Charlottesville's colored community without disrupting the white community's version of peaceful and ever-so-gradual integration. Some thought the whole Billy Sprouse mess would be relegated to old news within the week.

But this was not to be.

Jack Forester watched as Billy Sprouse was led into the courtroom handcuffed and shackled and flanked by two of Sheriff Bredlo's larger deputies, with Joe Smiley, attorney for Billy Sprouse, walking somberly a few steps behind. As the entourage was seated at the defendant's table, Jack could see Billy's hard smile as the defendant turned to the courtroom spectators as if taking in his own celebrity. Whatever else was on Billy's mind, it was clear to Jack that this was probably the most attention he'd ever gotten, and he was clearly enjoying it. *Is it the handcuffs around his wrists with a chain leading to the shackles around his ankles, enhancing his already dangerous profile? Is it the fear in the darting eyes of those who look at him and then quickly look away as he catches their eye with his black-eyed stare? It is all this,* thought Jack, *that appeals to Billy, most especially the fear he inspires.* Billy turned and stared hard at members of the jury. Some quickly looked away, and Billy smiled.

You fool, thought Jack looking over at the defense table and Billy Sprouse. *All your bravado is going to help me cook your goose, starting with your behavior in the city jail over the weekend. Everybody,* thought Jack, *including the jurors, seems to know something about the fire Billy Sprouse had started in the city jail.*

Chapter 29: Fire in the City Jail

The previous Sunday—*just yesterday,* thought Jack—Billy Sprouse had wanted to show his fellow inmates just how tough he was. Jack had heard all the particulars from the cops who were there and the inmates alike. The conversations were repeated almost verbatim.

"I'm gonna beat the crap out of that nigger-lovin' deputy Freddy Dunlap," he had told Joe Harper, his cellmate. Harper was awaiting trial for assault and battery, another barroom fight he had started.

"Now why and how are you going to do all that?" asked Joe Harper, unimpressed. The six-foot-two, 250 pound Irish American had been in jail a dozen times for a variety of violent crimes, including a manslaughter conviction for beating up his best friend, apparently over a girl, so badly that he had been hospitalized for a week before regaining consciousness. The friend had never been the same since. None of it seemed to bother Joe Harper, who, at the age of thirty, had obviously not changed his ways.

"Yea, Billy, tell old Joe what you gonna do. You're not a bad ass; you're just a loudmouth punk." Harper laughed as he watched a sea of anger well up in Billy's eyes. Billy was still holding onto the bars while Joe was sitting calmly on the floor with his back against the wall. *You don't want to piss off this young punk too much*, Joe thought. He *might come back at you with a shiv in the night.*

"I'll tell you what I'm gonna do, Joe, and don't call me no punk. I'm gonna get that deputy by starting a fire."

Joe laughed again, "How you gonna do that, Billy?" Billy turned away from the bars, looked at Joe, and smiled a cold, hard, soulless smile. He answered, "Remember when we came in from the last exercise break and I stumbled against Sheriff Bredlo's desk?"

"Yea, I guess I do," said Joe.

"Well, I picked up his Zippo lighter." Billy produced a silver monogrammed lighter and flicked it, creating a large orange-red flame. "I'm gonna get him in here by setting the mattress on fire, and then I'm gonna beat the crap out of him."

"Why?" asked Joe simply.

"Cause he said what I did to them niggers was wrong and he hoped I got twenty years for it. I'm gonna mess him up."

Joe considered this last statement. Then he responded in kind. "Well let me tell you one thing, Mr. Bad Ass. If you mess him up while I'm in this cell, it'll probably cause me trouble, and I swear I'll kill you with my bare hands right here if that happens. You read me, boy?"

Billy felt fear rising from the pit of his stomach. He hadn't felt fear, or any emotion except anger, in a long time. The fear froze his thoughts momentarily.

"I said, do you read me, Billy Boy?" Harper started to get up as if to make his point with his fist right now. What the hell did he care anyway?

Billy quickly responded as he sought to cover his fear with anger and guile.

"Hey, I got you covered Joe. This don't concern you, and I won't let it. Next time they call you for interrogation or whatever, while you are out of this cell, that's when I'm gonna do it, okay? So you can relax."

"Yeah, all right then." Joe Harper sat down, back against the wall, closed his eyes, and appeared to be taking a cat nap. He knew that little prick would not try to sneak up on him now. Billy just wanted to show old Joe that he could be bad, too. Joe did feel a momentary twinge of pity for poor old Deputy Fred Dunlap. *But hey, that's not my problem*, he thought, drifting away into a dreamless sleep.

And so it had been. That Sunday, the day before Billy's trial when lawyer Tim Timmons had come to speak with his client Joe Harper, that was the day

Billy Sprouse had chosen to start the fire.

As soon as Harper had been walked from the cell to the visitor's room, Sprouse activated his little beat-down party. He cut open his mattress with the shiv he had made, exposing the flammable cotton interior. He waited about ten minutes, until he heard Deputy Fred Dunlap open the door to make his rounds of the cells. As soon as he saw the deputy entering his area, Billy Sprouse lit the mattress stuffing with the Zippo lighter and said calmly, "Hey Deputy, I got a little problem in here. Somehow my mattress caught on fire. Would you look at that?" he said pointing to the smoldering mattress with black smoke billowing up.

Deputy Dunlap, seeing the growing fire hazard, quickly inserted the skeleton key to unlock Billy's cell door, rushed in, pulled the mattress away from Billy, and started to stamp out the small fire.

"Shoot, Billy, this ain't anything. All you gotta do is just smother it out." As he quickly extinguished the fire, Deputy Dunlap turned to Billy and said, "Now why did a country boy like you start this fire, Billy, and how did you do it? You lookin' for some more attention or something?"

"That's right, nigger lover. And you're it." Billy hit Deputy Dunlap hard with a right uppercut that he uncoiled with lightning quickness. As the stunned deputy struggled to recover from the blow, he tried to reach for the gun in his holster. Too late. Billy hit him twice more, knocking him to the floor. In some kind of maniacal fury, Billy kicked the deputy in the head and shoulders as Deputy Dunlap curled into a fetal position and covered himself as well as he could.

"What the hell's going on back there?" yelled Sheriff Bredlo as he and two other deputies rushed in to find the source of the commotion. When they reached Billy's cell he was standing quietly, smiling, his bloodied knuckles wrapped around the bars. Behind him lay Deputy Dunlap in a heap, moaning but barely conscious.

"What the hell did you do to him?" yelled Sheriff Bredlo as one of the deputies struggled to unlock the cell door.

"Why, Sheriff," said Billy, "I found out Deputy Dunlap was a nigger lover, so I had to give him a beat-down."

"You son of a bitch," yelled Sheriff Bredlo as the door flew open. "Let's give Billy Sprouse a taste of his own." The two deputies grabbed the unresisting and still smiling Billy Sprouse.

"Take that smile off your face, punk." The Sheriff hit Billy hard behind the left ear with his billy club, and Billy slumped. Bredlo hit him on the left temple and Billy fell to the cement floor of his cell.

"You two give him a little stompin', but don't leave no marks. He's got to go to court tomorrow." Sheriff Bredlo dragged a groggy but now awake Deputy Dunlap out of the cell and down to the sheriff's office. He left the other deputies to finish beating Billy Sprouse.

Deputy Dunlap was less hurt than he had appeared

at first. He collapsed on the sheriff's couch. "How the hell did he get you in that cell?" asked Sheriff Bredlo as he propped Dunlap up.

"He started a fire with his mattress. I had to go in and put it out."

"But how did he start the fire?" the sheriff wanted to know.

"With this," said Dunlap, showing Bredlo his own lighter. "I found it in his cell before he hit me from behind." The sheriff had been looking for his lighter since it had gone missing earlier that day.

"Why, that little son of a bitch! May he rot in Hell."

"I think he's already there," said the deputy softly.

Jack had gotten word that both General Cartridge and Joe Smiley had been informed of Billy's jailhouse fire episode. Jack wondered at the time if they would use the incident to claim police brutality and gain the jury's sympathy for their 'poor country boy,' but he knew on that first day of the trial that Billy had blown it all with his belligerent posturing and that the jury would see the starting of the jailhouse fire for what it was, another violent crime committed by a vicious offender. *So*, thought Jack, *the General and Joe Smiley will probably let that strategy go.*

Chapter 30: The Right to a Speedy Trial:
Day One, Opening Statements

Whatever rights may not have been observed in the due process of defendants in 1959, the right to a speedy trial was not among them. Billy Sprouse waited fewer than two weeks in the city jail before trial, and Judge Donald Stevens had allotted just two days on the docket for the trial.

Judge Stevens had a crowded docket, and he believed in keeping things moving along—swiftly and in an orderly fashion. He ran a tight courtroom. Whether you served as an attorney for the commonwealth or for the defense, you'd best not drag out your opening statement or your interrogation of the witnesses. If you did, Judge Stevens would cut you off at the knees. Jack knew this from years of experience. He wondered if Joe Smiley had done his homework on the judge.

Sitting at the commonwealth's table at the front

of the packed courtroom, Jack turned slightly around to get a quick take on the mix of spectators. He could see Mickey's father, Michael Courage, sitting on his own in a distant corner. He recognized some of General Cartridge's people, including Alex Ramos, the General's personal enforcer and security man. Jack was sure that Ramos would be providing his boss an in-depth report, not only on the trial, but also on who was there and how they responded to all its twists and turns. *Just like a bad Santa*, thought Jack, *Alex Ramos will be taking his notes and checking them twice to see who needs to be dealt with after the trial.*

The usual contingent of senior citizens with interest and time on their hands were present, but so were a fair number of business people who had taken time off from work to view the spectacle of white trash gone bad and to see for themselves what the trial might mean for their still confused and slightly confrontational relationship with the colored folk. For many of these merchants, the hardworking black person represented considerable income, and their stores had become dependent on receiving a healthy share of it.

There was also a large contingent of Charlottesville's black citizens seated in the de facto segregated area in the left rear of the courtroom. Their unusually large number represented strong support and a kind of empowerment of the families of Lucius Johnson and Roy Amery, as if to say, "We will not be intimidated this time, and we will have justice in this courtroom."

They were determined that this trial would proceed differently than the trial five years previously of Willie R. Jefferson, a retarded black man convicted of raping a white prostitute who had seduced him in order to steal his wallet. It had all taken place right here in Charlottesville. The man had been convicted on her word against his, partly because his disability made him unable to speak properly for himself. In a world where even consensual sex between black and white was often considered rape, a young retarded person sat on death row in a prison near Richmond, his appeals exhausted, awaiting execution.

For the blacks present in the courtroom on this day, the Jefferson case represented the worst of the white man's justice, and, as their leaders had said in their churches, in their taverns, and at other meeting places, they were determined not to let that sort of injustice spin out here. The commonwealth's attorney had told them in Ebenezer Baptist Church not so long ago that with patience, they would have real justice for Roy Amery and for the memory of Lucius Johnson. The black leaders and their followers were here today to witness that justice and *nothing less.*

Of course there was the usual contingent of low-end rednecks and white trash who believed smugly that the only place for a nigger in the courtroom was as a janitor or defendant. They were here for the entertainment value only.

There is no reasoning with these people, thought Jack. *One can only try to protect the rest of society from them.* In 1959, white trash feared the upward mobility of blacks and what it might mean to their status in society's pecking order as they saw it. They felt threatened and afraid, and they hated blacks for their own unacknowledged fear of them. That hate was present in the courtroom as they scowled at the large black group being allowed to sit and attend the court proceedings. *Yes,* thought Jack, getting ready to present his opening statement, *we'll need to keep a sharp eye on that group.*

Jack's opening statement was simple, factual, to the point, with just a little bit of gristle for the jury to chew on. Facing the jury and pointing to the defense table, he began. "Billy Sprouse, the sullen young man you see there in handcuffs, has been charged with kidnapping a sixteen-year-old Negro, Lucius Johnson, with the intent to extort money. He is also charged with felony murder in that he was directly responsible for Lucius Johnson's death; Lucius Johnson hung himself while trying to escape from his captors. Mr. Sprouse's partner in these crimes has already pled guilty to charges related to this incident. He will testify to the facts as I have stated them."

Jack continued, "We will, furthermore, prove that Billy Sprouse was the ringleader of the two perpetrators, and that it was his exclusive determination to kidnap and hog-tie Lucius Johnson against his partner's wishes. The 'accidental' hanging was a direct result of Mr. Sprouse's actions, and it occurred while he was in the process of committing the felony of kidnapping;

therefore, his actions were the proximate cause of Lucius Johnson's death. Accordingly, we will prove that Billy Sprouse is guilty of felony murder."

Jack concluded by saying, "We will show that Billy Sprouse has shown no remorse for causing the death of Lucius Johnson neither at the time of his arrest nor any time since. The evidence will further show that Mr. Sprouse, on the night of Monday, July 13th, 1959, sought to terrorize perfect strangers just for the hell of it. At the time, Mr. Sprouse, drunk and a little high, was trying to raise the level of terror he was causing to a new high. It was a thrill crime. In this trial we will prove not only guilt on all charges, but also malice of intent that will dictate the maximum sentence the law will allow. Thank you." Jack nodded gently to the jury and returned to the prosecution's table.

Joe Smiley for the defense quickly got up, strode over to the all-white jury, and smiled broadly at them. He was dressed in a dark blue pinstripe suit, a white shirt, and a power-red tie, his elevated cordovans raising his doughboy silhouette a full inch beyond his natural five foot five. With his swept-back blonde hair, his extended jaw line, and crinkly blue eyes, he appeared a somewhat stunted Aryan poster boy. It was apparent as Joe Smiley began his opening statement that he was impressed with himself; it remained to be seen if the jury would feel the same way.

"Well, good morning, ladies and gentlemen. It is an honor to be in your courtroom today to defend young Billy Sprouse. It is apparent to us all that he made some mistakes and some bad errors in judgment last July 13th, but, as we shall see, the cause of his roughneck action was not a wanton desire to harm or abduct the two Negro boys in question. Rather, his actions were the direct result of immoral advances that Lucius Johnson and Roy Amery made to him and to his friend Mickey Courage."

There was a collective gasp from the black section and even a look of surprise from the white spectators.

Smiley continued, "We will show that these colored boys got into the car Billy Sprouse was driving voluntarily and for immoral purposes. There was no kidnapping.

"We will further show that young Mr. Sprouse was so outraged that these Negro boys would even think that he would respond to homosexual advances that he decided to teach them a lesson. Now he may have taken this lesson too far, and while he does now regret the accidental hanging of Lucius Johnson, it is our contention that Lucius Johnson brought it on himself by his own morally reprehensible advances to my client.

This charge drew a series of excited whispers and sent a buzz of anticipation through the courtroom. Judge Stevens slammed down his gavel and growled, "Order! I will have order in my courtroom!" Immediate quiet prevailed.

Joe Smiley looked closely at the jury. He continued, "Mr. Sprouse may be guilty of simple assault, even of false imprisonment with extenuating circumstances, but here in this court he is being charged with kidnapping and felony murder. Given the immoral solicitation of the two Negro boys, Mr. Sprouse's outrage is understandable. He may have overreached, but this in no way justifies the commonwealth's attorney misrepresenting the facts of the case in order to create charges of kidnapping and felony murder. We will prove that. Ergo, we will prove Billy Sprouse is not guilty of any of the current charges as stipulated by commonwealth's attorney Jack Forester." As he spoke Jack's name, Joe Smiley pirouetted in his elevator shoes to point at the commonwealth's table, then turned back to the jury and, in a carefully crafted afterthought, stated, "I know it's an election year, Jack, but let's not throw away the life of a youthful offender for your own political gain."

The courtroom erupted, and Jack was about to respond in kind, when he realized that was just what Smiley had intended. Fortunately, Judge Stevens intervened first.

"Sit down, Mr. Smiley!" he roared, and, turning to the court stenographer, continued, "Strike that from the record. Mr. Smiley, you are out of order and you know it. Any more inappropriate and irrelevant aspersions directed at the commonwealth's attorney and I will hold you in contempt and have you thrown out of my courtroom. Is that perfectly clear, Mr. Smiley?" Judge Stevens leaned over the bench and held Joe Smiley in a menacing stare.

Smiley responded quickly and meekly, "Yes, sir,

Your Honor. I apologize to the court."

"And to Mr. Forester?" continued the Judge.

"And to Mr. Forester," said Joe Smiley quietly.

Jack looked over at the jury which had keenly followed the smack down the judge had delivered the slick out-of-town lawyer. It was a good start that the judge had so publicly discredited the defense tactics. Now perhaps this all-white jury would also see through the defense's attempt to demonize perhaps through their own prejudice. *If so*, thought Jack, *then there is a decent chance that I can get justice for Roy Amery and the family of Lucius Johnson. Maybe I can achieve justice acceptable to black and white alike and achieve a little peaceful social evolution for Charlottesville.*

The judge was looking hard at both attorneys. "All right, Mr. Forester, call your first witness. By the way, I want to make it clear to both the commonwealth and to the defense: I will not tolerate any histrionics in my courtroom. Save that for your closing arguments. Does everyone understand that?"

Jack and Joe Smiley nodded dutifully.

"All right, proceed. Your first witness, Mr. Forester," the judge intoned.

"The prosecution calls Roy Amery to the stand."

And so it began. The stage was set for high drama in the packed courtroom. Amery was an eyewitness as well as the second victim of the crimes, and could testify to the actual events leading up to Lucius Johnson's hanging death. His credibility would probably determine whether Billy Sprouse was guilty of kidnapping or of something quite different, as Joe Smiley would attempt to prove. Jack was worried about the tactics Smiley would use to discredit Roy Amery. He wondered if his preparation of Roy had been sufficient. Jack had said, "Stick to the facts. Just be honest, keep your eyes on me as best you can, and don't let Mr. Smiley fluster you. I'll be right there with you, so it's okay to be nervous, but don't let him scare you. Don't worry." But Jack knew that Roy would worry, and Jack worried too.

Chapter 31: Roy Amery Interrogation

Roy Amery, dressed in his Sunday best, a slightly tattered white cotton suit, white shirt, and red bow tie, approached the witness chair. He looked younger and smaller than his seventeen years. He also looked a little nervous, but Jack knew from his meetings with Amery of his resolute determination to represent and defend the memory of Lucius Johnson.

Roy sat down in the witness chair and quickly glanced out on the sea of faces; then, as Mr. Forester had instructed him, he looked only at the commonwealth's attorney.

"All right, for the record, what is your name?" said Jack.

"Roy Amery!" said Roy, almost shouting it out.

"All right, Roy," said Jack gently. "Now what was your relationship to the diseased, Lucius Johnson?"

"He was my cousin. And my friend," said Roy.

"Do you recognize the defendant, Billy Sprouse, sitting over there?" Jack pointed at the slouching figure at the defense table. He was apparently trying to give Roy Amery the evil eye.

"Yes, sir, I do," said Roy, staring steadily at Sprouse and pointing directly at him. "That's him sitting right there." Jack moved slightly to his right so as to cut off eye contact between the parties. He didn't want the latent prejudice of a member of the jury to be awoken or for any juror to think the witness was acting uppity.

"All right, tell the court what you and Lucius were doing and where you were going on the night you met Billy Sprouse."

"We was headed over to see Charlene Morris. She's my girlfriend. Charlene had her cousin with her. She had come up on the bus from Gum Springs. That's why I had asked Lucius to come along, so he could meet her."

"And when did you meet up with the defendant?" Jack asked.

"Well, we was talkin' and walkin' fast, uh, down Peach Street," answered Roy. "We were both pretty excited about meetin' up with the girls, and all of a sudden this car stops right in front of us and two white guys jumped out and grabbed us for no reason."

Jack glanced over at the defense table and noticed Billy Sprouse's sullen expression. Billy wasn't winning any brownie points with the jury. That was good. Jack also noticed Joe Smiley's sardonic smile. Joe Smiley was gazing at the jury knowingly. Jack wondered what the little big-city lawyer had up his sleeve, and why he was not peppering Jack's interrogation with objections or protests. That worried him. Judge Stevens broke into his reverie.

"Mr. Forester, do you have more questions for this witness, or are we all to just imagine what happened next?"

"Uh, no, Your Honor, I was just observing the mood of this court room."

"Have you finished observing?" This brought a few chuckles from across the courtroom, which seemed to please Judge Stevens.

"Well, then," Judge Stevens continued with the slightest of smiles. "May we continue with the testimony of this witness?"

"Uh, yes, sir, Your Honor." Jack turned from the judge back to his witness and continued. "All right, Roy, you say the defendant and his friend jumped out of their car and just grabbed you for no reason. Is that right?"

"Yes, sir."

"You'd never seen them before that night?"

"No, sir, we'd never laid eyes on them before they jumped us."

"All right, Roy. Now take your time, this is important. Tell the jury exactly what happened next."

"Well, I broke away from the one guy who had grabbed me and started to run off. But that guy there—" Roy pointed at Billy Sprouse.

Jack interrupted, "For the record, Roy, are you pointing at the defendant?" Jack walked over to the defense table and stood by Billy Sprouse.

"Yes, sir," said Roy. "He had Lucius in a headlock with one hand, and Lucius couldn't get away. He yelled at me that he had a knife in his other hand, and that if I didn't come on back, he'd slit Lucius' throat right there."

"What happened next?" asked Jack.

"Well, I wanted to run away, but I couldn't leave Lucius like that so I came back. Then they forced us into their car, me in the front seat with the other guy and Lucius in the back seat with that guy." Roy pointed again to Billy Sprouse. "When I looked in the rear view mirror, I could see he was still holding a knife to Lucius' throat. They drove the car on down to some old shack at the edge of town. They stopped the car and told us they was gonna let us go after we gave 'em all our money, but when they found out we only had about two-fifty, that guy, Billy Sprouse, got real angry. Then he told the other guy to let me go, but if I didn't come back with twenty-five dollars—'party money' I think he called it—if I didn't come back within an hour, he was going to kill Lucius, 'slit his throat like a pig at the slaughterhouse.' Then they set me free, and I took off running, yelling that I'd be back and not to hurt Lucius."

Roy went on to tell Jack and the courtroom how he'd run all the way back into town, borrowed money from his girlfriend Charlene, and hurried back to the shack at the edge of town where the white boys had been holding Lucius. "But they was gone. The door was open to that beat-up old cabin and when I looked in all I could see in the moonlight was this crumpled body on the floor. He had a piece of rope around his neck. I knew right away it was Lucius." Roy erupted from his softly spoken testimony and yelled toward Billy Sprouse, "You left him hanging like a piece of meat, you honky bastard." Roy tried to look past Jack his friend's murderer, but Jack intentionally blocked his view.

There was subdued murmuring in the courtroom; everyone feared Judge Stevens' retribution. Judge Stevens looked down at Roy Amery as he said, "Strike that last statement from the record. Mr. Amery, you will confine your answers strictly to facts related to the questions asked, or I will have you thrown out of the courtroom, do you understand?"

Amery nodded quietly.

Jack was surprised that Smiley had not raised a protest on legal issues concerning Roy's outburst, but there was none. Did Joe think it actually played into the prejudice of the jury? Perhaps.

"All right, Mr. Forester, finish with your questions for this witness."

"Thank you, Your Honor."

"Take your time, Roy. Now tell the jury what you did after you saw the body of Lucius."

Roy turned his head towards the twelve white faces of the jury and continued. "I didn't know what to do. Lucius was already dead, but I knew I had to get some kind of help. The only thing I could think of was to get to the police station and tell 'em what happened, so I ran all the way back to town."

"Did you go to the police station?" Jack asked.

"Yes, sir."

"Whom did you talk to?"

"I think his name was Sergeant Carter."

"Do you see him in this courtroom?"

"Yes, sir." Roy pointed to a large, red-haired, uniformed man, sitting in the gallery, apparently waiting to testify. "What did he do?"

Roy continued. "He listened to my story and told me that he and his men would go out and look into it right away."

"And then what happened?"

"Well, by then it was the middle of the night, so Sergeant Carter had one of his men drive me home. I wanted to go with them back to where Lucius was, but Sergeant Carter said that wasn't necessary. He said they would come by my house the next day and pick me up for further questioning. He said that one of the boys that might have done what I told him about had already come in to confess and that the police were already out looking for the other one." Roy looked down at his trembling hands. "I got back with the money as soon as I could, Mr. Forester, but they had already killed him."

"All right, Roy. Thank you." Jack smiled at Roy to let him know he had done a good job. "Your witness, Counselor," said Jack as he walked past Joe Smiley and sat down at the commonwealth's table.

Smiley got up slowly and smiled broadly at Roy Amery for all the jury to see. Then he walked quickly over to the witness chair and began his interrogation.

"Well, Roy, I bet you were pretty excited when you and Lucius went out that night," he said with a big grin.

"Well, yes, sir, I guess we was. I sure was lookin' forward to seeing—" Roy was going to say, "Charlene and her cousin from Gum Springs," but Smiley cut him off.

"You were looking forward to getting out on a hot summer night for a little fun, am I right?"

"Well, yes, sir, I guess so," said Roy quietly.

"And you and your buddy Lucius were looking for a good time, right?" Smiley asked.

"Well, I was lookin' forward to seeing Charlene and Lucius wanted to meet her cousin—"

Smiley cut him off again. "Just answer the question yes or no. You were looking for a good time, right?"

Roy hesitated and Smiley bored in. "Right, Roy?"

"Well, I guess so," said Roy softly.

"And that's when you spotted those two white boys in their car at the corner of Peach and Rafferty."

"Well, that's when we first saw 'em," agreed Roy.

"Now, when you four met up, Mr. Sprouse over there," Smiley pointed at his client, "the defendant, will testify you tried to come onto him like you and your buddy wanted to fool around with them. That's what happened, right?"

There were loud murmurings and a couple of loud guffaws, which Judge Stevens quashed with a bang of his gavel. He swept the gavel in an arc from one side of the courtroom to the other as he said, "The next person who raises his voice in my courtroom without my say-so gets thrown out. The second person who raises his voice and disrupts my courtroom will be cited for contempt and then thrown out."

Speaking directly to the gallery, the judge continued, "So if anybody thinks you won't be able to control yourself, you'd better get out now." Everyone in the courtroom seemed to freeze in place. There was absolute silence. Nobody left.

"All right then," continued Judge Stevens. "You people out there in the gallery are going to shut up and listen. Right? That's good." Now Judge Stevens turned his attention to the defense table. "As for you, Mr. Smiley, when you ask a question of a witness, don't cut him off before he gives you his full answer. Let him finish. Are we clear?" Smiley nodded quickly and looked furtively over to the jury to see if they had been able to grasp the innuendo of his previous question.

Up until the most recent question of Roy Amery, Jack had held his fire in the hope that the judge would not; he knew that a rebuke from the bench would be far more effective than his own objection.

"All right, continue, Mr. Smiley," said Judge Stevens.

"Well, let's see, Roy. You and your buddy came up on Billy Sprouse and Mickey Courage on that hot July night and you were just a walking and a skipping along, right?"

"Well, we was walkin'," said Roy steadily.

"You was just a' walkin'," Smiley mimicked Roy softly. Then, much louder, he continued, "I bet you know what Mr. Sprouse is going to say. He's going to testify that you and your buddy walked right up to their car and asked them if they wanted to, you know, 'get it on'."

"No, sir," said Roy. "They just jumped out of their car for no reason and jumped us before we even knew what was going on."

"You sure you didn't go up and make some kind of immoral suggestions, and that's why they jumped out of their car and grabbed you?" asked Smiley.

"I don't know what they was thinking," said Roy evenly. "All we wanted was to get to Charlene's house. They just jumped out of their car and started beating on us for no reason."

"Uh huh," said Smiley in a mocking tone. "Uh, now Roy, you said earlier you had broken away and had started to run. So tell us again why you came on back."

"Because that defendant over there," Roy pointed at Billy Sprouse. "He had a knife to Lucius' throat and he said he'd slit it if I didn't come back."

Smiley looked at Billy Sprouse, to whom Roy had just pointed, and said in a voice intended for the jury, "You know, Roy, you don't have to point to the defendant; everyone else knows who he is, even if you have to point at him to find him."

"Objection," said Jack Forester. There were amused, but muted, giggles coming from the white trash contingent in the courtroom.

"Objection, Your Honor," Jack repeated. "Counselor is being argumentative and is badgering the witness."

"I agree, Mr. Forester," said Judge Stevens. "Mr. Smiley, you are trying my patience. You may think you can get away with your snide gratuitous innuendos in a small southern town, but such is not the case in Charlottesville. Your job is to interrogate the witness, not to try to humiliate him. If you continue these tactics, I will hold you in contempt, and things will go very badly for you. Now do you read me?"

"Yes, Your Honor," said Smiley, glancing over to the jury to see if he had won any support with his tactics. A slight smile appeared on his face.

Judge Stevens, who had been looking at Smiley, turned to the jury and continued. "Attorneys in my courtroom will show respect for all witnesses presented, even if they do not exhibit this same respect for themselves. I expect you in the jury to accord the same respect to all witnesses as you do to my courtroom as a whole. I trust you understand me." The jury nodded like a bunch of poppies blowing in the wind. Meanwhile, Smiley was standing mute in the knowledge that he had become, however briefly, the object of the court's scorn. He knew that to say something in righteous protest now would jeopardize his well-conceived plan to beat the charges against his client. He reddened and awaited the judge's further instruction.

"So, Mr. Smiley, are you ready to proceed in accordance with the will of this court?"

"Yes, sir, Your Honor."

"Do you have any more questions for this witness?"

"Yes, Your Honor, I do."

"All right then, you may proceed."

"Thank you, Your Honor," said Smiley.

"With caution, Mr. Smiley."

"Yes, sir, Your Honor."

Joe Smiley resumed his questioning of Roy, with some caution.

"Okay. Now, Roy, you said earlier you escaped and started to run away. Is that right?"

"Yes, sir," said Roy.

"So tell us again why on earth you came back?"

"Because the defendant had a knife to Lucius' throat and he said he'd slit it if I didn't," repeated Roy.

"Did you actually see a knife?" Smiley wanted to know.

"I couldn't see it from twenty yards away when he yelled at me to come back."

"So how do you know he had a knife?"

"'Cuz I could see it in the car when he had it to

Lucius' throat."

"And how could you, being held in the front seat, see into the back seat?"

"I saw it in the rear view mirror."

"You saw the knife in the rear view mirror?"

"Yes, sir."

"So you didn't actually see the knife, only a reflection in the rear view mirror of what appeared to be a knife."

"He had a knife," said Roy steadily.

"So you say," said Joe Smiley. "But let me ask you one more time, did you ever see the actual knife?"

"No, but I know he had it."

"But you never saw it, is that correct?"

"Yes, that's what I said," said Roy.

"Then you don't *know* he had a knife."

Roy started to speak, but Joe Smiley continued. "No more questions for this witness, Your Honor."

"All right, the witness is excused." As Roy was leaving the witness stand, Smiley turned to the judge and said, "Your Honor, I would like the record to show that there was never any knife recovered in this case."

"Any objection from the commonwealth?" asked the judge.

"No objection." Jack had no choice. Though he was certain Billy had had a knife as Mickey Courage alleged, it had not been recovered. Point to Smiley.

Joe Smiley looked meaningfully at the jury and started to return to the defense table. Then he turned back to Roy. "One last question, Roy. How do you feel about Mr. Sprouse today?"

"I hate him for killing my best friend."

"So you say. And how did you feel about him when you first met up with him that night?"

"I didn't feel anything but fear. I was scared of him and his partner."

"You sure you didn't feel any other way about him?" asked Smiley, with a tight smile.

"What do you mean?" asked Roy.

"You know Roy, excited, err, wanting to fool around with him."

Jack stood up immediately to object. "Your Honor, those last questions as posed by Mr. Smiley are unfounded, misleading, and inflammatory."

"I agree," said Judge Stevens. He immediately said to the court Stenographer, "Strike those last two questions. The jury will disregard." Then he turned to Smiley. "Do you have any further pertinent or relevant question for this witness?"

But the damage had been done. Jack knew it, and Joe Smiley knew it. The immoral advances innuendo had been put out there for any juror to grasp onto if he were looking for a way to justify, or at least ameliorate, the charges against the defendant.

Smiley had no more questions and Roy stepped down glaring at him as he passed by. This only pleased Smiley, and Jack knew it. Both attorneys were called out of their musings by Judge Stevens. "Call your next witness, Mr. Forester."

"The commonwealth calls Mickey Courage, Your Honor." Straight from his weekend stay at Sheriff Shotwell's home, Mickey Courage appeared through a side door. He was dressed in a yellow sweater and gray slacks and escorted by a Louisa County sheriff's deputy, who led him up to the witness stand.

After Mickey was sworn in, he sat down quickly and faced Jack and the sea of faces behind him. "Mickey," Jack asked, "what was your state of mind before you and Billy encountered Roy Amery and Lucius Johnson?"

"We had been drinking and sniffing glue, and Billy said he wanted to go out 'Coon hunting,'" said Mickey.

"What exactly is Coon Hunting?" Jack asked.

"Billy said it was like you roust a couple of colored

boys, scare the hell out of them, and then let 'em go, but I had no idea when we ran into these guys that Billy would pull a knife and hold one for ransom."

"Now, Billy," said Jack, "this is important. What was your state of mind at this point?"

"When I saw Billy put the knife to the one kid's throat, I was as scared of him as they were. I didn't know what he was going to do."

"Okay," said Jack, "so who tied up Lucius in the rafters?"

"Billy did," said Mickey, "so he wouldn't escape before his friend came back with the party money. But neither one of us thought he would try to get away and fall off the rafters and hang himself. That was just a tragedy for everyone," said Mickey.

"Especially for Lucius Johnson," said Jack.

"Yes, sir," said Mickey Courage, looking down. "I'm so sorry for what we did and for what happened."

"All right, Mickey. Thank you for your testimony." Jack believed that Mickey had come across as both truthful and remorseful. Now if he could just hold up against Smiley's cross-examination. Jack turned toward the defense table and said, "Your witness, Counselor."

Again, the diminutive Smiley leapt up like he'd been shot out of a cannon. He trotted toward the witness stand, talking the whole way.

"Well, Mickey Courage, you're sorry about everything and all, but it was all Billy Sprouse's fault, right?"

"No, sir, I didn't say that," said Mickey.

"But you did say that it was Billy's idea to roust those two colored boys after they came on to you."

"It was Billy's idea to kick 'em around, yes. But they never came on to us."

"So you say. Now you have already struck a deal with the prosecution in exchange for your testimony, is that right?"

"Yes, sir," said Mickey.

"So it would be in your best interest to say what they want, whether the colored boys came on to you or not, isn't that right?" asked Joe Smiley as he leaned in on the witness stand where Mickey was sitting.

"Mr. Forester told me to tell the truth. That's all I had to do, and that's what I'm doing."

"So you say," said Smiley pulling back from the witness stand.

"And they didn't come on to us, ever," said Mickey firmly. Smiley snapped to attention at this last voluntary statement and said in a loud voice, "I did not ask you that."

Judge Stevens cut him off. "But you implied it, Mr. Smiley. Now move on. Do you have any more questions for this witness?"

"None," said Smiley, raising both hands as if to dismiss Mickey Courage for unacceptable testimony.

"The witness may step down," said Judge Stevens. "Call your next witness, Mr. Forester."

Receiving virtually no rebuttal from Smiley, Jack called Sheriff Bredlo, Sergeant Carter, and other officers. They testified to the facts of the case. Smiley seemed almost bored with the proceedings as he chewed on the eraser end of his pencil while raising only minor objections. Through testimony given, Jack felt he had successfully laid out all of the elements, factual and otherwise, to sustain charges of kidnapping and felony murder. He was a little concerned at the lack of resistance from the defense table but felt he had built a nearly airtight case. He also believed he was prepared for any last-minute surprises Smiley might have planned.

"Your Honor, the prosecution rests."

"All right," acknowledged Judge Stevens. "Now, Mr. Smiley," said Judge Stevens looking at his watch, "it's about eleven o'clock. Would you like to present your case now, or would you rather I recess the court until after lunch?"

"Uh, no, Your Honor. I'd like to proceed now. I only have one witness to call."

It appeared that Judge Stevens had been looking forward to an early lunch. He leaned down from the bench, almost as if to blame Smiley for lack of decorum, and continued, "Well, Mr. Smiley, you may proceed, but keep in mind that we will break for lunch at twelve o'clock sharp, whether or not you are ready. Got me?"

Jack could see that Smiley realized he may have made a tactical error with the judge, for, as Jack and every other local officer of the court knew, when Judge Stevens asked you whether you wished to recess for lunch, he was saying *he* wanted to recess for lunch. Apparently, though, Smiley felt it more important to proceed now and risk incurring Judge Stevens' wrath than to delay the testimony he wanted to present to counter the testimony of Mickey Courage.

Consciously avoiding the judge's stare, Smiley looked around as if he had dropped something on the floor.

"Is it still the defense request that we proceed *now*?" intoned Judge Stevens.

"It is, your Honor," Smiley answered meekly.

"Then let's get on with it," growled Judge Stevens. "Call your next witness."

"Thank you, Your Honor," said Joe Smiley. "The defense calls Billy Sprouse."

Chapter 33: Billy Sprouse takes the Witness Stand

As his name was called, Billy Sprouse quickly stood up, still handcuffed but unshackled, and walked up to the witness stand, strutting and looking around as if he were the long awaited star of a Western Movie. Apparently no amount of coaching from his defense team had convinced him to act contrite or remorseful. This was his moment and he was going to have it.

Before the trial began, Joe Smiley had offered Billy a coat and tie, even a suit "which he could keep." Smiley had pleaded with Billy to cut his scraggly long hair short in an all-American crew cut. "Please," pleaded Smiley, "keep in mind that how you dress and act this week could make the difference in whether or not I can get you off."

Initially, Billy blew him off. "You work the trial, city man, but don't tell me how to look or act. This is my show." Apparently, though, Smiley had convinced

Billy that a little cooperation could make the difference between twenty years in prison for a felony murder conviction and getting off with a couple of years and probation. Billy was moderately impressed, so he had his hair cut, although in a spiked crew cut with grease, courtesy of the barber at the jailhouse. He wore the suit pants he had been given, but not the jacket that came with them. His white dress shirt was open, with a thin black tie dribbling down and the sleeves rolled up to reveal sinewy muscles and a homemade tattoo.

Despite Smiley's persuasion, I bet this is not the way Billy looked yesterday at the dress rehearsal. I bet he sandbagged Smiley a little bit, thought Jack. *Well, good for him, and good for us.*

And so it was. As Billy completed his strut to the witness stand, the jury saw him for what he was, and for what he wanted them to see.

Jack watched while Joe Smiley murmured to himself as he hurried up to interrogate his witness, probably wondering how he could minimize Billy's self-presentation.

"Okay, Billy," said Smiley to his client. "You know you've been charged with kidnapping and second-degree homicide. Tell the court again how you plead."

"It's a load of crap," said Billy looking straight at the jury.

"Can you be more specific?" said Smiley quickly to avoid any language censure from the bench.

"You bet I can," said Billy.

"Good. Now tell the court how you met up with those two colored boys on the night in question."

"Sure, I can do that," said Billy, holding his arms wide open as if welcoming the court into his coming story.

"We was just doing a little drinkin' and foolin' around. It was hot, and I started sniffin' on this glue I got off a guy—Mickey did, too—you know, to get a little extra buzz on. Well I tell you, it did make me feel pretty wild." Billy looked over at the jury and offered a leering smile. There was a slight giggle coming from the white trash corner of the courtroom— slight, because no one wanted to get kicked out of the courtroom. By now there wasn't a spare seat in the house, and people were passing messages to the overflow crowd just outside.

Jack got a note from one of his assistant DAs that there were over two hundred people standing around the courthouse square, mostly white on one side and black on the other. Jack knew how important it was that both sides see justice in the court's verdict; that it could be the difference between violent or peaceable assembly.

It's all in my hands, thought Jack as he listened intently to the rest of Billy's testimony.

"So anyway, I seen this '55 DeSoto with the keys in the ignition. We decided to take it for a little joyride and just leave it somewhere when we was done with it." Billy giggled slightly as he continued, "Shoot, we've done it a bunch of times." Even Smiley's eyes rolled at this last remark, but he decided to let Billy get it all out, thinking that this latest criminal revelation might actually work towards his newly developing strategy.

"Anyway," continued Sprouse, "I do believe even Mickey was gettin' a little scared of me, and that made it even more fun. Yeah, I think he was. Well anyway, there we was, right at the corner of Peach and Rafferty, and I saw those two spooks walking in our direction."

"Watch your language young man," said the judge.

"Huh? Okay, those two niggers—" There were renewed muted guffaws coming from the white trash section.

"Mr. Sprouse, you will refer to that race as Negro or colored in my court. Otherwise, I will hold you in contempt and throw you out of my court. Do I need to have your attorney explain to you what that means?" Joe Smiley mouthed "No, sir," to his client. He looked a little desperate.

After a pause, Billy answered, "Sorry, Judge," showing his best broken-toothed grin. "I never know what to call 'em."

Judge Stevens looked hard at Billy Sprouse as if trying to ascertain whether the witness was being contrite or playing to the crowd. He decided to let it go for now. "You'd best be very careful with your language in my courtroom from now on, Mr. Sprouse.

All right. Continue with this witness, Mr. Smiley, but with caution."

"Yes, sir, Your Honor."

"Okay, Billy, you're in this car, you're a little high. What happened then?" asked Smiley.

"Well, let's see," said Billy stroking his chin for obvious effect. "Oh, yeah, we was kinda stopped at Peach and Rafferty when we seen these two, uh, colored boys walking towards our car."

"Okay, Billy, I've got some very important questions, so please answer them carefully." Again, Jack caught Smiley's eyes pleading with Billy for cooperation, probably to stick with whatever script they had cooked up before they came into the courtroom that day.

"Uh, now you say they came up to *you*."

"Yeah, that's right."

"And you were parked at the time?"

"Kinda. We had just pulled over. I was gonna take a leak in the hedges by the side of the road—" there were scattered snickers in the gallery—"when I saw these two, err, colored boys coming our way."

"Now the prosecution says you jumped out of the car and started assaulting these boys. Is that how it all started?"

Billy smiled broadly. "No, sir. Those boys came right up to our car and started struttin' their stuff."

"What do you mean, 'strutting their stuff'?" Joe Smiley asked.

"You know," began Billy. "They started comin'

on and sashaying all around."

There were loud murmurings in the courtroom before Judge Stevens silenced them all with the sound of his gavel, then said, "I will have silence in my courtroom. Now continue, Mr. Smiley."

"Thank you, Your Honor. Now Billy, you say they were sashaying around. What happened then?"

"Well one of them, I think it was the one that hung himself, asked through the window if I wanted to get it on."

"Then what happened?"

"Well," said Billy, slowly for effect. "That's when I realized they must a thought we was homosexuals too. Now that made me mad—Mickey too—so we just sorta got out of the car and beat the crap out of them, you know, to teach 'em a lesson."

"So why did they then get in the car with you?"

"Oh, yeah, that," said Billy as if just remembering now. "I decided they could make it up to us for thinking we were queers by givin' us a little party money. So we dragged 'em in the car to mess with 'em a little more, you know, scare 'em and then let 'em go after they gave us money to buy a little more booze. It wasn't no big thing. Just havin' a little fun on a hot night in this crummy little town."

"But you never meant to hurt them?" asked Smiley.

"Shoot no. We was just havin' a little fun."

"And you never meant to kidnap anybody?"

"Heck no. We was just holding the one boy 'til

the other one got back with the party money."

"All right. Now tell the court in your own words all that happened leading up to Lucius Johnson's unfortunate hanging."

"Okay. I got you, Coach," said Billy Sprouse leaning back in the witness chair. He crossed his legs and looked first at Joe Smiley and then to the jury as if to let them in on his story of the 'bad-ass night.' It was evident to Jack, observing, and probably to the jurors too, that Billy was actually proud of his actions that night and did not mind who knew it.

"Okay. So anyway, after we got 'em in the car and drove around, you know, just messin' with their heads, we was gonna let 'em go, but then I realized they only had a couple a bucks to contribute to our party money and it made me mad again. So I got the idea to drive to this old abandoned shack on the edge of town where I hang out sometimes. Now the deal was that Mickey was gonna let his guy go to get more money, while we held on to his buddy just to make sure he'd come back. Shoot, it shoulda been no big deal. Soon as the one came back with ten or fifteen dollars, we'd have kicked 'em both in the butt and let 'em go. Like I say, it wasn't no big deal."

"All right," interrupted Smiley. "Did Mickey Courage go along with all this?"

Billy smiled, but it was not a nice smile. "Well, let's just say he didn't try to stop me."

"So you'd say he was a willing accomplice."

"A what?"

278 ALDEN E. C. BIGELOW

"That he agreed with your plans."

Billy was not about to share the glory.

"I said he went along with it all, but it was my show."

Smiley visibly blushed. *Apparently*, thought Jack, *the plan had been to make Mickey equally culpable, but Billy just couldn't help himself.*

"Okay," said Smiley quickly. "Let's move on. You drove out to the old abandoned cabin with the two colored boys. Exactly what took place then?" 'Exactly' was the code word that Smiley had used when preparing Billy for trial to alert Billy to answer the question *exactly* as they had rehearsed it in the city jail interrogation room.

"What's that?" asked Billy, to let Smiley know he recognized the signal that it was still his show. "Let's see. You want me to tell exactly what happened just like we talked about in jail." Then, to Smiley's horror, Billy gave an elaborate wink to the jury and continued. "Yeah, well, let's see, I told Mickey to let the one guy go so he could come back with the money. Then we'd free his buddy. That was the deal. I told him I'd slit his buddy's throat if he didn't, but I don't think I woulda."

"Right," interrupted Smiley again. "Now did you really have a knife to his throat, Billy?" Smiley looked at Billy Sprouse hard, hoping for the right answer.

There was a pause. Then, "Oh, shoot no. I got long fingernails, sharp. I just had the top of my middle fingernail jammed against his throat so he's think it was the tip of a knife." Again turning towards the all-white jury with a slight smile, Billy continued, "But it wasn't."

"You had no knife, did you?" asked Smiley slowly.

"Heck no. I didn't need no knife to scare those boys."

"Okay, fine," said Smiley. "Now, let's move on. Did you tie up Lucius Johnson at the cabin?"

"Yes, sir, I did."

"Why?"

"Why, to keep him from gettin' away before his friend came back."

"How long did you figure that would take?"

"I don't know, maybe forty-five minutes."

"And then you would have let him go?"

"Shoot, yes. Soon as we got our party money, we was done with them. Already had our fun."

"And that's all it was?" Smiley wanted to know.

"Yeah. Just havin' a little fun."

"So what happened to Lucius Johnson?"

"Well," said Billy slowly. "I took him up the ladder to the rafters, and tied him up pretty good with some rope I had up there. Then I tied one end to a cross beam above him so he wouldn't think about getting away. Then Mickey and I went outside to drink a little rotgut I had hidden from when I had been there a week before. It couldn't a been more than ten minutes before we went in to check on that old colored boy and there he was, dangling from that rope. He musta fallen off the rafter and hung hisself.

Shoot, I told him not to try to get away."

Jack could only imagine the vile KKK abominations that Sprouse's casual recounting of Lucius Johnson's lynching must have evoked in the minds of the black spectators and wondered what Smiley had been thinking.

Smiley interrupted again. "So, Billy, what were your exact thoughts at that moment?"

"I thought, 'dumb Nigger,'" Billy mumbled under his breath. But then he continued as he had rehearsed it with Smiley. "Oh, I felt real bad that he had gone and accidentally hung himself. We didn't mean for anything like that to happen. Sorry about that." Billy smiled at the jurors, some of whom seemed to turn away in disgust. The courtroom was cold and silent. It was apparent to all that Billy's callous apology was anything but.

"All right," said Smiley. "Thank you Billy." Then turning to Jack he said, "Your witness, counselor."

Jack got up to begin his cross-examination of Billy Sprouse. He started to walk toward the witness chair but stopped in midstream as he took in the jury's obvious repugnance for this witness, for this defendant. At the same time, Jack was aware of the glint in Billy's eyes. It was as if he were primed and ready for a verbal dogfight.

"I have only a couple of questions for the defendant, Your Honor."

"Proceed," said the Judge.

"Billy, do you recognize this pocketknife?" asked

Jack, holding up an old and scarred wood-handled Barlow pocket-knife.

"Yeah, but that ain't mine."

"But you had it on you when the police picked you up, didn't you?"

"Yeah."

"Well, how did you get it?" Jack wanted to know.

"I took it out of Lucius Johnson's jeans pocket when I checked to see if he was dead," said Billy Sprouse matter-of-factly.

"You stole this knife (Jack was holding the knife up high for all to see) off the body of a boy you had just caused to kill himself?"

"Hey, it wasn't like that," said Billy, momentarily flustered. "I mean it wasn't like I stole it or nothing. I mean he was already dead. He wasn't going to use it no more."

"So let me get this straight," said Jack. "Because Lucius Johnson was already dead, a death which you caused, but because he was already dead, you didn't actually steal the knife. You just sort of liberated it. Is that what you're saying?"

"Yeah, something like that." Billy looked again at the jury with a little smile, as if to say he was glad that part was all cleared up.

Now Jack turned to the judge and said, "I have no further questions for the defendant, Your Honor. In his own way he has already answered them all."

Now it was Billy himself who looked stunned. His show was over just when he was getting warmed up.

"The witness may step down," said Judge Stevens.

Billy looked a little shell-shocked as he was led, still handcuffed, back to his chair at the defense table. He looked over at Jack as he sat down, almost as if he knew it was all over for him now. Then Joe Smiley leaned over and whispered, "You know, Billy, that was some pretty pigheaded testimony." Billy felt the old anger of the shunned outsider again. "But you know, it just might work to your advantage."

"Mr. Smiley," said Judge Stevens, "call your next witness."

Joe Smiley jumped up, looked from the judge to Jack Forester and then slowly to the jury. He smiled broadly and said, "Why, thank you, Your Honor. The defense rests."

Again there was a buzz and a mild commotion at the seemingly abrupt ending to a fragmented defense presentation for Billy Sprouse. The gavel banged as Judge Stevens intoned, "I will have order in my courtroom. Well, fine, Mr. Smiley. Right then," said Judge Stevens, extracting a pocket watch from his vest pocket and looking at it for all the court to see. "It's eleven forty-five. We'll break for lunch and reconvene at two o'clock sharp. Then, Gentlemen," he said, eyeing both Jack and Smiley, "we'll have closing arguments. With any luck we should have this case in the hands of the jury by three. That's good. All right. Court is adjourned until two o'clock."

Again it was clear that Judge Stevens wanted to keep this case moving along. The gavel banged again.

Jack watched as the courtroom emptied. There was nothing unusual at first. The jury marched out single file, relatively impassive. The white spectators chatted away, almost as if heading out at a movie's intermission, but anticipating the second half. Only the black spectators were totally silent. There were angry eyes looking back at the witness stand from which Billy had testified. They were headed out to share their thoughts, their anger, with all their black brothers waiting in the courthouse square. Jack knew that only a proper conviction and sentencing of Billy Sprouse could head off demonstrations or riots or worse, and he knew how dependent the required unanimous guilty verdict was upon the persuasive strength of his closing argument.

Chapter 34: Closing Arguments

At two o'clock sharp on that hot July afternoon, Jack presented his closing argument to the jury.

"Well, Ladies and Gentlemen, now that we've heard it all, let's break it down. The defendant admits he leapt out of his car with Mickey Courage and assaulted Lucius Johnson and Roy Amery. He says it was because these two colored boys had proposed immoral acts to them and that is what provoked them into committing the assault. Billy Sprouse further claims that the colored boys 'came on to them.' Now this has never been proven or even corroborated by anyone else, including his partner. In fact, Mickey Courage admits there was no provocation at all by the colored boys. Billy and he had just decided to kick a little butt when they ran into them, just for the hell of it."

Jack continued, "Further, Mr. Sprouse himself admits that, after assaulting Lucius Johnson and Roy

Amery, he and Mickey Courage dragged them into the stolen car to scare them a little more. He also admits taking them, against their will, to a remote cabin at the edge of town, where he admits to holding Lucius Johnson captive while freeing Roy Amery to go get some party money. All this was corroborated by his very own testimony. The assault, the kidnapping to extort money, it's all there, Ladies and Gentlemen, by Billy Sprouse's own admission.

"Then there are the felony murder charges against Mr. Sprouse. Billy Sprouse has admitted he tied up Lucius Johnson in the rafters of this cabin with the end of the rope attached to a ceiling crossbeam, so he couldn't escape until his buddy came back with the party money. Well, a terrified Lucius Johnson *did* try to escape, and, in the process, fell off the rafters and was hung by the very rope with which he had been tied to the cross beam by Mr. Sprouse."

Jack continued, "In other words, Billy Sprouse was the direct cause of Lucius Johnson's death by hanging, which transpired while Sprouse was in the commission of felony kidnapping for extortion. Now, the Virginia statute defines death caused directly or indirectly by a perpetrator during the commission of a felony as murder. It is only because we will assume that Billy Sprouse did not *intend* to kill Lucius Johnson when he tied him up that we have reduced the charge from first-degree murder to felony murder."

Jack said emphatically, "But, Ladies and Gentlemen of the jury, after you separate everything out, you now see that all the elements of these crimes of which Billy Sprouse is charged have been proven by testimony of the defendant himself. And no matter what false justification he has offered, and no matter what sympathy you might feel towards the defendant because of his background or lack of upbringing, you must remember this: he knowingly committed the crime of kidnapping for the purpose of extorting money, and by statute he is guilty of felony murder for causing directly or indirectly the death of this victim while in the commission of the felony crime of kidnapping."

Jack walked right up to the jury box and locked eyes with each juror, slowly looking at each, one by one. Then he said, "Ladies and Gentlemen, you must do your duty. There is only one conclusion. As proven by his own testimony, Billy Sprouse is guilty of both charges beyond any reasonable doubt. Billy Sprouse and his partner assaulted Lucius Johnson and kidnapped him for extortion. In the process, they killed a young man guilty of nothing more than the misfortune of running into two young punks who thought it would be fun to mess up a couple of colored boys. Now Lucius Johnson lies dead in his grave, never to see his parents again, never to have any more life, because Billy Sprouse wanted to have a little fun, do a little kidnapping, do a little extortion for money, and, oh yeah, he caused Lucius Johnson's death in the process. You have heard the deep remorse that Mickey Courage has shown for his part in these crimes, but, do you think Billy Sprouse showed remorse when he found the lifeless body of Lucius Johnson swinging from the rafters? Do you remember what Billy Sprouse did first? He pulled Lucius Johnson's knife from the pocket of his lifeless body. And remember Billy Sprouse's explanations to you in his earlier testimony: 'Well, Lucius Johnson wouldn't need it any more, so it wasn't like I was stealing.' That's some remorse, Ladies and Gentlemen. And now we know, he is not only guilty of the crimes as charged, but he has no remorse for *any* of it, including causing the death of Lucius Johnson."

Jack stepped back two steps so he could gaze upon the jury as a group and concluded his closing argument. "As sure as Lucius Johnson, an innocent victim of Billy Sprouse's one-night rampage, lies dead in his grave, so you must now do your duty and find Billy Sprouse guilty as charged."

Jack backed off slowly from the jury box, letting his words sink in. Then, he turned and walked back to the commonwealth's table and waited for Smiley's closing argument.

Joe Smiley stood up slowly, turned, and smiled in Jack's general direction. He walked over to the jury box, hands clasped behind his back and head down. He was silent. He arrived at the box, turned and leaned his behind against it, and gazed outward towards the judge and Jack and the courtroom of spectators. It was as if he were seeing the courtroom just as the jury did, almost as if he had become one of them.

Suddenly, he turned around to face them, from inches away. He slammed the flat of his hand against the jury box railing.

"So that's it, Ladies and Gentlemen of the jury. Two white boys get a little high, a little boozed up. They get into a fight with two colored boys who came onto them thinking they were homosexuals. Now let's see, then they got a little out of hand in their high jinx, and they decided to hold on to one of the colored boys until the other one came back with a little party money. We all pretty much agree with this set of facts. Now we also know if it had stopped there, if the other colored boy had come back with the money, they would have let 'em both go and it would have been over. Neither the cops nor the commonwealth's attorney would probably have ever heard about it. Just a couple of juiced up white boys getting in a minor late-night scuffle with two colored boys who themselves were just out looking for a good time."

Joe Smiley continued, "But everything changed when that one colored boy went and accidentally hung himself trying to get away. Billy didn't plan on that, Mickey Courage didn't either, and certainly Lucius Johnson didn't. It was just a tragic accident. That's all it was. I know it is tragic for Lucius Johnson and his family, but Billy Sprouse didn't murder him; he didn't even want to hurt him. It was just a case of redneck high jinx gone bad."

Joe Smiley had a sly grin on his face. "Now we do

know a little bit about the partner of Billy Sprouse. So what about Mickey Courage? He's already cut a deal with the commonwealth's attorney. You can bet he didn't settle for a murder conviction or even kidnapping in his deal. I hear he got involuntary manslaughter and false imprisonment for his 'lesser' role in these offenses. Lesser role, indeed."

Continuing, he said, "And that's the issue, Ladies and Gentlemen of the jury. Mickey Courage was as responsible as my client for what happened that night. In the end I agree it became more then red neck hi jinx, and I agree they should be punished accordingly."

In a loud voice, Smiley said, "But let's be clear, I agree with the commonwealth's attorney that, just as Mickey Courage may be guilty of false imprisonment and third-degree extortion, the same applies to his equal partner Billy Sprouse. Nothing less, nothing more. Now, from what I hear about Mickey Courage's plea agreement, he's going to spend something like three years in prison and three years on probation after that for his crimes against Lucius and Roy Amery. Well, that sounds fair. Billy Sprouse and Mickey Courage were equal partners in these crimes, and Billy didn't make Lucius Johnson hang himself any more than Mickey did, so there you have it. If that man over there—Joe Smiley pointed in the general direction of Jack Forester, "—is willing to cut that deal for Mickey Courage, then why not the same deal for his partner, my client, Billy Sprouse? Well, why not? They were in it together from the very beginning."

He continued. "So now I'm going to say something radical to you. I said I agreed with Mr. Jack Forester over there. I do believe Billy Sprouse is guilty of bad judgment, false imprisonment, and second-degree involuntary manslaughter, just like Mickey Courage, and that's what you should find him guilty of. Unfortunately, the charges before you here today, kidnapping and felony murder, are much more severe, and they are inappropriate. And if these charges are inappropriate for Mickey Courage, they are just as inappropriate for Billy Sprouse. In addition, I believe the current commonwealth's charges as leveled against Billy Sprouse are fueled by the commonwealth's determination to make an example of Billy Sprouse, who, unlike Mickey Courage, wouldn't cooperate to save his skin, and whose lack of education and family support rendered him unable to take advantage of the system as his partner was able to do."

Jack stared hard at Smiley, who had just leveled this clearly twisted argument, but Jack could not object to a closing argument; he could only hope that what he'd said in his own closing argument was strong enough to stay on the minds of the jurors against Smiley's bombast.

Smiley concluded his line of reasoning by saying, "So I say to you Ladies and Gentlemen of this jury, go ahead and find Billy Sprouse guilty of false imprisonment and second-degree involuntary manslaughter. And give him Mickey Courage's deal. Send him to prison for three to five years and put him on probation for another three years, just like his partner. Now that is appropriate. That is acceptable to my client," at this, Billy Sprouse at the defense table looked up bug-eyed, but said nothing, "and we accept that finding."

Some of the jurors looked confused, not understanding what they could or could not do to reach such a verdict if such were their desire. Of course, Joe Smiley knew, and he was more than willing to address the issues of their concern.

Jack listened intently as Smiley resumed.

"Oh, wait a minute, you *can't* do that," resumed Joe Smiley. "You have only one choice, guilty or not guilty of the crimes of which he is accused. Well, we already know what the prosecution thinks of these offenses. Look at what they gave Mickey Courage, Billy's partner. And if Mickey Courage is not guilty of felony murder or kidnapping for extortion, then neither is Billy. It's as simple as that. He's not guilty of these charges as specified. Now your only choice is to find him not guilty of them."

Jack observed Smiley reading the faces of the jury and responding accordingly.

"Now I can see your concern," Smiley said. "Don't worry, Billy Sprouse will not get off scot-free. Following your verdict of not guilty, Mr. Forester over there will most likely refile charges appropriate to the crime. And my client will most likely accept a plea bargain similar to that of Mickey Courage. Justice will then be served in this case, but appropriately, not by the commonwealth's desire to send a message to the community of Charlottesville." Jack sat grimly through these innuendos and implied accusations against himself and his office. His jaw was visibly clenched and his face reddened in anger, but he knew that his turn would come again shortly, after Joe Smiley's masterful manipulation of the facts and circumstances had ended.

"But," said Smiley, pirouetting and once again facing the jury head-on, "of these charges as presented to you today, Billy Sprouse is not guilty. As the commonwealth determined for his partner, the level of the offenses as committed simply do not rise to the level of the charges of which he is accused. You must not let Jack Forester throw away the adult life of a disadvantaged, misguided white boy just to make some kind of liberal, integrationist-type statement to the community. You must find Billy Sprouse not guilty of both of these specific charges. I trust you to make the commonwealth apply real justice in this case.

"Thank you." Joe Smiley waved a sweeping hand past each juror as he backed off toward the defense table, slightly stumbling as he knocked into his chair with his heel. He quickly sat down as a couple of chuckles were heard somewhere in the courtroom.

* * * * * Rebuttal * * * * *

Jack smiled to himself as he stood up to make his rebuttal. It was probably one of Smiley's finest performances, he thought, only slightly marred by his stumble at the end. But now it's my turn.

Jack walked quietly over to the jury box, turned, looked back at Joe Smiley at the defense table, and reengaged the jury. "Nice try, Mr. Smiley. You say that Billy Sprouse might have done something wrong, a consequence of youthful high spirits, which resulted in some bad judgments. You make him sound like the reluctant boy scout who steals the camp canoe to paddle down to the girl scout camp and bad things happen along the way, things which are just out of his control. Something like that, right? He's just a rebel without a cause. Do you like that metaphor, Mr. Smiley? Yeah, maybe Billy Sprouse is just another James Dean with a twist. Right? Wrong!!" Jack slammed his hand down on the front frame of the jury box as he looked at each member of the jury. He had their attention now.

"That punk over there," said Jack, pointing at the slouching, scowling Billy Sprouse, sitting next to Joe Smiley, "—and that's what he is, a callous, remorseless punk—just for the hell of it, he decides to steal a car, go joyriding, go find some unsuspecting black kids, and 'mess 'em up'."

Jack continued, "Remember what Mickey Courage testified that Billy Sprouse said he wanted to do? He wanted to go, quote coon hunting, unquote. Remember that? And what did he do after stealing that '55 DeSoto for a little joyride? He drove it to a black neighborhood looking for victims. And he found them—two totally unsuspecting, totally innocent victims who were on their way to meet some girlfriends. That stuff about Lucius Johnson and Roy Amery coming onto them we know is bogus; it has been completely refuted by the surviving victim, and discredited by the testimony of Billy Sprouse's own partner."

Jack pointed at Billy Sprouse again and continued, "Now I want you to remember Mr. Sprouse's demeanor during his own testimony. He was actually embarrassed when talking about the alleged homosexual advances as provocation for what he did to these young men. It was obvious that he felt uncomfortable telling that cooked-up story because he didn't want anyone of you to get the wrong idea and think *he* was a homosexual. That's probably why you didn't buy it either. And now remember how proud he sounded when talking about the actual assault, and how he had everybody scared to death, even his partner? Oh yes, he wanted to let you know just how tough he is, and scary: a young man to be feared. That's what he wanted you to believe, and I guess that's what he got. I mean, look at him over there. Is that a young man full of remorse, or someone who would do the same thing again if we let him out on the streets any time soon?"

Billy Sprouse turned his head toward Jack and stared at him with venomous eyes. It was a look not lost on the jury, as they were right in his line of vision, just behind Jack. Joe Smiley quickly leaned forward in his chair to block any further interaction between

Billy and Jack and the jury behind Jack, but he knew the damage had been done.

Jack turned around completely to face the jury. He had his back to Billy Sprouse and his attorney as if dismissing them from any further proceedings.

He continued, "So our tough young James Dean wannabe, our hopped-up thrill- seeker, Billy Sprouse, assaults and terrifies two young black men totally without provocation. He forces them into a stolen car with his reluctant partner, Mickey Courage, and drives them to an abandoned cabin on the edge of town; where he holds Lucius Johnson hostage while freeing Roy Amery on the condition that he return with party money. He tells Roy that, if he does not return with the money, he will slit Lucius' throat like a stuck pig."

Jack said, "So, Ladies and Gentlemen of the jury, what we have here is false imprisonment with the intent to extort. Well, that's kidnapping, plain and simple; therefore, there can be no doubt that Billy Sprouse is guilty of kidnapping. That's count number one."

Jack continued, "As to the second charge of felony murder, it was during the time period when Mr. Sprouse was in the process of committing this very same felony kidnapping that an understandably terrified Lucius Johnson, who had been tied up by Billy Sprouse, tried to escape. He hung himself accidentally by the same rope with which Billy Sprouse had tied him up."

Jack slowed down to make his next point clearly. "Now the law is very clear on this with respect to the crime of kidnapping. A perpetrator whose kidnapping victim dies as a direct or indirect result of his actions and while in the commission of a felony—in this case extortion—is guilty of the murder of that victim. If we believed that Billy Sprouse actually meant to kill Lucius Johnson, we would be seeking a first-degree murder conviction. We do not. But we do believe that Lucius Johnson's hanging death, though not specifically intended by Billy Sprouse, was certainly an indirect result of his actions while in the commission of felony extortion. The law calls that felony murder, and that is what Billy Sprouse is guilty of, beyond a shadow of a doubt!"

Jack continued by talking about Mickey Courage. "Now, you may wonder about the difference in culpability between Billy Sprouse and Mickey Courage, who pled to lesser charges. There are three differences. First, Mickey Courage cooperated with the commonwealth. He told the whole truth. Secondly, he agreed to testify against Billy Sprouse. Without that testimony, we might not have been able to prove beyond a reasonable doubt the charges of which Billy is guilty. Finally, remorse; Mickey Courage is sincerely sorry for his actions of that night, overwhelmed with guilt, and sorry for the death of Lucius Johnson. He has expressed it to us, to the Johnson family, and in his testimony before this court. For all this, we have given Mickey Courage some consideration."

Jack then said, "And, finally, Ladies and Gentlemen of the jury, in comparing the guilt of the two perpetrators of the crime, remember that Mickey Courage is a juvenile and entitled to certain protections under state law not afforded to Billy Sprouse, who is an adult."

Jack continued, "By contrast, consider Billy Sprouse, an adult offender, who has shown no real remorse—who, in fact, seems to revel in telling you about his very own orchestrated night of terror. Remorse? Here's a man who stole a pocketknife from the pants pocket of the body of the boy whose death he had just caused. Is this the action of an offender who deserves consideration of any kind? I think not. Consider that we have already shown him to be guilty of the charges as specified, kidnapping and felony murder. He has demonstrated no remorse, offered no cooperation with the law. To add insult to injury, we have all seen him at that defense table and on the witness stand. He exudes a certain kind of perverse pride in the terror and devastation he caused. Billy Sprouse wants you to know he is a tough guy, a man to be feared, a man who asked for no consideration. Would you want him on the street any time soon terrorizing our community again?"

Pointing at Billy Sprouse again, Jack finished his rebuttal. "Show him you *do* fear him on our streets with our wives and sons and daughters. Remember who caused the hanging death of the innocent and terrified Lucius Johnson, and remember who rifled through the pockets of his still hanging body so he could steal his knife. It's that surly little character over there." Jack pointed at Billy Sprouse, who was strangely staring down at the floor.

Has Smiley gotten through to him, or is he actually remorseful, thought Jack? *No, I think he's actually a little scared.*

Jack turned back to the jury and concluded, "Find him guilty as charged, and I hope later you will give him the maximum sentence he so richly deserves."

Jack thanked the jury and returned to his chair at the commonwealth's table.

Chapter 35:
The Judge Instructs and the Jury Deliberates

It was three o'clock sharp, on Monday, July 27th, 1959. As the judge had wanted, as he had expected, closing arguments had been completed on time—on the judge's time, just as Jack had anticipated.

Judge Donald Stevens gazed from the bench to the jury box and instructed this all-white jury on the work before them.

"All right. Listen up, Ladies and Gentlemen. You've got a heavy duty before you, deciding the guilt or innocence of Billy Sprouse. These are serious crimes of which he has been charged: kidnapping with intent to extort money, and felony murder by causing indirectly the death of a hostage while in the commission of a felony. If found guilty of either or both of these charges, Billy Sprouse will spend a significant portion of his adult life in prison. For now, the severity of his punishment, if he is found guilty,

cannot influence your determination of his guilt or
innocence. That is a separate issue, and it is only a
consequence of your finding, not a consideration of
it, so be clear on that."

The judge continued, "You have already listened
to closing arguments from the defense and from
the commonwealth. Each strove to convince you
that their interpretation of the very same facts as
presented must yield the opposite finding than the
other seeks. The defense worked to persuade you
that there is insufficient evidence to convict their
client of the *specific* charges as presented, while
the commonwealth argued that there is more than
enough evidence to convict him on *all* charges beyond
a reasonable doubt. Meanwhile, the defense argued
"not guilty" or at least "not proven guilty." Well, for
the defense and for the commonwealth, that is their
job, equal and opposite, to persuade you he is guilty
or to persuade you he has not been proven guilty.
Yes, that is their job, Men and Women. Each argues
for a different finding based on the same evidence
that has been presented to you, each with his own
interpretation. As I said, that is their job."

Looking directly at the jury, the judge said, "But
now they are finished and it is up to you. You are
the ultimate deciders, and that is *your* job. You are
about to deliberate on the guilt or innocence of
Billy Sprouse. You must separate the facts from the
innuendo, from the emotion, from anyone's wishful
thinking. You must separate the wheat from the

chaff. In other words, you must determine the facts of the case, stripped of prejudice, intimidation, and orchestrated confusion. And you must apply only those facts as you determine them to the charges as follows:

"On the first count of kidnapping with intent to extort money, do the facts show that Billy Sprouse held Lucius Johnson by force in order to extort money from his friend Roy Amery? Yes or No.'

"On the second count of felony murder, did Billy Sprouse cause directly or indirectly the death of his hostage during the commission of a felony? Yes or No.'

"On both charges, you must decide if the facts as presented merit your finding on each of the charges. Now don't worry about how the law is applied to your findings. That is the job of the court."

The judge finished his instructions by stating, "Meanwhile, if you have any questions about the facts of the case or what the law is as it relates to this case, or if you need additional transcripts of the testimony for any part of this trial, say the word and the bailiff will get it to you. If you have questions on how the law applies to the facts of this case, or on any other issues you cannot resolve, you may send me a note and I will assist you in any way that does not affect your objectivity in reaching your findings."

The judge gave one last piece of advice. "Stick to the facts. As for the overall testimony, discuss it, deliberate it, be open to other views, but don't bully and don't be bullied. Each one of you twelve jurors is as essential as the others, for you must reach a unanimous verdict of guilt or innocence. That is your job. And you must work together to do it. Take whatever time you need to do it. Right. Thank you again for your service. Now, let's get to it."

At a nod from the judge, the bailiff led the jury out of the courtroom to begin their deliberations. The courtroom was adjourned and quickly emptied.

Ralph Tierney turned to Rex Alston as they and their fellow jurors were led out of the courtroom to the little A-framed brick cottage next door which served as the jurors' deliberation quarters. "Hey, Rex, did you see those white-sheeted klanners out in Court Square? Man, we don't need *them* up here."

"Yeah, I saw them, Ralph. I also saw those colored people carrying signs, saying, 'Billy Sprouse must Pay,' and 'Justice for Lucius Johnson.' What the hell's that all about? I don't like what's going on with our colored folks."

"Well maybe if we do our job as jurors, we won't have to worry about it." It was Rick Flowers, a known liberal in town. In fact, every juror knew all the others; it was a small town, and the jury pool was pretty well restricted to white voters, and further restricted by the selection process of both the commonwealth and the defense.

The walking conversation continued. "Yeah, well, I'm sure not going to have any uppity Negroes dancing in the street with a picket sign telling me what to do," said one of the jurors.

"Okay, Ladies and Gentlemen," said Deputy Joe Craddock. "Through this door right here there's a table and plenty of chairs. The bathroom is right down the hall. I'll be right outside if you need me or if you need to get anything from the judge."

The Deputy continued, "Let me know when you're done. I know the judge would like to get this verdict in by the end of the day. Of course, it's up to you; you take as long as it takes." The Bailiff smiled and closed the door, and the twelve jurors sat down at an oval knotty pine table to begin formal deliberations.

"Okay," said Ralph Tierney. "First thing is to elect a foreman by secret ballot."

"Hell," said Rex Alston. "You know we're all going to vote for you, Ralph."

"Yeah, you do have a way with words," someone added. Ralph was publisher of Charlottesville's only major daily paper, the *Daily Progress*.

"We'll vote by secret ballot," Ralph said, "And Rex, you collect 'em and count 'em."

Five minutes later Rex had counted all the ballots and, as everyone would have predicted, Ralph was elected with a count of 11-1. "Well, that's good," said Ralph. "But just remember, any verdict we render in this case has to be unanimous, that's twelve to zero."

After a small murmur of understanding, the jurors began discussion of the facts, charges, and testimony in the Billy Sprouse trial. The discussion, the arguments, the negotiation and cajoling continued for two hours, but by four thirty, on the third ballot, the jury had reached the required unanimous verdict.

The importance of Billy Sprouse's testimony was best summed up by Rex Alston, as he discussed it with jury foreman Ralph Tierney in the jury room. "Now I wasn't going to be pushed around by the liberals on this jury. And I know lots of good old boys who get a belly full of booze can do dumb things, but not like this. That Sprouse boy messed up a colored boy bad, kidnapped him for the idiotic goal of party money, and then ended up killing him—even if it was by mistake. And he showed no remorse—nothing. That's what really got me. He just seemed proud of it all."

Rex continued, "And last Sunday, I hear he caused trouble in the sheriff's jail just trying to show how tough he is. Oh yeah, we all heard the scuttlebutt about the big bad tough guy giving the finger to us and to our town. Well, that was it for me. We all knew he was guilty of both crimes. It was just a question of whether the charges were excessive in light of the facts of the case. Well, I don't see any need for leniency given his attitude combined with his actions."

Tierney responded to Alston's argument by concluding, "We need to send a message to him and to the community at large. We are not going to tolerate any unprovoked assaults on our citizens, colored or white. And for those who would thumb their noses at our system of Justice, those who would show no remorse for their crimes, but rather revel in the harm and anguish they have caused their victims, we all agree that they deserve the full measure of the law and its consequences. The message is clear: a similar justice awaits any other hooligan who is contemplating any night of terror on any member of our community."

They had all come to a similar conclusion, some of the jurors more reluctantly than others, but nevertheless, they had done so. "This is not a matter of white versus black. Perhaps that is an issue for another day, but, in this case, the colored people will see that the justice system works for them too," concluded Ralph Tierney.

"OK, Ralph," said Rex Alston. "Stop your speech. We've all just rendered a unanimous verdict for guilty on both counts. You don't have to convince us all over again."

The bailiff returned, having received and carried their message to Judge Stevens that they had reached a unanimous verdict, and led the jurors across the little courtyard into the Charlottesville General District Courtroom. They took their seats in the jury box as the bailiff carried their written verdict to a smiling judge Donald Stevens. Jack Forester was seated at the commonwealth's table. Across the way were Joe Smiley and his client, and behind them a packed courtroom. All awaited the reading of the verdict.

It was four forty-five as Judge Stevens studied the paper on which the verdict had been written. Jack knew the judge was pleased with the timing; the trial would indeed be over by five p.m. or before. It had all been orderly and timely, and Judge Stevens was a man of time. He handed the slip of paper back to the bailiff, who carried it back to the jury foreman.

"Is this your unanimous verdict?" Judge Stevens, asked Foreman Tierney, who looked down at the paper again.

"It is, Your Honor," he said.

"Please read it to the court," intoned Judge Stevens. "On the first count of kidnapping, how do you find?"

"Guilty, Your Honor."

"On the second count of felony murder, how do you find?"

"Guilty as charged, Your Honor."

At this, the courtroom erupted in cheers and clapping on one side. An ominous sound of boos and hissing could be heard from some of the spectators on the other side.

"Order! Order!" yelled Judge Stevens. "I will have order in my courtroom. Bailiff, throw out anyone who doesn't sit down and shut up right now."

Billy Sprouse stood up, shaking free of his guard and shrugging off a limply grasping Joe Smiley. He pointed at the jury with his hands still handcuffed and screamed out, "You're all nigger lovin' bastards and you can all go to Hell."

Almost simultaneously, two city policemen and a deputy from the sheriff's office grabbed him. They all fell to the floor as he struggled to free himself. Two more city detectives joined in the melee before they were able to subdue a grimly struggling Billy Sprouse.

He was shackled again head to foot, and a piece of tape was put over his mouth and wrapped around his head.

In the jury box, Rex Alston turned to Ralph Tierney on his right and said, "To think I was almost feeling sorry for that little prick. Why, they should lock him in jail and throw away the key. He's not fit to be free in society."

"Clear the courtroom," said Judge Stevens, who seemed personally offended by the breakdown in decorum. He waved his gavel in the direction of Billy Sprouse and said, "I hold you in contempt of court, Billy Sprouse. Bailiff, I want that man kept in solitary confinement, handcuffed at all times, until he appears in court again. I suspect that will be about eleven tomorrow morning. The jury will reconvene at nine to discuss and determine Mr. Sprouse's sentence. I would expect to see you, Mr. Sprouse, and you, Mr. Smiley, as his lawyer, at eleven. I will render my decision on sentencing, having received the jury's recommendation at that time. When you are brought in, Mr. Sprouse, you will be shackled. There will be no tape covering your mouth; however, one outburst from you, and I will have your mouth taped so tight that all you'll be thinking about is your next breath." Judge Stevens paused for a moment and then concluded, "Now get him out of here."

The handcuffed Billy Sprouse, flanked by two Sheriff's deputies, was quickly led out of the courtroom. The jury filed out, across the courtyard square to the jury quarters, where they were dismissed until nine o'clock the next morning. Ralph Tierney looked around at the whites on one side of the square, with the white-sheeted Ku Klux Klan in their midst, and the silent angry eyes of a large number of black people on the other side and could only think, *Please Lord, don't let the callous, thoughtless actions of two white punks, and mostly Billy Sprouse, don't let their selfish actions tear our town apart. I pray the verdict we render will be enough justice for everyone.*

And just across the way, standing in the doorway of his office, was Jack Forester, watching it all with very similar thoughts.

Chapter 36: Sentencing

Court reconvened at eleven on Tuesday morning, July 28th, 1959, fifteen days after the crime was committed. The jury, who had reached their sentencing recommendation, had already been brought back to the courtroom and were seated in the jury box. Jack noted that the jury had reached their verdict pretty quickly, and thought that this was probably a good thing for the prosecution. Billy Sprouse's courtroom outburst and scuffle with the law from the day before had not won him any sympathy from the jury and had probably hastened the deliberations and unanimous findings in the penalty phase of this trial.

"Mr. Foreman," said Judge Stevens to Ralph Tierney, standing in the corner of the jury box. "What is your sentence recommendation on the first charge of kidnapping?"

"We recommend a maximum sentence of fifteen

years."

Throughout the courtroom, there were murmurs of disbelief at the severity of the sentence. Billy Sprouse was, after all, only eighteen.

"Order. I will have order in my court." Immediately, the courtroom went deathly quiet. They had all seen the consequences of disrupting Judge Stevens' court.

"And on the charge of felony murder, your recommendation?"

"Your Honor," responded Ralph Tierney. "We recommend a maximum sentence of ten years for the felony murder of Lucius Johnson."

As was the custom, Billy Sprouse had been standing facing the judge during his sentencing.

"Billy Sprouse, do you have anything to say before I impose final sentencing?"

Jack watched as Billy Sprouse turned slightly to look around the courtroom, winked at some of his people, then gazed past the jury and finally back to Judge Stevens. It was immediately apparent that he was not going to take the advice of his lawyer, Joe Smiley, to throw himself on the mercy of the court. "It could save you a lot of jail time, Billy. Wise up," Jack heard Smiley say directly to his client. But Billy wasn't going to wise up. In many ways, this courtroom drama, starring himself as a mean James Dean, was the best role he had played in a hardscrabble life of denial. No, this was still his moment and he wasn't going to let that fast-talking midget lawyer from

Washington talk him out of it.

Looking straight into the judge's eyes, and smirking slightly, he answered the judge's question. "I ain't got nothing to say to this court, Your Honor, not a damn thing."

An eerie silence fell over the courtroom at this last profanity, but Judge Stevens decided to let it go, as he knew there was plenty of other punishment about to come Billy Sprouse's way.

"All right, Mr. Sprouse. Now, you shut up and listen if you don't want to have that duct tape reapplied to your mouth. And you'd better listen well if you want to have any major portion of your adult life to enjoy outside of the penitentiary."

The judge continued, "The jury has recommended a maximum sentence of fifteen years for the crime of kidnapping. I'm going to amend that to ten to fifteen years. The jury has further recommended a sentence of a maximum of ten years for your crime of felony murder. I will amend that to eight to ten years. Finally, there is the contempt of court issue, which you so richly deserve for your actions in my courtroom yesterday. For that, I will sentence you to one year. The two other sentences will run concurrently, but this last year is to run consecutively. That means you will serve a minimum of ten years in the penitentiary for the kidnapping and felony murder charges. Then there is the one-year sentence for contempt of my court, and I will grant no parole on that one."

The judge concluded his sentencing, "Now listen

carefully, Mr. Sprouse. What this means is that you will be eligible for parole in eleven years. You'll be twenty-nine then, and maybe you will have learned from this lesson. Maybe not. But for our community of Charlottesville, the message is clear: any violent and premeditated terror acts committed without any provocation on the citizens of our community, black or white, will not be tolerated, and, as you have just learned, Mr. Billy Sprouse, will be dealt with most severely."

Sitting at the prosecutor's table, Jack remarked to himself how completely Judge Stevens grasped the gravity of the situation and what could be at stake even in Billy's sentencing. *Judge Stevens is a lot more than form and lunch breaks*, Jack thought. He wondered how well the General would take the conviction and sentencing, how he would react to this defeat of his strategy. All this Jack noted as he watched Smiley, his chin down and looking even smaller in stature.

Meanwhile, Billy Sprouse had been standing stiffly in handcuffs and with clenched teeth listening to the judge's sentencing speech. He had regained his belligerent attitude. He looked as if he would break something or someone if given a chance, and that was the way he wanted to look. Three deputies were standing around him watching his every move, while Billy stared straight at Judge Stevens with a scowling smile of defiance. This was not lost on Judge Stevens.

"Mr. Sprouse, I discern from your demeanor that you have not learned much about the American system of justice, nor do you show much respect for it. That's too bad. Your behavior yesterday, your defiance today, and your apparent lack of remorse for causing the death of Lucius Johnson leave me with little sympathy for your position. I can only tell you that your attitude had best change quickly in the penitentiary if you wish to survive the minimum eleven years you are about to serve. I can further assure you that you will soon find amongst your fellow inmates far more vicious and far tougher people than you could ever imagine in your wildest dreams. You're still a punk acting out. There you will find really bad people who will have their way with you unless you cooperate, really cooperate."

Now Judge Stevens looked down from the bench square into the eyes of Billy Sprouse. "You savvy what I'm saying, Mr. Sprouse?"

Billy Sprouse almost inadvertently looked down, as if suddenly realizing the impact of Judge Stevens' words. Then he looked up as if to reengage the judge, but he couldn't, and the whole courtroom sensed what Billy felt: fear of the unknown, of what and who was to come his way—soon.

"All right then," said Judge Stevens with a sphinx-like smile. "Get Mr. Sprouse out of my courtroom and down to his new home in the state penitentiary. Let's see, it's eleven thirty on Tuesday, still time for me to go home and mow my lawn. Good. Court is adjourned."

The news spread quickly and once again Jack watched it all from the front window of his office. The courthouse spectators spilled out onto Court Square. Here could be seen the picketers representing Lucius Johnson's people. There were members of the 'troublemaking' NAACP, the National Association for the Advancement of Colored People, seen by most local whites as a white liberal and uppity black socialist agitation machine. For many blacks, it represented a voice against discrimination that they had not had before.

Across the square from these demonstrators, there was a different kind of group headed up by the hooded and much feared Ku Klux Klan. There were competing signs, "Justice for Lucius Johnson," "Free Billy Sprouse," and "Keep the Negro in his place"— signs that seemed to wave angrily at each other from across the square. Between the two groups of demonstrators were a few nervous policemen hoping it would all stay peaceful.

Just off the square in Jackson Park, a large crowd of Charlottesville residents had gathered on this sunny Saturday morning to see what would happen. Some people had brought picnic baskets, and blankets were laid out in the grass as children climbed up the stone statue of Stonewall Jackson on his horse to get a better look at it all or just to sit on the horse with ole Stonewall, the South's second most famous soldier.

It was not unlike the annual Fourth of July atmosphere in Charlottesville with parades and clowns and other entertainment, though the focus here was far different. People were not celebrating the annual rebirth of their country, but rather gathering in a mostly impassive way to see which way the results of this trial would carry the day. Would the Negros get uppity? Had Billy Sprouse gotten the justice many thought he deserved? Would there be a violent confrontation? Would there be blood on the streets between the two opposing groups on the square?

Among the spectators in Jackson Park, many of the blacks and whites stood impassively, almost shoulder to shoulder. These were people who knew and worked with each other five days a week in places like the local mills and manufacturing companies. Their working comradeship cut across color lines. They watched the Klanners and their supporters and the NAACP and Lucius Johnson demonstrators, and they waited for a sign. And then it came.

Jack walked out of his office and leaned against his door to get a better vantage point. Things were getting tense as he listened to the Klan speaker ratchet up his rhetoric. "They gave Billy Sprouse twenty years, just 'cuz some dumb nigger boy went and hung himself. They blamed it all on him. Hell, Billy wasn't even in the shack when it happened. And they convict him of murder. What's going on around here? Bunch of liberals and nigger lovers got your tongue?" It was Dickie Slayton up from Klan headquarters in Greensboro, North Carolina. He had come to help out, perhaps to incite all those hard-working white people, and perhaps those not-so-hard-working, who felt threatened or displaced by the rise of the Negro in his community.

"Hey! I'm tellin' you white folk out there," he screamed out from his bullhorn, "it's the beginning of the end for all hard workin' white folks in Charlottesville if we don't stand up for Billy Sprouse, if we don't show the Negro that he can't push us out of our rightful place in Charlottesville society. First, this court shanghais justice and sends a white boy to the penitentiary, just 'cuz he got a little rowdy with a couple of uppity Negro boys and things got a little out of hand. Hell, if those colored boys had stayed out of his way, nothing would have happened. And that's the way it used to be. Now the white boy is going to jail for up to twenty years on a trumped-up murder charge. The next thing, my friends, the court and the

Feds are going to push these Negro people into your neighborhoods just like they're doing in your public schools. Pretty soon, they'll tell you the Negro has a right to be in your club, or your neighborhood bar, or your church. And it's not just about Negro invasion, it's about the loss of all your community rights—hell, even your private right of association. Do you want all that? Because if you don't, you better stand up against this abomination of a court trial. It may be your last chance to stand up for your rights before they're all taken away."

Meanwhile, across the square, a similar bullhorn was used by Roy Amiss of the NAACP to make his points to the gathering crowd. "Is twenty years enough for the murder of Lucius Johnson? You know that Billy Sprouse will be out in less than ten. Let's show these crackers that we want more than just a piece of justice, that we want the full measure of justice!"

Slowly, almost imperceptibly, the whites and blacks in Jackson Park began to separate from one another, to pull apart as they were galvanized by these two agitators. Where there had once been a mixed milling crowd of curious friendly spectators there were now two camps, all white on one side and all black on the other. There were over one hundred people in each camp, and both camps were beginning to get worked up, just as their two speakers had intended.

There was apprehension, an expectation of bad things to come. Mothers began to walk their children away from the park. Within groups, there were the ne'er do wells, the out of work crowd, the white trash, and the other whites—mostly men now. For them, of course, it was an opportunity to have a little fun at the expense of the black brother whom they feared was going to pass them by, if he had not already done so, in the pecking order of Charlottesville economic society.

One of the locals marching with the klan shouted out to whoever would listen, "Hey, that nigger wasn't kilt by Billy Sprouse. He probably hung himself when he realized he couldn't join the party with Billy Sprouse and that Mickey Courage fellow." It was an even more twisted version on an old racist joke, but it yielded the desired results, hard laughter and cackles of agreement from one side, the NAACP bullhorn on the other: "Maybe we should let *Billy Sprouse* jump off a rafter with a short rope tied tight around his neck. That would be real justice, an eye for an eye, not this cracker justice."

Curiously, neither exhortation seemed to move the black and white crowd watching from Jackson Park. It was as if they knew, instinctively, that neither speaker spoke *their* truth, but attempted instead to agitate them, to manipulate them for one side or the other, and they did not like it. Then Louisa County Sheriff A. P. Hill, who had been watching from across the square, walked over to Lucius Johnson's father, shook his hand, and said, "Mr. Johnson, I am very sorry about your son."

Almost as if by signal, though there was none, Junius T. Jones, the black philosopher king, friend and advisor to Jack Forester, emerged from the group of black spectators. He walked directly up to A. P. Hill and said loudly enough for many to hear, "Sheriff, we can't let no outside agitator tear our community apart. Our Negro people got a measure of justice today. We will work for more justice with the white people we trust and the black people we know. We have no need for outside agitators." Bits and pieces of their public conversation filtered throughout the park and gradually, imperceptibly, blacks and whites coalesced until they were almost one group again. There were some handshakes, even some hugs between black and white who had already stood together in the workplace and now they stood together outside of it.

Sheriff A. P. Hill and Junius T. Jones walked up to the man from the NAACP, the man with the bullhorn. Gently but firmly, Junius reached out and grabbed the bullhorn from him. Startled, the NAACP man started to pull the horn back, but then he saw that eyes from everywhere were fixed upon him. They all seemed to be saying the same thing, "You'd better give up the bullhorn." Reluctantly, he did. Junius T. Jones lifted the instrument and spoke his mind as he always did. He was talking to black and white alike; he was talking to Charlottesville.

"People, we have just been through a bad time together, and one of our fine young black men was killed in the process. Now the rule of law has spoken and on some level justice has been served. Maybe Billy Sprouse didn't get all of what he deserved, maybe he did. We may continue to argue over that. But he did get a fair trial, a fair hearing of the facts, and the lies and false innuendos were separated from the truth by the workings of this court. So I say that Lucius Johnson got the justice he deserved, and for what he did, Mr. Billy Sprouse has been put away for a long, long time. It was justice in our community for a young black victim, and it came despite the meddling of these two outside groups. I say now that we politely ask both of these groups to leave—klanners and the NAACP—both of them. And I invite them to leave right now. Charlottesville still has a long way to go to get to racial harmony, but we can do it peacefully, and we can do it without any more interference from either of these two groups. Now, will you join me in urging them to leave?"

"Yeah, go agitate back in North Carolina where you came from," said a white in the crowd to the hooded Ku Klux Klan.

Then a black man pointed towards the NAACP group and said, "Why don't you go march on Washington where you can do some good?" Similar thoughts could be heard from the voices of the spectators in Jackson Park. Then there were angrier affirmations of the need for the klan and the NAACP to leave the square, and the spectators began to move in as one toward the outside demonstrators.

The official NAACP representative grabbed the bullhorn back from Junius T. Jones and cried out, "All right, I think we've made our point here. I think we can all go home now."

The KKK leader was more reluctant to disband, but he was not stupid. His eyes darted nervously across the angry crowd moving ever closer to him and his fellow klanners. "All right, men, let's march on down Jefferson Street," he said, as he began moving at a slow trot. Briefly, he turned for one last fusillade at the crowd, "Charlottesville whites, you're going to need us back here one day soon. You mark my words." Then he and his men trotted off out of harm's way, some tripping on their sheets as they fled. Someone from the onlookers bid the klanners a final farewell as he yelled, "Yeah, we could use you next Tuesday. That's garbage pickup day, in case you left one of yours behind." General laughter in the crowd followed this remark, and the tension was broken.

Both outside groups seemed to have disappeared as if they had never been in Jackson Park or on the courthouse square. For the next hour, blacks and whites, individuals and families, milled about together, shaking hands and laughing about the abrupt departure they had precipitated of both the NAACP and the KKK. For one brief moment on a sunny Tuesday morning on July 28th, 1959, the Charlottesville community, black and white, had come together for a common cause, peace in their community, control of their town, and a chance to work for equal justice for black and white.

Perhaps it is an outward and visible sign of a fragmented society coming together on equal grounds for their common good, thought Jack as he continued to look out the window. *Justice for Lucius Johnson has been served despite interference from the likes of one General Samuel Cartridge.* But Jack also knew the current modus operandi of the General would be to punish or neutralize all those who opposed him—people like himself. For this reason, Jack had concern not only for himself but for those around him.

Chapter 38: Jack Goes Home

Jack had kept himself incommunicado after Monday afternoon's verdict, staying at his house with Jack the dog and letting the phone ring, as it did many times. He had even resisted the ever-present temptation to call Sally Fretango.

Today, though, Jack had watched from his office as the crowd dispersed following sentencing. He'd seen the NAACP and the KKK evicted from Jackson Park and marveled at the subsequent civilized intermingling of the integrated crowd that remained. Today Jack wondered if the Billy Sprouse trial would mark a watershed in Charlottesville's path to racial harmony. Jack did not know for sure what it all meant, but he had witnessed both the NAACP and the Ku Klux Klan stand down in the face of a united interracial crowd. This was something he had not seen before in Charlottesville society. It was a start. And

Jack felt good about this particular case and verdict secured in the name of Lucius Johnson, a justice that should bring some solace to his family.

What about himself, his political future, he wondered, now that he had thwarted General Cartridge's efforts to make the Billy Sprouse trial a showcase for white over black? Far from preserving the racial pecking order, the verdict exemplified racial equality under the law, thanks in no small part to Jack's efforts.

"I'd say the all-powerful General Samuel Cartridge is sticking pins in a Jack Forester doll right about now," Jack chuckled to himself. "And I'd say that's about it for my political aspirations. Oh well, I didn't want to be a congressman anyway."

Jack went back into his office, gave a slightly bemused Alice a big hug, and slipped out the back door to a small parking lot. He got into his old Chrysler convertible, which today he had decided to drive to work. He put down the top and drove home slowly so that he could enjoy the heat of the bright July sun. It was a beautiful day, and he was going to go home and hug his dog, and he was going to call Sally Fretango.

It was just past one o'clock as Jack turned the convertible into his driveway. He stepped out of his car. There was Jack the dog, sitting on his haunches at the top of the front porch steps behind the fenced yard. But he was not looking at his master; he was looking behind him, barking intently, and the hairs on the ridge of his back were standing up. Jack turned around and saw first the great white Lincoln Continental pull up and park just behind him in his driveway, and then, emerging from within almost as if he had materialized from thin air, stood Alec Ramos, chauffeur, body guard, and *comme il faut* of General Samuel S. Cartridge.

"Hello Jack, long time no see. The General would like to have a few words with you, if you don't mind."

Jack looked at the muscular figure, who stood six foot three and looking cool in dark glasses and a tropical tan suit. "Say, Alec," said Jack. "I see a bulge in your breast pocket. Are you carrying a concealed weapon?"

"Well, you *do* have a sharp eye, Jack. As a matter of fact, it's a Smith & Wesson 38 special, and I've got a license for it. Care to see it, Mr. Commonwealth's Attorney?"

"Not at the moment. I'll let you know, Alec."

"Good. Well, the General's waiting. Could you please step into the back of the car? He'd like five minutes of your time, if that doesn't impose too much on your schedule."

Jack looked at Ramos, and then back toward Jack the dog. "Okay, Alec, but you stay outside where my dog can keep an eye on you. Three's a crowd on the inside, if you know what I mean."

Ramos hesitated briefly, then smiled and said, "But of course, Jack. I'm sure the General wouldn't have it any other way." He moved to the rear of the

Continental and opened the suicide door so that it pulled wide toward the rear of the car. This Lincoln Continental feature of the fifties made for an easy entry point, but the door was prone to fly off in crashes, hence the term 'suicide door.'

How appropriate, thought Jack, as he started to step in, stopped, and turned towards Alec Ramos. "By the way, Alec, I've instructed my dog that if I'm not out in five minutes, he is to jump the fence and tear you apart."

On hearing his master's voice in the general direction of Alec Ramos, the dog emitted a low menacing growl and showed his teeth.

"Well, that's just fine, Jack," said Ramos with a steely grin. "If you're not out in five minutes, I'll explain it to your dog." He patted the breast pocket concealing the 38 special. *It's all just verbal jousting*, thought Jack, as he lowered himself into the back seat of the great luxury car. *Or is it?*

Jack sat down quickly and turned to his right to face General Cartridge, who was dressed in a white linen suit, a blue pinstripe shirt, a red string tie, and a broad-brimmed white linen planter's hat. Here was the kingmaker himself, who, at seventy-six, still looked fit and agile. His pale blue eyes seemed to surround one's being while piercing any protected facades to the very core of one's thoughts and fears. Jack imagined Cartridge as a cobra, hypnotizing its prey before swallowing it whole. This cobra, however, was smoking a large cigar whose pungent aroma permeated the rear cabin of the vehicle while some of its exhaust smoke trickled out the slightly cracked window to the right of the General. The other windows were sealed so that the air conditioning generated by the still running engine could keep it stale and cool for the General. Jack pushed the automatic window button to his left, but it was locked.

General Cartridge looked over and smiled, "Humor me, Jack. I can't stand the heat, and I like a good Havana cigar. Just give me five minutes, and I'll let you escape into the fresh air again."

Jack turned to face this enigmatic old man, who controlled almost all political life from Charlottesville, to Richmond and far beyond. "Now, what could you possibly want from me, General?" asked Jack. "I think I've shown you that I am not one of your good ole boys, so what could we possibly have to offer each other? Let me be blunt, General. Why have you and your bodyguard chosen to pay me a surprise visit today, of all days?"

"Let me assure you, Jack, that while Alec does provide me other services on occasion, he is solely my chauffeur today. As to why I am here today, dear boy, it is to congratulate you on your smashing courtroom victory in that Billy Sprouse affair and to ascertain where you plan to go from here. Maybe we can be of mutual assistance in good and legitimate ways. Call this a brief exploratory visit to determine if you will let me actually assist you in your political career. In return, you might be of some assistance to me, but only in those areas that fit your beliefs and standards, and, of course, not in those that do not."

Jack raised his hand, as if in dismissal of a familiar diatribe, and started to get out of the car. He felt Cartridge's claw-like hand on his shoulder. "Wait, Jack, hear me out. I asked only for five minutes of your time. Is that too much to grant a dying old man?"

"Dying of old age, or dying of disease?" asked Jack coldly as he slumped back into the softness of the Lincoln's black leather seats.

"Well, you don't beat around the bush, Jack," chuckled the General, "but I've always known that about you, honest and candid to the point of being blunt. That's good. Most of the time, I don't worry about how things stand with you. But you wear it on your sleeve, which is not always good if you want to win in the political world. Let me answer your question. First, yes, I am dying of old age, I suppose, as are we all, but I'm dying more immediately of lung cancer. Though my friends at Universal Leaf in Richmond would deny it, I think that fifty years of smoking their cigarettes, long before I gave them up for the occasional Havana cigar, have brought me to this. My doctors told me last week that I have between twelve and eighteen months before I go on to the next level. What the hell, better to know and plan ahead than to have death sneak up unawares or to have life just wear you out. So, being the vain man I am, I concern myself with my legacy—more specifically, my political legacy."

The General continued; "But first let me thank you for educating me as to the evolving nature of mankind. Quite frankly, I always thought that the Negro was a necessary though inherently inferior segment of our southern society. I suppose that particular prejudice has been embedded in white man's psyche since our ancestors first brought the Negro from West Africa in chains as property, chattel whose sole purpose was to serve the white man. As we know, the black man as slave became almost immediately an integral part of our economy. But with the invasion of the North in our war for the right to secession, and with the postwar intrusion of reconstruction politics on our way of life, the Negro was reborn as an unlikely constituent. He became politicized and manipulated by outside forces for their own nefarious purposes."

Jack was unable to get a word in edgewise as the General continued his monologue. "It took the South many decades and the help of a few Supreme Court rulings, like *Plessy vs. Ferguson* in 1896, to set things right, to rejustify segregation and the rightful social order in our society. And then along came *Brown vs. the Board of Education* in 1954. That damn secret communist from California, Chief Judge Earl Warren snookered us in the *Brown* decision. That desegregation foolishness started the Negro unrest all over again."

Turning to look directly at Jack, the General said, "You know, Jack, until recently, I just did not get it. I believed that they are not like us whites, that they think differently, look differently and are satisfied in different ways. But you made me realize one thing in the way our little old southern town has responded to the events of the Billy Sprouse case. Charlottesville, as a whole, respects the Negros' right to justice more than they fear being integrated by them. Now that showed me something, and I am a practical man. It showed me what my dear friend J.T. Dixley tried to convince me of at a little private meeting we had in the executive room of Farmington Country Club just this week. The modern-day integrated Negro is here to stay and over time he will gain all the basic rights of association. It is ironic that these very same white, blue-collar people who originally had felt so threatened were the first to accept that fact."

The General continued, "Now, for me, it's always been a matter of pragmatism, more than the people's idealism and doing what's right. I want to do what works for me and my political machine. The Negro as a practical matter represents a fifteen percent of the electorate, a voting block that I intend to control and utilize. Quite simply, I intend to offer the Negro, through my representatives, what he wants, while at the same time not alienating my white voter base. It will be like walking a tightrope, but I believe that, with people like you Jack, it can be done: good for the Negro, good for Jack Forester's political future, and good for the Cartridge political machine. And you know, Jack, the Billy Sprouse trial is what showed me the light."

General Cartridge began to restate his case. He was warming to his own monologue. "What I saw today in Jackson Square was illuminating. The Negro race has become its own people, not to be toyed with by the KKK or manipulated by the NAACP. Most importantly, in our own community, you have shown me, together with an all-white jury, that our own society now accepts that the Negro should have equal rights under the law, and more importantly, that these rights should be respected and protected in this community. Now I'm smart enough to predict the next steps, the inevitable integration of black and white on every other level: economic, political, social—I mean jobs, schools, clubs, churches, the works. Like it or not, it's all coming, and the Billy Sprouse verdict showed me that a major portion of our citizenry accept, or will accept that condition or will be made to do so soon thereafter."

"General Cartridge," Jack said, finally succeeding in intervening, "I appreciate this evolution of your philosophy on the social pecking order of things, and I'm glad to be a small part of it, but, at the risk of being rude, where is all this going and how does it concern me?"

"Easy, Jack," said the General with a slight rasp. "Give me my remaining two minutes' indulgence, and perhaps you'll understand my point."

"Two more minutes, General, and then I'm going to get out of your car and go feed my dog," said Jack. "He's been working hard trying to look after me and

protect our property from the likes of Alec Ramos."
A faint but continuous rumbling growl could be
heard even through the closed car windows. General
Cartridge could not repress a chuckle. "Man's best
friend, eh, Jack?" asked General Cartridge.

"My best friend," said Jack.

"Yes, well, I won't keep you from delivering him
his reward, so I'll get to the point." General Cartridge
was not accustomed to interruptions. "I *know* what
you can do for me Jack. Here's what I can offer you
in our proposed partnership." A million things raced
through Jack's mind as he anticipated the General's
proposal. After the trial, the General's desire to
control his future was even stronger. Freedom and
power were always within the deep pockets of a
man used to having his way and to lesser men doing
his bidding in return for economic and political
support. Jack knew that, within this framework, he
could pursue his own political career from DA to
congressman and probably on to governor, when
the General determined it was his time, with almost
certainty of success. The thought was intoxicating,
almost, for the price was that he would always be
in the General's debt, always on call to the iron fist
within the velvet glove. And he would have to comply
on demand, not unlike the allegorical farmer in "The
Devil and Daniel Webster." Lost in his own thoughts,
Jack barely acknowledged the raspy drone of the
General's persuasions. Suddenly, he heard a tapping
on his window.

"Jack. Is that you in there? I decided that if the mountain won't come to Mohammed, well, I guess I decided to play the Mohammed role. Are you in this great white boat of a car? I can't tell through these smoked windows. Very sinister. And who is that imposing man with sunglasses standing at the front of this sharkmobile and watching me so intently? And why is Jack the dog growling at him from behind the fence? Too many questions? Jack, are you in there?"

Smiling broadly, Jack opened the door a crack, as the General still had all of the windows locked save for the one to his right cracked to filter out his cigar smoke. Jack wondered why he had not also locked the doors to prevent his escape until the General allowed it. *Probably an oversight*, thought Jack, as he stared up at the beautiful and welcome sight of Sally Fretango.

"Hello, my darling. What a delightful surprise—and perfect timing. I'll be right with you."

He turned back to the General who was momentarily silent in the face of this unwelcome intrusion. "Sorry to cut you off, General, but I'm getting out now. I've got my best girl and my best dog waiting for me. I must rescue my dog from Alec Ramos, whom he really doesn't like, and rescue my girl from Alec Ramos, who might like her too much." As he got out of the car, Jack winked at the startled General and leaned back to make contact with him. "You need to get another boy for your job of rising lieutenant from Charlottesville. It ain't me. The price of fame and glory under your direction is too high. I've seen what you've done with your own son, your rubber-stamp Governor and gofer. You've used him and abused him at your whim, and for that very same compliance, you award him none of the respect he still craves from you. It's a conundrum, isn't it General?"

Jack continued, "But then, none of your people really have your respect, General, because you control them. And, that's the way you like it. But I'd watch out for your man Alec Ramos. I think he chafes under that control; he might act out on you one day. Just a thought."

Jack finished by saying, "Oh, but I digress. I'm not your boy. Nope. I'll just have to see what I can do on my own. By the way, Sheriff A. P. Hill is still looking for the two out-of-town snipers who came looking for Mickey Courage and got run off by him and his deputies. You wouldn't know anything about that, would you? Because, while I'm still commonwealth's attorney, I'll prosecute the criminals who instigated that crime to the fullest extent of the law. That's anyone connected to the crime, even you." Jack noticed the General's mouth had momentarily dropped open. Jack smiled, "Well, gotta go now."

He slammed the door, took the broadly smiling Sally Fretango by the hand and walked the length of the great white Continental, past the sinister Alec Ramos who was returning to the driver's seat of the vehicle. Alec Ramos took off his dark glasses and glared at Jack and Sally as they escaped through the gate and up to a delighted friend who was pounding his tail in anticipation at the top of the steps.

Jack turned once more to see the driver's-side door slam behind the disappearing figure of Alec Ramos. With the windows darkened in such a way as to reveal no one inside, the car resembled a ghost ship on wheels as it backed down the driveway, peeled its own tires, and sped off into the distance. "Well. There goes my chance of having a regional career and beyond in politics," said Jack—mysteriously, or so he thought to a bemused Sally Fretango.

"Maybe not, Jack. Besides, you have more than enough to do right here in Charlottesville. I'm going to help you in every way I can. And then we'll see what comes next!"

"Hey, who are you really, my girl?" said Jack, his arm around Slly's waist. Together with Jack the dog, he escorted her through the screen door of the white clapboard cottage at 1717 Rugby Avenue and into the natural cool within, out of the ninety-five degree heat outside and away from the lingering residue of General Cartridge.

"It's about time Jack the dog and I get to know you a little better." Jack pulled Sally to him and held her tight. He could feel her warmth and her figure, and her sweet strength. He kissed her lightly. She looked up and said, "We've got all day, Jack, and maybe the rest of our lives."

"At least!" laughed Jack.

Chapter 39: Denouement — Main Players

Roy Amery: Graduated from Charlottesville's all-black Burley High School and attended North Carolina AT&T. In 1963, he married his childhood sweetheart, Charlene Taylor, and moved to Reidsville, North Carolina, where he took a job as Production Line Manager for the Domino Textile Manufacturing Company.

Lucius Johnson: Killed in the Billy Sprouse/ Mickey Courage 1959 kidnapping, he was considered by many one of the early martyrs of the civil rights movement leading up to the civil rights legislation of 1964.

Mickey Courage: Served thirty months of a three-to-five year sentence and was paroled for good behavior in 1961. He moved to Culpeper, Virginia, where he got a job as a mechanic trainee at the Baldwin Chevrolet dealership. In 1962, he married

Culpeper native Cheryl Delgano. The couple have one child, Michael Courage III.

Billy Sprouse: Sentenced to a total of ten to fifteen for kidnapping, eight to ten for felony murder, and one year for contempt of court with earliest possible parole in 1970. He petitioned the Virginia Supreme Court of Appeals in 1960 for a writ of *habeas corpus* attacking the validity of his conviction. Essentially, his court-appointed lawyer claimed that Billy Sprouse was wrongfully accused of kidnapping rather than of the appropriate charge of false imprisonment or illegal detention.

It is interesting to note that, in his original petition, Billy applied as a pauper for a court-appointed lawyer, listing his net worth as twenty-five cents. In March of 1961, his appeal was rejected by the court.

In September of 1962, Billy Sprouse was killed while playing touch football in the prison yard of the Goochland state penitentiary. He was gang-tackled after catching the football, and never got up. A five-inch homemade shiv was found buried in his lower abdomen. Apparently, Billy's behavior at the state penitentiary was no better than it had been in the Charlottesville jail. Billy Sprouse was twenty-one.

General Samuel S. Cartridge Senior: Died of a massive heart attack, brought on by other health complications, in December of 1961. One of Virginia's largest state funerals was held at St. Stephen's Episcopal Church in Richmond. Eulogies included that of his son, Samuel S. Cartridge Jr., who expressed the sorrow of all Virginians on the passing of one of the most selfless and dedicated public servants the state had ever known. It was rumored that the eulogy had been largely written by the ex-governor's secretary.

Jack Forester: Courted, got engaged to, and married Ms. Sally Fretango in the six-week period immediately following the Billy Sprouse trial. A small wedding was held at 1717 Rugby Avenue. Alice Dillon, Junius T. Jones, Joseph L. Johnson, Sheriff A. P. Hill, Jack's two children, and Jack the dog were in attendance. Jack the dog was the best man.